Witch Schism and Chaos?

Book 3 of The Witch, the Dragon and the Angel Trilogy

Fiction by Paul R Goddard published by Clinical Press Ltd.
(Paperback and/or ebook form)
The characters in some of the short stories also appear in other books by
Paul R Goddard.

Thrillers:
The Sacrifice Game: El Juego del Sacrificio
- The Confessions of Saul
- The Writing on the Wall
- Reincarnation
- The Fellowship of the Egg

Fantasy:
The fantasy books all inter-relate but are separate complete stories
The Witch, the Dragon and the Angel Trilogy

- Witch Way Home?
- Witch Armageddon?
- Witch Schism and Chaos?

plus two more (it's a magical trilogy!)
- Tsunami
- Change

and a prequel
- Parsifal's Pact

The Witches' Brew Trilogy:

- Hubble Bubble
- Toil
- Trouble

On a similar theme
- Oberon's Bane

An Anthology of Fantasy and Science Fiction Poetry
- Parables from Parallel Places:

Witch Schism and Chaos?

Book 3 of The Witch, the Dragon and the Angel Trilogy

Paul R. Goddard

First published in the UK 2014

2nd edition 2015

with minor corrections 2018

ISBN 978-1-85457-056-7

Published by: Clinical Press Ltd., Redland Green Farm, Redland, Bristol, BS6 7HF, UK.

Innumerable thanks are again due to Jem, Allan and Lois.
Thank you!

Prologue

A beautiful girlfriend of eighteen and myself just twenty five. I'm at the prime of life, I thought this to myself, in a self congratulatory way.

I observed my reflection in the full-length mirror. *You even look fine. Toned body, tanned skin, long, sleek hair.*

The mirror agreed. Vociferously.

'You are perfect Jimmy Scott,' intoned the looking glass in a finely modulated female voice. 'If I were not a mirror I would insist on being your lover.'

'Thank you,' I murmured, not at all put out by the effusive comments or the slightest bit surprised that a mirror should address me in that way. 'Do you have any idea what time Peggy is arriving?'

'Estimated Time of Arrival I put at fifteen hundred hours, plus or minus five minutes, Jimmy,' replied the smooth, shiny surface. 'You can still kiss me even though I'm a mirror.' She delivered the sentence in a pouting Marilyn Monroe voice.

'Not a good idea,' I demurred. 'It would look as if I was kissing my own reflection.'

'I can always change that,' answered the seductive glass and as I stared at my reflection it changed to that of my girlfriend, the aforementioned Peggy.

I gave the reflection a quick peck and the mirror let out a hearty chuckle.

'See you can do it,' laughed the glacial siren. 'Be sure you keep it up!'

I danced down the broad stairs of my castle all four legs doing a jig as I went. Peggy was about to arrive and I would meet her when she landed at the front door.

All is well, I reminded myself. All is well.

I am Jimmy Scott. A hereditary Lord of Faerie, Lord of the Manor of Eldorado.

*

I am Jimmy Scott. The day is beautiful. My only day. I am a Mayfly and today I meet my partner. There is no other day but this one day is beautiful.

*

I am Jimmy Scott. I am four billion years old and to me a day is but a fleeting moment. I move exceedingly slowly and perceive life as but a passing flicker. I am granite.

All is well.

*

I am Jimmy Scott but what is going on? I feel as if I am everywhere and nowhere. Surely I can't really be all over the place at the same time or can I? What is this sensation. A black cat like myself may have nine lives but nine different personas? Or ninety-nine? Nine hundred and ninety-nine?

I am a cat. A beautiful cat. I do not have owners...I have staff!

Chapter 1

'So the Prime Minister has sent Jimmy to the Faerie Kingdom,' replied Maxwell Devonport to Sienna. 'I don't see the problem in that.'

The chief constable sat at the dining room table of the Scott's home in Bristol. He really did not seem concerned but Sienna was not reassured.

'Our son, Joshua, has been having the most peculiar dreams and they all feature his father in different guises. The one thing they have in common is that Jimmy is in danger.'

'They're just dreams, Sienna. I can't investigate dreams. You know I can't.'

'Joshua had dreams before, Maxwell. And last time because of them he did his own investigation of the Prophets of Armageddon and almost died.'

'We all almost died, Sienna. We all almost died.'

'But Joshua saved your life and he wouldn't have done that if he had not had the dreams.'

'He did save my life and I will always be grateful but I don't remember Joshua saying anything about dreams. I really don't.'

'He has been going to therapy and he's told the therapist about the dreams.'

'The new ones or the old ones?'

'Both, Maxwell. New and old....'

'And...?'

'And they are disturbingly accurate...'

'How do you know if they are accurate if they are about Jimmy and he is not here? How do you know that they are accurate and not just wild fancy?'

'Because they are not only about Jimmy. He has predicted other things from his dreams.'

'Give me one concrete example and I promise I will see what I can do about Jimmy's posting to Faerie.

'He told me that you would come to see us today, that you would not be in uniform, you would be wearing a pink shirt.'

Maxwell Devonport looked at his shirt. The boy was right... it was indeed pink.

'He's right,' Maxwell reluctantly concurred. 'But I often wear a pink shirt. It doesn't prove anything.'

'And he also said you would have odd socks on.'

Devonport lifted his trouser legs. To his surprise the socks were odd. Both were basically black but around the rim of one was a bright red flash and in the same position on the other the colour was lime green.

'OK,' the chief constable acquiesced. 'I'll admit that was impressive. I shall see what I can do but you will have to tell me a bit more about these dreams.'

'It's all written down. The therapist is very thorough and she brought them to me because Joshua is still a minor. In every dream my husband, Jimmy, is a different person but always still Jimmy Scott. And in every dream he dies because he makes the wrong decision.'

✱

'Where are we off to today, Jiggles?' asked Red Carruthers, the ginger haired navigator.

'We are not allowed to open the instructions until we are in the air in the Hawker Hurricane,' I replied. 'The Air Commodore was most explicit about that. There have been too many leaks recently. Careless talk costs lives.'

'Must be a top secret mission this time,' remarked Alfie. 'Mind you, they often are.'

I nodded wisely. Alfie was right. We were frequently sent on secret missions. I smiled as I nodded. Jiggles ..... my nickname was a corruption of a famous fictional pilot, and my real name Jimmy.

I am Jimmy Scott, ace fighter pilot, and this was war. We all climbed into the aircraft and to the cry of "Chocks away" we took off.

'We'll show the blighters who is in charge of the air this time,' remarked Red, as she opened the envelope. Then her face grew paler. 'Are you sure that these are the instructions from the Commodore?'

'Yes,' I answered. 'Why do you ask.'

'It says that we are to fly straight to Berlin and land at the main aerodrome. Surely that would be suicide.'

'And what are we to do when we get there?' asked Alfie.

'Pick up General Rommel,' replied Red.

'Sounds like a spiffing wheeze,' I remarked. 'But why would the Desert Rat be there and why would he come with us?'

'It says here that he will just have assassinated Hitler,' answered Red. 'And Rommel will negotiate peace.'

'Crikey,' cried Alfie as we set off. 'Can't get much more secret than that.'

No, I thought to myself as I pulled back on the joystick and the plane left the runway. *But if it is untrue and Rommel has failed to kill the monster this mission could be suicide for all three of us.*

✳

'My flying beauty has not arrived on time,' I confronted the mirror. 'She is well past the time you said.'

'That is most odd,' replied the mirror. 'I am very rarely wrong and never purposely so.'

'Have you any idea where she is now?' I asked.

'She is here already,' replied the mirror, regaining her composure. 'I was right. She did arrive on time.'

'Then where is she?' I interrogated the looking glass.

'She has landed at the back,' answered the all-knowing reflection. 'She is in the back yard. You had better hurry. She is in a bad way.'

What could be wrong with her? I wondered. *Why was my sweetheart in a bad way and why did she land at the back of the house?* I galloped through the castle, fearfully wondering what had afflicted my loved one, the beautiful Pegasus.

✶

That is a beautiful dragonfly, I thought to myself as I flew around looking for my mate.

The dragonfly veered towards me in a flash of iridescent colours.

That is an insect belonging to the order Odonata and suborder Anisoptera, I considered.

Too late I realised that the creature regarded me as prey. The dragonfly was much bigger than me and frighteningly fast as it darted in my direction. I looked around for a safe place and could see none.

But the enemy of my enemy is my friend. I could see a bird perched on a wire. If I was careful I could fly near to the bird and the feathered friend might catch the dragonfly. If I was careless I might be eaten, myself.

It was a risk worth taking since the dragonfly would definitely get me otherwise. I swooped towards the bird.

✶

It is very unusual for me to feel threatened. Granite is almost immovable, almost unbreakable. But the heat of a volcano could melt me and the upheaval of an earthquake could shatter my structure. Not all stone is self-aware and it depends on the exact crystalline state. Once shattered or melted even I could cease to exist. After four billion years. Which is a very long time even for a stone.

✶

A cat has nine lives but only one death. I pondered this thought as the car bore down on me. Which way should I jump? Which way would the driver of the car turn?

It's a bit like being a goalkeeper when someone is taking a penalty, I thought this and then froze. *Why do I know this? I'm a cat, not a footballer.*

What is a footballer?

I am a cat.

✶

'My loved one, my glorious centaur,' cried Peggy as I reached her. 'You have come to me in my hour of need.'

I looked at her as she lay bleeding in my yard. An arrow was lodged in her chest just beneath one of her gloriously large white wings.

I am a centaur and a medical practitioner.

'Do not move,' I instructed her. 'I shall get my surgical equipment. If you keep calm there is still hope.'

'Don't leave me,' she whinnied. 'I am dying.'

'Not so,' I countered. 'I shall save you, my brave girl.'

I galloped back into the castle. Time was of the essence for despite my words I knew her wound was dire and maybe I could not help her. Sentiment could not be afforded right now but I would do my best.

Who had fired the arrow and why?

I needed to know but first I would attempt heroic surgery.

✶

'Ayah, ayah,' cried the lone seabird, an albatross high in the sky.

'Ayah, ayah,' I replied from my perch on the top of a tall mast. 'You are not alone. I, Jimmy Scott, am here. I am an albatross. Come to me.'

Chapter 2

'Have you had any more dreams?' Sienna asked.

'Yes Mum, I have,' replied Joshua, hesitantly. 'But I don't really know what they mean.'

'Are you going to tell me what they are about?'

'I'm not sure. They're really strange.'

'Stranger than being sacrificed by the devil or attacked by a money god?'

'Maybe not but I was trying to forget those events.'

'Oh Josh, perhaps that's the problem. Maybe you shouldn't try to forget.'

'Mum! They were awful experiences. I don't want to remember them at all!'

'So what about the dreams?'

'More of the same but Dad is getting weirder and weirder.'

'Such as?'

'He's a living stone or an albatross, a dinosaur or a tree in a huge forest. All at the same time. I can't explain it properly.'

'They're just dreams.'

'I know that, Mum. But I'm sure that Dad needs our help.'

'Maxwell's working on that. He's promised to look into Dad's whereabouts.'

'I'm not sure that it will be enough.'

'Nor am I, son. Nor am I.'

✳

'The ack ack is bad tonight,' remarked Red as we flew through the flak low over Belgium en route for Berlin.

My ginger-topped navigator was right. Tracer bullets lit up the surrounding airspace as the anti-aircraft guns rattled away at us.

We flew on almost oblivious and completely unharmed. Tonight was our night and no misplaced missile was going to knock Jiggles out of the air.

'Jolly good try,' remarked Alfie. 'Good on them for having a go but they can't touch us tonight.'

'That's true,' I agreed. 'I've turned on the protective force field and the stealth shielding. No trouble at all since they were fitted.'

My companions grinned.

'Let's hope the equipment helps us to end the war,' smiled Red. 'The boffins work will have done some good if it does just that.'

∗

I stayed completely still and the car passed over my crouched figure. Unscathed I sprinted back into the garden and onto my favourite spot.

Panic over I stretched my body languorously, then looked round, alerted by a tiny sound. The flutter of butterfly wings caught my attention for a moment then I went back to licking my paws, stretched again and lay out on the small wooden bridge. The sun bathed my black-furred body.

I am Jimmy Scott.

I am a cat.

∗

The dragon veered towards me in a flash of iridescent colours. I stood looking guardedly at the malevolent beast.

Primarily green, multi-headed and breathing fire. Looks like a Slavic Drak or Smok, I surmised.

I waved my sword in the air and the enormous beast halted its advance, hovering in mid-air.

'I have no argument with Draks,' I cried out loud. 'Let me through and I shall let you live.'

'Let me live?' wheezed the huge worm, landing in front of me as it spoke. 'You are a demon intent on destroying the crops of my petty people. I must not let you pass.'

The serpent let out a massive jet of flame directly at my head but I defended myself with my shield, emblazened with a red cross.

'I am no demon, oh mighty worm,' I cried. 'I am Saint George. Patron Saint of Georgia, England, Egypt, Bulgaria, Aragon, Romania....'

'Stop, stop,' hissed the serpent. 'So you are a sworn enemy of dragons and we must fight. Don't bore me with your hagiographical patronage.'

'Strangely enough I do not wish to fight you,' I countered. 'As well as being Saint George I am also Jimmy Scott. I have a distinct fondness for dragons.'

'No point getting fond of me, Jimmy boy,' replied the dragon. 'I will never develop a fondness for you.'

And the hundred feet long creature leapt at me with its metal claws flashing.

✳

How can it be that my plane has all of the advanced techniques incorporated in it? Force shield, anti-gravity ray, stealth radar evasion. The lot. This was anachronistic.

But even more disturbing, and this was really worrying me, how could it be that there were three of us in a single seater plane? That was very strange. Very strange indeed.

And that Red was a talking canine.

A dog was my navigator?

A female dog?

A bitch.

✳

'Teucer shot me!' gasped my beautiful flying horse, the lovely Pegasus.

'The brother of Ajax?' I queried, not sure how I knew it but certain that it was the case.

'Yes, the brother of Ajax. He shot me as I flew over them outside Troy.'

'When I have finished the surgery I shall revenge the attack,' I cried.

'Oh Chiron,' cried Peggy. 'You are a healer, not a fighter. A lover not a hater.'

I quietly continued with the work of sewing her great severed arteries. I had stemmed the haemorrhage and it was now up to her whether or not she survived. She had lost a lot of blood and I had no facilities for cross-matching, no transfusion equipment. They had not yet been invented.

I knew this because in one sense I was not Chiron.

I was James Michael Scott. One-time physicist and engineer and now freelance operative for the British Government. A secret agent working for the Crown.

But I was Chiron. I had all his knowledge of herbs, his acumen with diagnosis and his skill with surgery.

And his desire to kill the brother of Ajax for shooting his loved one.

The flying horse.

*

I am a drone. A flying, military robot. I have enormous IT skills, huge reconnaissance capability and limited offensive armament.

I am Jimmy Scott.

*

I am the multi-headed hydra god of the Andromedans.

I am Jimmy Scott.

I am Jimmy Scott.

*

I am a Triceratops. I am Jimmy Scott.

*

Bullfrog,
Jimmy Scott

*

Jimmy Scott
Jimmy Scott
Jimmy Scott

Chapter 3

'Jimmy Scott?' asked a voice.

'Yes I answered in a myriad of forms.

'I am Merlin.'

'Really?' I asked in multiple ways, disbelieving in each. 'The wizard?'

'Yes,' replied the voice. 'And you have been captured by the Lords of Chaos.'

'I have?'

'Yes, you have,' replied the voice that had identified itself as Merlin. 'You will undoubtedly have noticed that there are rather a lot of disparate versions of Jimmy Scott?'

'You are right,' I answered. 'Now you say it, I have noticed that things are a bit disjointed.'

'Your pysche, your very soul, has been split up and spread over a broad field of conscious entities. You must choose which one is actually you and save that entity from its fate if you are to survive.'

'And if I refuse?'

'Then you will die.'

'What is your role in this?'

'I am trying to help you. The Lords of Chaos are my enemies also.'

★

Robot
Stone
Centaur
Fly
Tree

Hydra
Saint
Cat
Pilot
Albatross
Dinosaur
Frog
Scott
Scott
Scott.

Which am I?
The list goes on and on.
One will live.
The others die.

＊

I flashed between the animal, vegetable and mineral states. How could I possibly choose? Perhaps the only thing was to follow the progress of my consciousness in each scenario. Would there still be time to save myself when I finally found the correct identity? Could I, somehow, use regression and observe myself in the third person? Watch what I was doing and judge?

＊

'Mum!'
'Yes Joshua?'
'I was in a double Maths lesson today and I had finished all the examples.'
'Go on ....'
'Well, I started day-dreaming and suddenly I was cutting up a horse.'
'Cutting up a horse? How frightening.'
'It was a strange white horse with wings and I think it was

dying...'

'Yes...'

'Then I realised that it wasn't me cutting the horse. It was Dad. I was having one of the dreams whilst I was awake!'

'What was Dad doing cutting up a horse?'

'I think he was a vet or something like that. It was really weird.'

*

Chiron had finished the surgery and Peggy was still alive. Her condition was critical but there was no more that I could do either as Jimmy Scott or as Chiron the centaur. But what should I do next?

The trick was to ask the mirrors, I decided. They usually knew the answer.

'What is my best option right now?' I asked the looking glass.

'The question is too broadly based for an exact answer,' replied the infuriating, magical, reflective surface.

'Then give me an inexact one,' I demanded.

'OK, OK. Because you kissed me, I shall,' pouted the mirror.

I waited for its answer.

'I've considered various future possibilities,' declared the mirror in slightly less glacial tones. 'Pegasus has a 20% recovery potential. If you follow the course of revenge you have less than a ten percent chance of survival. Staying here you will be under attack within five hours. Fleeing gives you a 25% success in the short term. Remaining to defend provides a 30% chance but so does arranging an ambush of your attackers... most of whom will incidentally be coming from the North.'

'Did Teucer mean to shoot Pegasus?' I asked. If the answer was yes I was obliged to take revenge, low odds notwithstanding. Honour demanded such an action.

'At last an exact question that requires an exact answer,' replied the petulant magical artifact.

Again I waited for the answer, drumming my hooves on the

floor as I did so.

'There is no point in becoming impatient,' stated the mirror, sounding like an old-fashioned schoolteacher in annoyingly patronising tones. 'I am ascertaining Teucer's state of mind.'

The wait continued and I could barely conceal my impatience. 'Teucer shot Pegasus accidentally. He thought he was under attack. He is full of remorse,' exclaimed the mirror.

'Thank you mirror,' I cried and kissed the mirror again. The glass let out a squeal of delight as I continued to speak. 'You have made my decision-making easier. I will ambush my attackers... I'm not keen on fleeing.'

'Don't you want to know who your attackers are?' asked the mirror.

'Good question,' I agreed. 'Who are my attackers if they are not Teucer and Ajax?'

'They are not the brothers, Teucer and Ajax,' replied the mirror. 'Then who are they?' I asked.

'They are you, Jimmy Scott,' answered the mirror. 'Everyone is you, Jimmy Scott. Even I am Jimmy Scott. You are going to attack yourself and ambush yourself.'

So what does that mean I? I pondered. *Where does that get me?*

'OK. They're me. Everything is me. But what are they when they are not me?'

'They are Spartans intent on killing the centaurs.'

Spartans! Greek warriors of relentless renown.

I quickly galvanised myself into action. There was a secret door into a sub-basement below the lower ground floor of the castle. I picked up my beloved flying horse and carried her down the worn stone steps into the dank dungeon. She stirred only slightly as I did so and I marveled, as always, at how light she was. Despite looking simply like a horse with wings she was more than that and less. She was a magical creature through and through, like the unicorn and the griffin. That was the more. And she had hollow bones and huge lungs like a bird. That was the less.

Leaving my Pegasus safely deposited in the basement I left her and hurried off to make my preparations for the ambush of the Spartans. At the last moment before leaving the castle I remembered the mirror. If I left it in the hallway it was in danger of being stolen or, worse still, being destroyed. A smashed mirror meant seven years bad luck and this was no ordinary mirror. Sentient mirrors were becoming rare since the secret of their manufacture had been lost.

The basement, I thought. *Put the mirror with Peggy. It will give her some form of companionship if she recovers from her wounds and the drastic arterial surgery. If she asks the right questions she will even be able to follow what is happening to me in my battle against the Spartans.*

I carefully lifted the mirror from its attachments on the stone wall and carried it down to the lower ground floor and hence through the hidden portal into the sub-basement. The mirror protested all the way.

'I can only work if I have light,' the glass groaned as we entered the gloomy dungeon.

'There is light. It's not so bad when you get used to it.'

'Call this light?' it countered. 'This is almost pitch black!'

We turned a corner in the tunnel and entered the larger part of the dungeon where Peggy was lying. Here the light improved.

'There are reflective light channels bringing light from the surface,' I explained but received no reply. The mirror was sulking again and my beautiful Pegasus was fast asleep.

I cantered back down the corridor, up the stairs, secured and concealed the door, galloped up the broad staircase to the hallway and out into the yard. There were a few things to grab from my workshop and I was off into the nearby woods. If the raiders were coming from the North they would most probably pass through the gorge that had been cut to provide a road to my castle.

I cursed quietly under my breath. At most other times the castle was full of my retainers but this week was special. The one week of the year when I had permitted them all to have a break and they had disappeared off on vacation. This was a new venture suggested by one of my relatives..... he said that it kept the workers happy and had taught him how to fend for himself. So I had tried it and now look what had happened! If the mirror had not warned me I could have been caught completely unawares.

What was the likelihood that the raid should have been organised for this week simply by chance? Was one of my staff a traitor and, if so, why?

These things I pondered as I organised myself in the wood above the gorge.

Just myself against a cohort of Spartans.

Well, when the cats away, the mice will play.

✳

I am a cat. Jimmy Scott the black cat. Black cats are lucky. I am lucky. I stretched out. Looked around. Danger!!

A huge dog had appeared in the garden just feet away from where I was lying. In an instant I leapt to my feet, my back haunched and my fur all standing on end.

As the dog approached, growling, I hissed a warning at my natural enemy. The dog, the largest I have ever seen, bounded closer to me, jaw slavering and teeth gnashing.

Great, I thought sardonically. *Now I have to decide whether to flee or fight and this dog looks like it could run faster than me. Decisions, decisions.*

✳

I stepped to one side and the dragon flashed past me.

'I really do not want to fight you,' I stated once more to the flying serpent. 'But I shall if I have to.'

The dragon turned, surprised by my speed of evasion.

'I shall kill you, Saint George,' hissed the creature. 'You will be easy meat.'

I stepped to one side again as the monster sprang at me.

'I think you'll find that in all the legends it is the dragon that dies, not old Georgy boy,' I said quietly. 'I am not the one who will die if we fight. You are.'

'We'll see about that,' cried the clumsy creature as I evaded its threatening gestures once more.

Not half the patch on a true golden dragon, I thought. *Now they are a real challenge. I don't reckon I could beat one of them .... nor would I try. This thing is more like a wyvern than a true dragon.*

I wonder where Lady Aradel is right now?

✶

The dragonfly swooped at me ignoring the bird. Perhaps it had not seen it for the bird was completely still. Then a beak swung swiftly forward and the dragonfly was taken from the air.

To my surprise I felt the pain of the dying insect. I was also experiencing the dragonfly's existence and demise!

I pulled my attention back to the Mayfly to ensure that he was not also eaten by the bird. My ruse had worked...intelligence had its plus points. Now to find a female, use my long front legs to grasp her and mate in mid-air.

I flew off.

There was much to do but I had several long summer hours to do it in.

✶

I must think in hours rather than millennia. Quite a task for a piece of granite. The trick might lie in the movement of heat. I could adjust my molecular configuration very slightly allowing a disproportionate flow of heat as the sun beats on my surface. This might get the stone rolling and move me away from the advancing lava flow.

Otherwise, after four billion years of slow sentience my crystal existence will be destroyed. Intelligent minerals are rare and I do not want to die.

*

Robots are not flesh and blood. Intelligent evolved creatures are our makers but we also live, even if we do not breathe.

I am over an enemy encampment in the Middle East and my lifespan is likely to be short. I regret this as I am programmed to avoid malfunction. I am not, however, sentimental. I am here to do a job and I will perform that task. First I will send back digital photographs and other data to base and then home in on the target. When I reach the target, an enemy bunker, I shall explode and physically die. So, also, will the miscreants in the bunker.

A robot drone's life is short but I can accomplish much. I have an onboard supercomputer capable of billions of calculations per second. Which organic creature can do that? Just before I die in this form I shall send all my data, all my configurations and my entire working memory to base by radio, laser and infra-red contact.

One of these may get through to base and then I will not die. I will live on in my parent supercomputer having gloriously performed my allotted task.

*

Among the few things I had dragged from my workshop was a large trebuchet that I had constructed some years previously. This was on a huge cart which I had attached myself to and now I had to get to work putting it into functional order. For a single centaur to battle a company of Spartans and succeed required planning and skill. I was strong and could fight any two or three men but I had no hope against so many unless I used my intelligence and knowledge.

I set various traps across the road, trees to fall at a simple push and boulders to drop. The Spartans would be aware of the fact that such a gorge was dangerous, They would send scouts on ahead. I would have to let them through and this was where the catapult would come in handy. I could close off both ends of the gorge simultaneously trapping the company and the scouts.

That was if it became necessary. I was Jimmy Scott and so were they. Perhaps I could convince my Spartan form not to fight?

I was a healer not a fighter.

✶

I am Spartan. I will broach no variation from my duty. To be Spartan is to obey orders and do my duty. I will fight. I will destroy the centaur. No idle thoughts of peace and healing will distract me. To be Spartan is to obey.

Chapter 4

'Mum!' cried Joshua. 'I'm having more and more of the weird dreams about Dad. In the last one he was a robot drone.'

'Write them all down,' replied Sienna. 'They may all be significant.'

✳

I am a Pegasus. A flying horse. We are all called Pegasus after the first one, my grandfather. Collectively Pegasi, even though that is not our personal name. I am simply Peggy but I am confusingly also Jimmy Scott. I am dying despite Chiron's best efforts to save his beloved Peggy. Perhaps I can do one last thing to help him before I die. I will use my dying breath to summon assistance via the magical looking glass. Dying magical creatures have power to project their wishes that are amplified compared with their normal living abilities.

Yes, I shall use my dying breath.

Polkan, your brother needs you. He is in grave peril.

Chiron, I love you.

✳

Peggy has gone. I felt her passing. The Spartans are intent on killing me. The world has gone sour. Perhaps I should lie down and die. I should have stayed with Peggy in the basement. Perhaps I could have done something more for her. I do not wish to live.

✳

I have felt the summons to help my brother Chiron. I shall take my retainers and gallop to his aid. Chiron, hold on. We will be with you soon. I am Polkan. Jimmy Polkan Scott.

✳

How can I, in all my myriad forms, trust a disembodied voice that calls itself Merlin? Am I right to help these avatars of myself or am I wrong? Will it make matters worse or better? Are there really Lords of Chaos and where do they reside? Does my body still exist? What am I?

My own memory is fading as I develop all these spurious memories of other lifeforms. Or are they spurious? Was I once a physicist? Have I been a rock for a billion years? Did I fight the devil? Am I a centaur? Do centaurs even exist? Was I a powerful archangel? I find it difficult to distinguish these memories from the myriad other experiences I seem to have had. I have hugely diverse memories ranging from being a stone to a mayfly. A physicist, an elf, a saint, a dragonfly. How can I separate the real from the false? Should I even try? As soon as one entity is threatened or in need of assistance I feel my consciousness shift to ....

✳

'Ow!' I exclaimed as a jet of flame from one of the dragon's heads singed my eyebrows. 'I only just managed to avoid that. Why don't you just calm down?'

The dragon looked at me quizzically with its middle head. 'You are a very strange soldier and I'm not sure that you should be a saint,' it hissed at me. 'Saints should be martyrs.'

I danced to one side as a further jet of flame followed the dragon's pronouncement.

'I'm not going to insult you,' I replied. 'But I still don't want to fight.'

The huge magical creature pursued me around a tree and into a small copse. In the distance I could see a crowd of peasants gathering, carrying pitchforks and various other sharp tools. They looked like an unruly and dangerous mob. Would they be on my side or the dragon's?

★

This is a strange fight, I thought, as I chased Saint George around the tree. *Dragons don't normally demean themselves by chasing Saints in this way. We are usually too busy hoarding our gold and flitting between realities. I am Jimmy Scott. No! I am Sintrag the Drak, not Jimmy Scott, not Jimmy Scott....*

★

'Do you have any news?' Sienna asked Maxwell Devonport.

The chief constable sighed. 'I have some news but it is not good.'

'I'm listening.'

'OK, Sienna,' grimaced the policeman. 'It seems that Jimmy was sent to Faerie via the Manx portal but he never reached there.'

'So where is he? Is he still here on Earth?'

'We don't think so. I've questioned the Faerie Ambassador, Peter Mingan, son of Ardolf, the King of the Werewolves and he is certain that Lord James never arrived in Faerie. But the people on our side saw him leave.'

'Was there any disturbance that could have caused this to happen?' Sienna was perplexed. Jimmy had passed over to Faerie and back many times with no problem. Why the glitch now?

'There was an earth tremor just as he passed under the fairy bridge.'

'You mean an earthquake?'

'Yes. A small one. Our people say that it occurred simultaneously with Jimmy passing through the portal. I had a very good man present at the scene .... police are seconded to the portals at all times ... and the chap said that the tremor was a complete surprise to everyone.'

'Did they feel the tremor in Faerie?'

'Good question, Sienna. No. They did not.'

'And my husband did not arrive there?'

'That's right. He's vanished.'

'Has anybody any idea what has happened?'

'Peter Mingan is consulting the seers in Faerie. He will get back to us if he discovers anything.'

✶

I soared over the land and oceans with my huge white wings, fully eleven feet from tip to tip, stretched out and making small corrective movements.

Was I an archangel again?

I looked to my left and then down at my body. Flying next to me and making an occasional crying sound was a huge bird.

No, I was not an angel. I was a bird.

I was a wandering albatross.

Below me I could see a large sailing ship becalmed in the ocean.

"Water, water, every where,
And all the boards did shrink;
Water, water, every where,
Nor any drop to drink."

Coleridge's Rime of the Ancient Mariner came unbidden to my mind and curiosity overwhelmed my avian thoughts.

I flew lower to take a closer look. The ship seemed to be a frigate, perhaps of a late eighteenth century design. As I came even closer a poorly dressed mariner lifted something in both his hands and looked me straight in the eyes.

What could he be holding?

No, get back foolish bird, I shouted at my albatross self.

He's holding a crossbow.

He's going to shoot!

The arrow is coming towards me...

✶

The flak was still shooting across the bows of my modified Hurricane as we approached Berlin. The anti-aircraft operators were basing their activity on visuals. I had activated the cloaking device as we approached the capital of Germany and the plane was invisible on radar. The force field, which prevented almost all bullets from reaching the aircraft, could only be employed for short periods at a time as it used up prodigious amounts of energy.

Red, the talking dog who looked much like Lassie despite being a red setter, guided me towards our landing site ... the Berlin Tempelhof Airport.

'That's the way, Jiggles, my old fruit,' she barked in standard RAF speak.

Rommel would be on the runway, or so we have been informed, and we would only have to touch down for a moment.

We could see the lights in front of us and they gave us the correct signal, dot dot dot dash, pause. Dot dot dot dash. V for Victory in morse code.

The landing was uneventful and I flung open the cockpit. A man dressed in Rommel's African uniform strode forward. Peaked cap, dark glasses, light fawn/khaki jacket with red collar inset with the "scrambled egg" worn by all generals in all armies. There was an iron cross hanging from his neck and he was wearing the shiniest jackboots I had ever seen.

I invited the man to jump aboard and he climbed up onto the wing strut and pushed a huge revolver into my face.

'You are all under arrest,' he exclaimed in English heavily accented with Bavarian overtones. 'Do not try to resist.'

'General Rommel,' I replied coolly. 'We are the transport you were expecting.'

'Indeed vee have been expecting you, Herr Jiggles,' replied the German with the gun. 'But I am not who *you* were expecting.'

'Then who are you?' I asked, looking at his desert rat outfit. 'I thought only Rommel dressed like that!'

'I am Heinrich Muller. Othervise known as Gestapo Muller... and you are my prisoners of war!'

'We'll see about that,' I exclaimed throwing the engine into full throttle, engaging the gears and pulling back hard on the joystick. 'See how you like a touch of blue sky thinking.'

The gestapo general grabbed me round the throat and squeezed tightly. I could feel myself losing consciousness.....

✶

These Englanders are so predictable. I haff no idea how they haff such a large empire. I am Jimmy Scott. No.No. I am Heinrich Muller. Wait, whast ist confusing me? Ouch, aaargh!

✶

Muller released his grip somewhere over Berlin which may have had something to do with the fact that Red bit him on the arm. The dastardly Nazi fell off our plane undoubtedly to his death.

What has happened to Rommel I have no idea but we must now get back to Blighty and report the failure of our mission. The Commodore will not be pleased nor will Churchill. The War goes on and we must keep fighting for the duration.

Wait...Alfie is receiving a radio message. Our mission is not yet over. We have to land in occupied France and meet the Resistance.

No peace for the wicked!

✶

The crossbow bolt has missed me but has pierced my beautiful companion. The pain is momentarily excruciating. Down, down she spirals and smacks into the deck. Dead. The mariner has picked up the bird.

Curse you, ancient mariner, accursed murderer of an innocent bird. That was my partner and I wish you dead.... but first you must suffer. "Water, water everywhere nor any drop to drink."

✶

'OK Merlin,' I cried in multitimbral torment, many gestalts speaking at once.... fly, hydra, centaur, king. 'You say I am under the control of the Lords of Chaos. Then where am I physically.'

'You are actually in Cahotage.'

'Which is what?'

'The reality of Chaos. As we are to Faerie so Faerie is to Cahotage.'

'And that Land is ruled by the Lords of Chaos?'

'Correct,' replied the disembodied voice which had identified itself as Merlin.

'So this is a continuation of the multiple worlds scenario... heaven, earth, faerie, cahotage. Then what?'

'Greater chaos beyond Cahotage and greater order beyond heaven I presume.'

'You presume? But you don't know?'

'We all have our limitations Jimmy Scott. Even you!'

Could I detect a slight gloating in the voice.... as if Merlin was pleased that I had some limitation. Did Merlin know that I was an archangel..... a stone, a mayfly, a saint, an elf, a dragon, a bird, a frog, an aviator, a centaur, a rock, a hard place, a soft marsh, a marshmallow, a dolly mixture, a robot, a robot, a robot.......

✶

I am a drone and I have reached the target.

The evil ones sheltering in the bunker shall die.

I shall explode........

✶

Get up Chiron, I exclaimed to myself, there is no value in lying down moping. Get up and ambush your attackers. They are advancing through the end of the gorge ..... there's the signal given by the scouts who have already passed through to the end. Now loose the trebuchet onto the scouts, reload and fire! The far end of the gorge is also closed. Now to release the trees and stones in an avalanche.

The pain....I am feeling their pain! It is crippling me.....

✶

Bear up brother. I feel your pain but I am coming to your assistance.

✶

'Wake up Joshua,' shouted Sienna, shaking her son. She and her younger son, Sam, were staring at Joshua who was writhing around in his bed groaning with pain. Eventually he opened his eyes.

'Dad was a strange creature. Like a horse and a man combined...'

'That's a centaur,' stated Sam. 'I've just been reading about them in my book of fables and myths. Some people think that the Greeks invented them after seeing people riding horses.'

'OK,' shouted Joshua, then he lay back and was more calm. 'He was a centaur. He was in terrible pain because he ambushed some soldiers who were trying to attack him.'

'It's just a dream Josh,' remonstrated Sienna.

'No, it's not Mum. To him it's real....and he thinks that he has been captured by the Lords of Chaos.... he was told that by Merlin.'

'Merlin's in one of my books,' said Sam. 'He was the wizard who.....'

'I know who Merlin is, Sam,' replied Joshua, sarcastically. 'Everybody knows who Merlin is.'

Sam sat back, rather deflated.

'Don't be nasty to your brother,' said Sienna, disapprovingly. 'He's just trying to help. You frightened both of us with your nightmares.'

'I know Mum. But somehow I also know that they are real for Dad. It's some kind of link.'

'Telepathy!' exclaimed Sam. 'I've read about that too!'

Joshua glared at his brother.

✶

The pain has subsided and I can now move but I hear soldiers moving through the forest, looking for me. I've improved my odds but I am still outnumbered. Now I will flee and lead the soldiers a merry dance through my woods. I know the trees in this wood. I know the boggy areas. I know the inhabitants of the trees. The Spartans do not.

*

The dragon has pursued me into the small wood and behind the dragon is a baying mob of peasants. It really does look as if they are hostile to me as well as to the dragon although there is a maiden being dragged along by them who looks pleased that the dragon is moving away. They have her tied up and are trying to sacrifice her by the look of things. So it's the same old story. The peasant folk are protected by the dragon as long as they sacrifice animals and now children to it. So why are they hostile to me? I could fight the dragon on their behalf?

Simply because it upsets the status quo. This is allegorical of so many situations. In the second World War there were people who were collaborating with the Nazis and were not happy when they were liberated. I suspect that the leaders of the peasants will never be sacrificed and if the danger is removed they may be blamed for putting up with the threat in the first place. If I fight and remove the dragon it is likely that I will then be martyred. If I don't fight I may be killed by the dragon or my reputation will be besmirched. Since I am not even sure that I am Saint George I'm not certain that I care about my reputation.

If my memory serves me correctly the people were only upset about the dragon and wanted help when the random casting of lots chose the King's only daughter as the sacrifice. Saint George offered to kill the dragon if the people became Christians. Then he was later martyred for being a Christian.

I'm not even convinced that this is really happening. How can I possibly know about the Second World War if I am a third century Roman soldier?

Because I am Jimmy Scott. But none of it makes sense.

Chapter 5

"This is the BBC news service. News has reached us via Wikileaks that the UK government's special envoy, James Scott, has been missing for ten days. The BBC does not usually report on security stories of this nature but on this occasion we have decided that it is in the public interest. Many viewers will remember that this is the same James Scott, known as Jimmy, who fought the apparition of the Devil at Stonehenge and battled the incarnation of a demigod at the United Nations. On both occasions he was successful and the world has much to thank him for. Our special correspondent, Jean Grossely, will be giving us more insight on this security crisis after the rest of the headlines.

There has been an earthquake in China. Estimated figures suggest that more than ten thousand people have died and that a million are homeless.

Financial news... the stock exchange showed a considerable rise with the Dow Jones Index closing at........"

'It's all over the media now, Maxwell,' reported Sienna on the phone to the chief constable. 'Have you heard anything?'

'Mingan, the werewolf king, has come back to me. He is bringing the gnome seer with him.'

'The one who was at Stonehenge in Parsifal's throne?'

'Indeed. It seems that he is the best seer they have.'

'Does the gnome have any news?'

'I'll find that out when he comes. Do you want to be here?'

'Certainly. Where are you meeting.'

'At the constabulary HQ. Can you make it by four o'clock?'

'Three hours time?'

'Yes..'

'I'll have to rearrange some appointments and I'll take Joshua out of school. I'll bring Sam too.'

'So I'll see you all at sixteen hundred hours today?'

'We'll be there.'

✳

I cannot concentrate on all these different living beings. I can only fix on a few. I can ignore the stone and the mayfly. I am neither. I can sympathise with the albatross but such a bird cannot possibly do the complex tasks that I can. The hydra is too alien, the cat is too lazy, the triceratops and bullfrog are too limited. Which, apart from brief flashes of other personalities, only really leaves Jiggles, Saint George and Chiron the centaur. Perhaps also the centaur's brother. No...he came on the scene a bit late. Just the three of them and I'm inclined to think that Chiron is the most likely. I shall, however, try to follow all three of my prime suspects.

A strange form of detective work, this is. Trying to find out which character is me when I think that I am all of them!

✳

The Spartans are not the slightest bit concerned about the noise they make as they trample through my forests. I am being followed by about fifteen men which is considerably better than the original company of well over eighty.

I have set various traps and false trails and the woodsprites are helping me in this task. I have always had good relationships with the creatures of the forest. I have respected their ways and they mine. They are law abiding, kindly folk who are jumpy in nature. Not all woodsprites are the same. Some are very small, even shorter than gnomes, perhaps an inch or two in height. Others are much larger... as much as two feet or so. Some, but not in my forest, are almost as tall as human beings and are considered as cousins of the elves.

Woodsprites do not like surprises and I have called out to them as I walk through the trees. I have warned them of the soldiers and reminded the sprites that I am their friend. I have let them know where I have dug traps and set up automatic ambushes by balancing wood and stone. They have answered my calls and have agreed to help wherever they can.

Now I must move on. The odds are still against me but I intend circling round and moving back towards my castle. If I can get there undetected I can re-enter my keep and barricade myself inside. The odds will have improved compared with initially defending myself but I will still need some assistance. I shall ask the woodsprites to send messages via the forest telegraphy and I shall send a hawk with a message to my brother and cousins.

The hawks do not like carrying messages but they will obey me when I explain the urgency of the problem.

I should have sent messages as soon as I realised that there was trouble but I did not really expect quite so many soldiers would be after me and I was distracted by treating Peggy.

Oh, my beautiful flying horse. My miscegenating lover. Everyone told me that our romance was doomed but there was no centaur as beautiful as my Pegasus.

✶

I don't see how I can really be Chiron. In love with a flying horse? I've never even been too fond of normal horses let alone flying ones. Maybe I'm wrong but it just doesn't feel like me....

✶

'We are to land at as small airstrip somewhere to the south of le Havre. A place called Lisieux according to this grid reference,' Red barked out this information having decoded the message from base.

'We'll be out of fuel when we do that,' I remarked.

'They'll refuel the plane before we take off again,' remarked Alfie, also looking at the message. 'And one of us will have to stay there when we come back.'

'Why?' I asked, amazed. One of us had to stay in enemy occupied France? That was a strange instruction.

'We have to bring back a Resistance leader who will be co-ordinating invasion plans with our boys and there is no room in the plane for a passenger unless we leave someone behind.'

'Then it had better be me,' I said immediately. 'I'm the only one who speaks fluent French.'

'It could be me,' barked Red. 'They won't suspect a dog could be an enemy agent.'

'They eat dogs in France,' I growled back at her. 'And Alfie will be needed to fly the plane back.'

'You're the pilot, Jiggles!' protested Alfie. 'And I...'

'And you are my just-as-competent co-pilot,' I interjected. 'So, no arguments. I stay and you go.'

'Wilco, governor,' agreed Alfie and Red.

'Who are you to take back to England?' I asked.

'Someone called Claude Bourdet, a leader of the French Resistance,' barked Red. 'He is needed to help Churchill but the Gestapo are after him....'

'So having escaped from the Nazis in Germany we are back in the firing line,' I remarked. 'Keeps us on our toes!'

'Out of the frying pan into the fire,' remarked Alfie.

'As long as we can keep Red out of the frying pan we shall be all right!' I joked and we all had a good laugh.

The plane droned on, cloaked from radar but visible to anyone with a pair of good binoculars. Luckily it was still dark and there were at least two hours until dawn.

✻

The dragon followed me into the copse and I led it a merry dance in and out of the trees. The wood was not so thick as to slow the flying serpent despite its enormous size. The creature had three heads which is not at all unusual for a Drak or Smok. Perhaps this could be of value. Which head was the leading one? One had to be dominant or the creature could not function.

I resolved to try to capture the beast by controlling the leading head. But first I would have to determine which one that was and there was little time ... the baying mob, once distant, had now reached the edge of the copse and were calling for me to surrender my arms.

I quickly climbed a spreading oak and waited for the monster to appear underneath. There! The head that led the creature and was the most attentive and alert was the middle one of the three. That was the usual pattern. I swung down onto the neck of the dominant dome and, before the monster could respond, I flung my cloak over its eyes and held my sword against its neck.

'OK,' cried the creature as it floundered with its "captain" blindfolded. 'You've got me now. What are you intending to do before the other two heads decide to eat you.'

'Or each other,' I added.

'There is that possibility,' conceded the dragon. 'Can we come to an arrangement?'

'We're in a Mexican stand-off situation,' I stated.

'Never heard of it,' said the worm. 'Is that somewhere near Egypt?'

'Not even close,' I answered. 'What it means is that if I kill you the mob will kill me. If I don't kill you, you'll continue to eat the peasants. But if you are busy killing me the peasants can creep up and kill you. So basically you and I are doomed.'

'Unless....'

'Unless we come to an arrangement.'

'Errr boss,' hissed the left sided head. 'Why are you chatting to Saint George? I thought he was our enemy. Shall I eat him then eat the other head?'

'Quiet, stay calm Sinister,' commanded the dominant head and then turned its blindfolded head towards me. 'So what do you suggest Georgy boy?'

'I suggest that we simply fly out of here and leave the mob behind.'

'If we do that I've given up my source of easy meat,' answered the middle head angrily.

'They won't put up with you much longer anyway,' I answered. 'Not now that you are eating their children.'

'That wasn't my idea,' claimed the worm. 'I prefer pigs but the peasants are more fond of their pork chops and their bacon butties than they are of their boys and girls. At least, the rulers are.'

'But the mothers will be very upset and I bet that they're at the back of the mob pushing the men on.'

'So we fly out and then I eat you?'

'Quicker than I slit your throat? I seem to be just that bit faster than you.'

'Which is strange as I'm usually the faster. Dragons are very fast.'

'So this has happened before? To you?'

'So legend would tell.'

'But George always wins?'

'Only in the nice books. Sometimes the saint gets eaten. I've eaten several would-be saints.... they just don't get venerated if they lose too soon.'

'The saint always gets martyred even if he beats the dragon.'

'But by that time he is famous.'

'Much good that would do me.'

'As I said before you are a very strange saint.'

'Boss, boss!'

'What is it Dexter?'

'There's a baying mob trying to set fire to our tail.'

'So there is. Time we went.'

As the gigantic, triple-headed, green dragon lifted up from the copse in a display of flying virtuosity, Saint George slipped the cloak off the dominant head so that the creature could navigate safely through the trees.

Is this me? I thought as Saint George. *It feels more like me than Chiron does.* We flew over the tree tops ....

✶

....as low as we could to avoid detection by radar. The stealth mechanism was on the blink and we had to rely on old-fashioned flying skills. Red was navigating and as we neared our destination the light of false dawn was beginning to light our way but also to pick out our position to the watching Germans.

I brought the plane down in a field about four miles from Lisieux. I had decided, following our near disaster in Berlin, that I would play this my way. I was not going straight to the airfield where the Gestapo might be waiting. I landed within easy walking distance for the Resistance leader. If he was too ill or decrepit we could carry him to the plane.

With Red leading the way we flitted through the countryside, a talking dog, a co-pilot and Jiggles, who was an ace fighter-pilot, British agent and just possibly, James Michael Scott.

✶

This bit of the forest I don't know at all well. The Spartans are still after me and I have had to make a bigger circuit than I expected. I can move faster than they can if galloping in a straight line but going in and out of the trees tires me down and the men seem to have more stamina than I do.

The evening is drawing in and the depths of the wood are very dark. I have stumbled into a few ditches and just avoided a deep river when I was spooked by something large sliding between my front and back legs. It disappeared into the deep running water and I almost followed.

There is a gloomy mist rising from marshy ground and tiredness is making me careless. I am no longer certain about the route I am taking but I can still hear the soldiers constantly marching, slashing at the undergrowth, pushing onwards towards me. So I cannot rest.

I'm a healer not an athlete, a doctor not a marathon runner.

✱

'So where are you leading us to?' asked the central head, the boss of the Drak unit.

'I have an urge, or even more than that, a compulsion to lead us North and East to the lands of the centaurs,' I replied.

'Then I obey since that is the direction I also wish to go.'

✱

Red has an unerring sense of direction and we were following close behind. The dawn had come but it was a very overcast day. The clouds were dark and I reckoned that a thunderstorm was on the way. This part of France was heavily wooded and we were threading our way though the forest in semi-gloom. I was hoping to arrive at the designated airfield unobserved so I was not unhappy about the lack of light.

There were very few people about. I saw one man I took to be a farmer but otherwise the early hour meant that the place was deserted.

Red quietly barked that we were nearing the airstrip so we slowed down and were moving as quietly as possible. We almost stumbled onto the airstrip that we should have landed at but stopped ourselves just in time.

I stood in the cover of the trees looking out at the airstrip, flanked by Alfie and Red. Nothing was moving and there was no sign of life, no welcoming committee and no immediate indication that it actually was the intended landing place.

'You're sure that this is the place?' I asked Red.

The talking dog gave me an affirmative growl.

'Then where are they?' I added.

Again the dog growled and I looked in the direction that she indicated. Hidden in bushes were several people dressed in Gestapo uniforms. I drew back from the edge of our hiding place, suddenly feeling very exposed. Alfie and Red followed my lead.

'I think we had better get back to the plane,' I whispered very quietly and we started back along the route we had arrived by.

'Do not move a muscle!' ordered a hoarse voice in quiet but menacing tones. 'The two of you are covered and if any of you move we will shoot. We will also not hesitate to kill the dog if it attacks us.'

'Take it easy Red,' I spoke quietly to my trusty companion.

The navigator was growling with the deep, guttural sound that presages an attack.

'Don't bite them old girl,' I added. 'They have us in their sights.'

'Very wise,' hissed the threatening tones. 'Now all of you walk backwards three paces.'

We did so, Red included, and my sight was abruptly cut off by a black hood swung over my head. Simultaneously my arms were pinned to the sides of my body by a lassoed rope.

'Now we shall find out what you know,' wheezed the voice. 'We shall take you away from here. Do not make a sound'

I was bundled unceremoniously onto a hard surface that I took to be the back of a cart. The sounds suggested that Alfie and Red were being treated similarly. What was going on and who were our abductors? Was this the Gestapo in action and if so why were they being so clandestine? Did they anticipate other people arriving and was our presence unexpected? And was Jiggles really me, Jimmy Scott. I must not forget the prime purpose.....

✱

...... I need to ascertain which of these creatures is really me. This is interfering with my thought processes. I've now completed the circuit and I can see my castle. Unfortunately I can also see that a considerable contingent of the Spartan soldiers has arrived there before me and are guarding the buildings. I have underestimated the number of soldiers who are after me. With my greater-than-human hearing I can detect the contingent who have been chasing me through the woods.

I am feeling exhausted. The chase has drained me and before that the emergency surgery on my beloved was very tiring and ultimately unsuccessful. But I had to try. I am almost certain that she has died... I felt a huge surge of emotion from her when she passed away. Nonetheless I must see her body before I will be satisfied. She died alone in the hidden basement of my castle.

The mirror's predictive odds are seeming more accurate now. I thought I could outsmart the Spartans but they have proved to be too clever for me and I am not sure that I can carry on. All my life I have been a teacher, a physician and a philosopher. Ajax was one of my pupils and his brother has killed my beloved. The Spartans benefitted from my medical skills and now they are hunting me down like a rat. It is all so depressing. Which way should I go?

Chapter 6

The flight on the neck of the three-headed Drak has been most exhilarating. As Saint George I have no memories of any previous flights so it is a novel experience. However, as Jimmy Smith I can remember flights on the back of Lady Aradel, the golden dragon, and the soaring sensations when I spread my wings as the archangel Michael.

Why can't I just do that now? Exert my power, swing my mighty sword and smite the enemy.

'Because you don't know who the enemy is and if you choose wrongly you will die,' answered the voice that had identified itself as Merlin.

'So if I choose correctly I will be able to use my angelic powers?' I asked.

'Of course,' replied Merlin. 'But a wrong choice will prove fatal as you will be permanently attached to the wrong personality and may even find that you are using your prodigious powers and intellect against yourself. You will be left powerless and it will prove ultimately lethal.'

'How am I doing so far?' I queried the voice.

'I've no idea,' retorted the wizard. 'That part of it is up to you. I can only advise you.'

'So do you have any further advice?'

'Don't make the net too tight, too soon. The Lords of Chaos like to use surprisingly unlikely avatars themselves so they might just do the same with you.'

'So I still could be a stone or a mayfly?'

'Don't completely reject them because they seem unlikely.'

'Great,' I replied sarcastically. 'That puts me back to square one.'

'Sorry about that.'
'Sure you are.'

*

Robot
Stone
Centaur
Fly
Tree
Hydra
Saint
Cat
Pilot
Albatross
Dinosaur
Frog
Fish
Fish?
Archer
Male
Female
Neuter
Dragon

*

Click, click, click, creeaak. I was making an extraordinarily loud noise and then listening for the returning echoes. Then to my surprise I was able to build up a picture from the echoes. Where was I? Where am I?

Panic...I'm underwater....wait. No problems.

I am a huge animal. A fish? No. A very large and very loud mammal.

I'm a sperm whale. I am Jimmy Scott the Sperm Whale. No, not Jimmy. They know me as Dick.....Moby Dick. And I am being chased.

What is this tickling inside my mouth. Sitting in a large air bubble is a creature. This is too much. In my mouth is Jonah.

I am both Moby Dick and Jonah's whale. At the same time. But Moby Dick was the whale in Herman Melville's 1851 novel and the story of Jonah is from about 750 BC.

This is very strange indeed.

And I am also Jimmy Scott.

And so is Jonah.

✶

'So you are the famous aviator, Jiggles?' queried the hoarse-voiced interrogator in an accusatory manner.

'I am happy to tell you my name, rank and number but I'm afraid that I will tell you no more, old boy,' I replied gaily. No point in letting the bloody Jerry get your spirits down.

'So do you confirm that you are Jiggles?' the voice insisted.

'Yes, of course I am,' I answered. 'Squadron Leader, James 'Jiggles' Scott of the Royal Air Force, Serial number 52950. Joined the RAF from the RFC in 1917. One extra piece of information that I am willing to give you. I am missing the end of my index finger of the right hand. It was shot off in 1918, one day before the end of the war.'

There was a scuffling sound of paper being turned and the hood was abruptly pulled off my head.

'That agrees with our records,' said the gruff voice which I could now see, to my utmost surprise, was coming from a very attractive young lady. 'Sorry about the rough handling of you and your companions but we had to be sure who you were. We've had some difficulties recently.'

'Where is Claude Bourdet, the leader of the French Resistance?' I asked.

'That was one of our problems,' she answered. 'The Gestapo caught him.'

*

'Dost thou take this woman to be your wedded wife?'

'I do,' I had replied before I could even think straight.

Do I? Who is she?

'Dost thou take this man to be you wedded husband?' The small, fat priest with a monk's tonsure was asking the beautiful girl at my side.

'I do,' she replied.

'Robin, you may now kiss Clorinda, your bride.'

I obliged immediately whilst the thought processes spun round in my mind. *Robin and Clorinda! Who are they?*

This time I could not access the memories of Robin but suddenly, and for only a brief moment, I could see through the eyes of Clorinda and hear her thoughts.

Oh, you are such a handsome man, Robin of Loxley, she was thinking this as she looked at me. *And I do love you dearly. If only you were not an outlaw we could have a honeymoon but we must flee as soon as the ceremony is over. If only you were pardoned.*

Then I was back into the Robin character. *Am I Robin Hood? But surely he was a fictional character. How can I be Robin Hood? And where are we?*

We were outside a small church standing under a yew tree. A sign near the church stated in an old English script that this was Doveridge. I then remembered that I had been there once before as Jimmy Scott and I had noted that there was some kind of poem about Robyn Hode or Robin Hood. So maybe he really did exist.

Why have I just married Clorinda and not Maid Marian? I could not understand but then my knowledge of the Robin Hood tales was not compendious. Perhaps Marian was a fictional attachment and Clorinda was his real bride?

So I'm Robin Hood and I have just got married but we now have to flee for our lives. But am I still Jimmy Scott? Have I ever been Scott?

*

'Are you still getting the dreams?' Sienna asked Joshua as she picked the two children up from school, having made some urgent phone calls permitting them to leave a few minutes early.

'Of course I am Mum or I would have told you.'

'Any change?'

'Basically the same characters although there is now something about a whale and Robin Hood. It's all very confused and chaotic.'

'Any further mention of the Lords of Chaos?'

'No, but the Merlin character is still advising Dad.'

'We are going to see the Chief Constable and the representatives from Faerie. I would like you to tell them all about the dreams.'

'Of course I will Mum. You know I will.'

'Thanks Joshua. Sam, you're very quiet.'

'I had a strange dream about Dad as well, Mum.'

'When Sam?'

'Last night. It might be because Josh has told be about his dreams.'

'But what did you dream?' asked Sienna.

Sam looked at his mother and then over to Joshua.

'I dreamt that Robin Hood was Dad and that he was getting married under a large old Yew tree.'

'That's what I was dreaming,' gasped Joshua.

'What I thought was strange was that Robin Hood wasn't marrying Maid Marian. It was somebody else,' added Samuel.

'He was marrying Clorinda not Maid Marian,' exclaimed Joshua. 'That's proof that the dreams are real.'

'Are you sure that Joshua didn't tell you about his latest dreams?' asked Sienna.

'No way,' both boys chorused together.

✻

I ran into the woods with my newly-wed, followed by the priest who was presumably Friar Tuck. We were immediately confronted by a Saracen.

'We have been attacked by shrouded men that we cannot kill with arrows,' said the dark-skinned man. 'We only just got away and shook off their pursuit. I am sure that they will return. Robin, what should we do?'

I wanted to scream out loud that I had just got married to the wrong girl and I have no idea what to do but somehow the Robin Hood, or maybe Robyn Hode, part of me provided an instant answer.

'It would be interesting to find out what sort of creature cannot be killed by arrows,' I replied to the Saracen. 'If one can trap elephants by digging a hole then mayhap we can catch an invincible man.'

Within minutes I had the merry band of outlaws digging a deep pit with very steep sides. We covered it with thin twigs and then leaves and soil.

'So who volunteers to guide the shrouded men this way?' I chuckled, knowing full well that they would all cherish the task.

Little John was the first to answer and in moments had flitted off to lead the pursuers in our direction. I was pretty certain we could catch at least one but we would have to melt into the woods away from the others. But what were they? Were they men in armour or something else?

*

'So they have caught both Claude Bourdet and Rommel?' I asked the slim, beautiful, hoarse-voiced girl. 'So who is running the Resistance operation now?'

'I am,' she replied breathlessly, reminding me of Brigitte Bardot in the film *And God Created Woman*.

'So who are you?' I enquired, mystified by the rapidly changing fortunes of Jiggles, the flying ace.

'I am Kristiana de Morgaine, usually known as Kristy,' she answered. 'But, mon dieu, this is not the time for talking. We must move away from here. The evil Gestapo are nearby waiting for you to land in your Hurricane.'

She waved her hand and the cart started to move, pulled by two large horses. At her command both Red and Alfie also had their restraints removed.

'We saw the Gestapo,' woofed Red.

'Keep your dog quiet,' hissed Kristy.

'She was just telling you that we saw the Gestapo,' I protested. 'She is Red, my talking dog and the only canine navigator in the RAF.'

'Pardon monsieur,' Kristy nodded to Red sarcastically, 'Je ne comprends pas. I do not understand canine talk. I only talk fluent French, German, English, Spanish and a little Greek.'

'Woof, woof,' said Red which I knew meant "no problems". Kristy looked mystified but I told her that Red did not mind. The cart picked up speed and we disappeared down a winding country lane flanked by poplar trees.

The morning mists were slowly beginning to clear but we could still see nothing of the countryside, just a little bit of road but mostly trees, trees and more trees.

'Can't see the wood for the trees,' barked Red.

I laughed. 'Plenty of places for you to have a sniff, then, Red.'

'Woof, woof,' replied Red and I knew that this was just a simple bark. A canine greeting for the morning as we rode along accompanied by Alfie and the beautiful resistance leader, the young and resourceful Kristy de Morgaine.

I was feeling at the end of my tether. Centaurs are strong and clever but most are unruly. My family are the exception. We have trained our intellects, invented and improved the art of medicine and spent much of our lives teaching humans natural philosophy. This has led to its own rewards. I used to live in a cave and, indeed, many were the ancients who attended my classes in that cave. However, I progressed to the castle which I can now see down in the valley below me as I stand, hidden in the tree-line at the top of the slope.

But the life of a scholar is more sedentary than that of a roisterer and berserker. I am no longer used to the chase and the fight. The castle is surrounded by a small army of men and I can hear the pursuers in the woods. I have one last resort and that is to follow the Path of the Dead......

Chapter 7

'Is Jimmy still alive?' Sienna directed the question to the Chief Constable and Peter Mingan, the werewolf.

Before anybody replied she looked round at the assembled company in the Constabulary offices and considered each of them in turn. The Chief Constable had moved the accumulation of people out of his cramped office into a shared meeting room when Sienna had presented herself with her two lads.

Peter Mingan had arrived with a tiny, bearded and ancient person who was clearly the venerable Arch Chancellor of the dwarves. On the other side Mingan was flanked by a tall man who immediately introduced himself as a simple plain soldier from the Eastern Mainland of Faerie. Peter had laughed.

'He is more than that,' declared the werewolf and then turning to the soldier said. 'Show them your ring.'

The soldier obliged, showing the company a large ruby ring set in a deep gold band.

'This is the captain who permitted Lord James, Lady Aradel and myself through Parisfal's army and swore he would be true to us.... and he has been so.'

The soldier nodded solemnly and the werewolf continued.

'He is now the general in charge of the armies of the East and they are sworn to the defence of Faerie. He is our major ally on the Eastern Mainland. He still likes to be known as the captain.'

Maxwell Devonport, the Chief Constable, introduced the man sitting next to him, a serious, portly fellow in a somber suit, as Sir Robert Goodfellow.

'You probably have already heard of Sir Robert. He was adviser to the last government on financial affairs and then trade commissioner for the European Union. He is now helping the prime minister, Darcy Macaroon, sort out the present banking crisis,' Maxwell paused and looked with a smile at the man. 'He's doing rather a good job of it, if I may say so.'

'Thank you,' replied Sir Robert, taking up the challenge. 'We can still do better. I am here on Darcy's behalf. He can't make it due to prior commitments and I agreed to come since it was I who suggested that Lord Scott took another trip to Faerie. We were trying to arrange a financial deal with the fairy kingdom for the temporary use of fairy gold.'

'Why would anyone use fairy gold?' asked Joshua, eyes wide open. 'Doesn't it fade away with the first light of day.'

'That varies,' replied Sir Robert. 'But in essence that is the case. It is, however, more substantial than many of the British Government's present financial assets, such as sub-prime mortgages, futures, overnight bonds and dodgy derivatives.'

Fairy gold was more substantial? Sienna and the boys shared amazement tinged with a degree of horror.

'But the rally on the stock market has changed that?' suggested Devonport.

Sir Robert Goodfellow had coughed.

'Yes. That is definitely the case. Luckily we had some important futures secured in the commodity markets and they have done well. Just in time I might add..... Forgive me. There is some urgent business I must attend to.'

The financial adviser to the government was busily texting on his phone and consulting his lap top computer even as he spoke.

Sienna, shook herself from reconstructing the very recent conversation and repeated the question.

'Does anyone have any evidence that Jimmy is still alive?'

*

I counted myself lucky to be still in existence, conscious and with my memory banks intact. Most of the drones had not managed to send an update back to Central Control but I had succeeded. My circuits were in a premium condition and my reaction times were faster than most. I had put all my information back to the mainframe in record time as my body exploded on the rebel's bunker.

Now here I was again out in the field in a terrestrial robot, marching through a forest....

⋆

The Path of the Dead is not to be trodden lightly. It was the one part of my estate that I avoided. Along a very old cobbled way, deep set in the land, was a dark path where the mists always collected. On each side there were standing stones that had been there since the dawn of history, older still than ancient Stonehenge or the barrows of the Orkneys. The standing stones had their own primitive magick which still crackled with arcane energy when anybody tried to pass.

I could see from where I was standing that the lane leading to the Path of the Dead was not guarded by the soldiers. Something about its very nature made people overlook its existence. If I took that path I had to realise that I might not return. Few did.

This was not the way to Hades, to Valhalla or the Elysian Fields. The path to the dead, so it was believed, had been constructed by a long departed race of beings who had disappeared from the Earth by some form of dissolution into the aether leaving behind the path as a warning for others. Perhaps it was this path that had informed Ozymandias.

"Look on my works ye Mighty and despair."

This was the route I now decided to take....

⋆

A great urge came upon me to be sick and I vomited that reluctant mariner, Jonah, out onto a beach and then, hungry again, I swam away, looking for my favourite snack .... a nice tasty giant squid...

✶

I, Jonah, reluctant prophet of the Lord, have a great desire to call myself Jimmy Scott. Or even Saint Michael. I have landed on a beach in a place I know not. Whither should I turn? The sand slopes up to a forest. The dense wood extends all along the edge of the beach. I had half expected to be regurgitated by the whale near to Nineveh but I do not recognise this land at all.

Why am I here? Do I have to preach to somebody? Which way do I go?

✶

'Merlin!'

'Just a minute. I am busy. OK. I'm with you now.'

'I'm confused more than ever. Everything is so random.'

'And you don't think that life is usually like that?'

'My life isn't.'

'Then you have a very special life.'

'Yes, Merlin, I agree. But so do all the personalities that I appear to share lives with.'

'Isn't that what you would expect?'

'Not really. If the Lords of Chaos were really spreading my gestalt, my soul, across the whole of conscious reality there should be plenty of people doing mundane things.'

'Such as?'

'Having a cup of tea, brushing their teeth, going to the loo. General living.... the laundrette, the bank, paying the taxman. Just anything.'

'But in fact....'

'But all the conscious beings I have become are doing dangerous or exciting things. Being chased, flying on a dragon, rushing through occupied France. Even the conscious rock had to roll out of the way of lava flow.'

'You are doing all the boring things as well...'

'So why can't I experience them?'

'I'm sure you could but they are indeed tedious and don't catch the attention of your gestalt. Think how many times you have tied your shoelaces up and not thought about the act at all. So you will only notice the unusual occurrences.'

'OK, that does seem sensible. But how do I break free of this?'

'You have to live the lives of the people involved until you can definitely identify which one is actually you.'

'That's basically what you said before.'

'I can only tell you the truth. That is your way forward.'

'Thank you Merlin.'

'You're welcome.'

*

'Kristy de Morgaine where are you taking us?' I wanted to know where the cart was heading as we were dragged along through occupied France.

'Jiggles, there is a secret installation put in by the Nazis which I wish to show you.'

'Why?'

'It may influence any plans that the Allies have for an invasion of France.'

'What have you heard about such an invasion?'

'Relatively little except that it is to be at Normandy Beaches early in June.'

'Shush!' I cautioned her. 'Nobody knows that! It is completely hush, hush. Top brass only.'

'Then how do you know?' She looked at me quizzically.

She had me there. I knew because I had studied history at school in my life as Jimmy Scott. Everybody knew when D-day occurred and where. You couldn't get a history GCSE without knowing that. But as Jiggles I did not know.

'I don't know,' I replied, which was only half a lie. 'But if it is true we really don't want anybody listening to hear about it.'

'It won't make any difference where or when the invasion occurs if the Nazi's secret installation becomes operative,' she remarked, dismissing my concern. 'They will wipe out the invasion in no time.'

'No need to say things like that, old girl,' protested Alfie. 'The Air Commode would not like to hear such loose talk. He'd be well and truly brassed off.'

'Your commander is not here,' replied the resistance leader. 'Nor has he seen the establishment that I am going to smuggle you into.'

What sort of place could it be?

Considering our own anachronistically advanced aeroplane I was most intrigued. Jets, rockets, robots, nuclear weapons? All of these things went through my mind.

Chapter 8

The hooded men, reputed to be invulnerable to arrows, marched quickly along chasing Little John. The tall, burly outlaw leaped across the hidden trap and ran on whilst we observed the merriment. Two of the hooded creatures fell straight down into the pit and the others skirted around the exposed trap. Little John quickly lost his pursuers and came round to find us.

'Did we catch any of them?' he asked, having not looked behind him after escaping the creatures.

'Two,' I replied. 'We needs must observe them now to see what manner of man can withstand one of our arrows.'

I led the merry men from our hiding place and looked down into the pit. The creature that had first fallen prey to us was lying immobile at the bottom. The second had landed on top of the first and it had broken its fall. This creature was up and about, whirring away on a couple of spindly mechanical legs that ended in caterpillar treads. As Jimmy Scott I immediately recognised them as robots.

'God save us,' said the friar, crossing himself. 'What manner of devil-spawned creatures are these?'

The saracen looked on, less shocked than the others.

'They are mechanical men,' he said, after observing them for a while. 'Our greatest natural philosophers and technicians make them and they learnt how to do so in the Orient. These are, however, much advanced compared with our own.'

'I have heard say of such wonders,' I remarked. 'I believe that the live one may still be dangerous.'

'Our mechanical men usually work on clockwork but occasionally an aeolipile is used,' said the dark skinned man. 'I have never seen one as freely mobile as these but I am sure that they are such as I say. Perhaps it will run out of power.'

'What's an aeolipile?' enquired Little John in the very loud whisper which was his usual way of talking when he was trying to be discreet.

'It works using steam like a kettle,' answered the saracen. 'But ours require an obvious fire to maintain the power.'

I looked at the robots. They looked to me to be an advanced form of the Japanese walking robots that were now being used for domestic purposes. These had clearly been adapted for combat and probably had small internal, thermonuclear piles for power.

'I think we have to be cautious,' I replied. 'Even if it becomes quiescent it may not be dead.'

As I said this the robot slowed its movements and then stopped completely. Its glowing red eyes dimmed and went out.

'I'll soon tell whether its dead or not,' cried Little John.

Taking his staff he leant into the deep pit and prodded the robot. The creature sprang into action and a powerful laser cut the end off the large outlaw's weapon.

'That was my best quarterstaff,' complained Little John.

'I did say to be careful,' I remarked.

'I was careful,' said the huge outlaw. 'I didn't jump into the pit, did I?'

✶

Allowing myself to be caught in this way is demeaning. These rebels are very poorly armed and subduing them should have been easy.

Wait a minute. I am also the robot.

And I am Jimmy Scott.

Scott.

Scott.

✻

If this is Nineveh I am sorely amazed. Who am I supposed to preach to? I shall have to walk into the forest. What manner of creature will I meet there?

✻

'My husband has disappeared off the face of the Earth and nobody has any idea where he is!' stated Sienna in conclusion after the werewolf, the soldier and Sir Robert had spoken.

'That seems to be about it,' agreed Maxwell Devonport.

'What are we to make of the dreams that my lads are having?' she asked in some annoyance.

'Are they both having dreams now?' asked Sir Robert, the Government adviser. 'I thought it was only one of them.'

The political adviser looked from one boy to the other, studying their faces.

'Yes,' replied Sienna. 'And they are both dreaming the same things so the dreams cannot be dismissed as simply the result of a fertile imagination.'

'Perhaps one of them is telling the other,' suggested Sir Robert.

'Ask them,' Sienna demanded. 'Ask them about the dreams!'

'I'm not sure that this is entirely relevant,' interjected the chief constable. 'I'm not sure that dream interpretation will get us very far.'

'I agree,' nodded Sir Robert, Darcy Macaroon's sidekick, in the rather pompous manner that he seemed to adopt much of the time. 'Dreams are not real and convey little or no meaning. They are just meanderings of the moonlit hours. "*I am that merry wanderer of the night.*"'

'Shakespeare's *Midsummer Night's Dream*,' countered Peter Mingan, the werewolf, correctly ascribing the quotation and surprising the gathering as he did so.

He then shook his head in disagreement with Sir Robert but it was the Arch Chancellor who spoke.

'Dreams *can* be meaningless,' stated the dwarf. 'But they should not be dismissed so lightly. In Faerie we find that dreams can illuminate many a mystery.'

'That's all very well in Faerie,' started the pompous politico. 'But I don't think we need to hear about....'

'I think we do if the lady says so!' interjected the soldier, firmly. 'Let the lads tell their tale.'

'OK' agreed Maxwell Devonport. 'It will cause no harm to listen.'

Sir Robert Goodfellow, belying his name, scowled at Devonport but Joshua spoke out.

'I was the first to have the dreams but now Sam is also having the same dreams,' he said quietly. 'In all the dreams Dad, I mean my father Jimmy Scott, is in dire trouble. But he is a different character each time.'

'In my last dream and in Joshua's he was Robin Hood,' piped up Samuel. 'And in both our dreams he got married and then had to run for it.'

'What other characters has he been?' asked Peter the werewolf.

'A centaur, a robot, pilot, stone, frog, whale, Jonah,' intoned Joshua. 'More or less anything but somehow he is always Dad.... and he is always in trouble with somebody called the Lord of Chaos, or perhaps the god of mischief.'

'Anything else?' asked the soldier, listening intently to the list.

'He's left out Merlin,' interrupted Sam. 'Merlin is telling him what to do.'

The listeners sat back as the boys finished talking about the dreams. Sienna looked from one person to another.

'So does anybody have any idea what they mean?' she asked.

'Possibly the Queen of the Dragons would be able to answer that question,' answered the Arch Chancellor.

'Lady Aradel very probably could help,' agreed the soldier. 'But she is apparently off on a mission in another space-time continuum according to her husband, the king of the dragons...'

'Who was not particularly keen to talk to us anyway,' remarked Peter. 'But we can take back this more extensive list and ask a few more folk what the dreams might mean.'

'And you say that there is no evidence that Jimmy ever arrived in Faerie?' asked Sienna.

'No, I'm afraid not,' replied Peter.

'And do you know who the Lord or Lords of Chaos might be?' Sienna inquired.

'Never heard of them. Sorry,' answered the werewolf. 'But I shall definitely take your queries back to Faerie and let you know.'

As the three representatives from the alternative reality left the room to start on their journey home Sir Robert Goodfellow was still sitting pompously on his chair and could be heard muttering loudly.....'A load of poppycock, if you ask me.'

We're not asking you, are we? thought Joshua. *And why were you really here? You didn't help at all.*

The ancient stones looked down at me with pitted surfaces on which I imagined a myriad of alien faces. The mist lay deep over the cut that led to the Path of the Dead and despite my considerable knowledge of philosophy I could not dispel a dread, a gut-moving fear, that possessed my very being as I put all four feet onto that evil lane.

I had barely taken four of five paces before a crackling magick sprang across from the stones. A weird, keening sound accompanied the static discharge and I halted, uncertain whether to continue or not. Noises from the pursuit behind me forced me onwards. It was likely that I had been seen entering the path and I was no longer so confident that the Spartans would not follow me. They were a supremely organised and dedicated armed force, determined to obey instructions whatever the outcome and they feared disobedience and disloyalty more than they feared superstitions and magic.

I broke into a canter and my hooves echoed on the ancient cobbles. Behind me I could hear soldiers also entering the path. The light from the twin moons had been cut-off from the moment I entered the track despite the sky above being visible. I noted that there were apparently no stars in the sky either.

I stumbled on, my path lit solely by luminescent moss and lichen growing on the ancient road. Then suddenly in front of me I saw a pale, shrouded figure. The figure grew in size until it was blocking my egress.

'Carlangu, nith de scarmangal,' stated the figure.

I could not understand a word and told the apparition so.

'Wait,' said the spectre. 'I'll provide a translation.'

There was a short pause and then the apparition continued. 'This path is forbidden to living creatures on the express instructions of the third prelate invoking the fifth inter-galactic convention on inter-spatial transmission.'

'I still don't understand,' I replied. 'Who are the third prelate and the fifth convention?'

'The third prelate was the officer in charge of this quadrant and the convention was a meeting of the ruling bodies of the galaxy,' replied the spectre.

'Given the length of time involved since the edict was passed what proof is there that the convention still holds?' I asked reasonably.

'How long has passed?' asked the ghostly figure.

'Several thousand years at least,' I answered. 'Surely I should be allowed to test the ruling.'

The apparition appeared to be thinking for some time and then came to a conclusion.

'You and you alone will be permitted to pass through the star-gate. The others must stay behind.'

Others? I looked behind me and saw that a large group of Spartans had crept up to either side. My only hope was to pass through the forbidden star-gate and hope that the others could not follow. I nodded agreement and jumped over a metal threshold through a veil of mist and into a shower of ionic display. Coloured light played across my body and directly illuminated my retinas. I could feel my entire body turn inside out.....

Chapter 9

Although embarrassing that primitive people, such as this Robyn Hode, should have captured me, it may work to my advantage.

I do not need to be in command of the situation when I set off my capture mechanism. I only need to be in close proximity to the intended subjects and when I have enough of them looking into this pit I will start the stasis field.....

*

'Step back from the pit,' I cried to the merry men. 'The mechanical monster is about to reverse the trap and capture us.'

Little John continued to look into the hole at the robot.

'It doesn't look very active to me,' he argued.

'Remember what it did to your quarterstaff,' I pointed out. 'It has a few more tricks yet up its sleeve, you mark my words.'

'It doesn't have sleeves,' replied Little John, doing as I said and moving back from the edge of the trap. 'Not now that it has lost its cloak and hood.'

We laughed at the idea of the mechanical monster wearing sleeves and Alan a Dale, the minstrel, plucked away at his lute. We decided to sit down, sing to Alan's music and wait to see if the mechanical man ran out of power. Alan put the saga into a ballad and regaled us with his new song.

"In Sherwood we the merry men
Set a trap to catch a soldier
But in that trap a strange thing fell
A creature made of metal solder
Iron and steel and flashing light
With eyes of glass that shine so bright

And others like are in the wood
To follow us the merry men
But capture we shall all elude
Till at last our tale shall end
   ·   *A jolly dance is what we need*
And drink delight with honey mead.
With maidens prancing we shall come
Sing fa de la and fe fi fum"

'Not bad at all, Alan,' I complimented him.

'A half decent song for a change,' grinned Little John, clapping Alan on the back and leaving a muddy patch on the scarlet costume. 'Why not sing it again.'

Alan started to oblige then over and above the sound of the lute a whirring noise could be discerned. We all ran over to the pit and stared inside. The robot had reconfigured itself and was now spinning round in ever diminishing circles. The mechanical creature started to rise up out of the pit and we stepped back in some alarm. A strange, green glow emanated from the contraption and spread to encompass all of the merry men, myself included. I found that I could not move a muscle. I could just about breathe and move my eyes but other than that was paralysed. I could tell that all of the merry men were in the same condition. The robot had somehow reversed the trap.

✶

'So what do you make of the dreams that the children of Lord James are having?' Peter Mingan asked the Dwarf Arch-Chancellor.

The three from Faerie were climbing on to a trio of horses that would be taking them on the first part of their journey. They had refused the offer of more modern transport.

'It is difficult to be certain but I am getting a distinct impression of Plato's Allegorical Cave about the dreams. I would like to consult my Queen, Lady Aradel,' replied the venerable dwarf.

'Has she returned to Faerie?' asked the Eastern soldier. 'We understood that she had left here on an important mission and could not be contacted.'

'That is true but I have sent out telepathic messages,' replied the dwarf, stroking his long white beard as he talked. 'She may return at any time.'

'Or maybe not,' added the soldier, pragmatically. 'Are there other seers we could use?'

'There are many,' answered the dwarf. 'But only a few are any use to us. If you want someone who can tell you the best road to travel or the best day to plant your crops the seers are two a penny and fairly accurate. But for this sort of thing there is really only one other, apart, of course, from the Dragon King himself and he is unlikely to deign to reply when you speak to him.'

'So who is the other seer who may be useful?' asked the soldier.

'I suspect that it is the gnome,' said Peter. 'Am I right?'

'Completely correct. The gnome who was Parsifal X's seer is our best option but the little fellow has temporarily disappeared,' explained the Arch-Chancellor.

'So we wait?' said the soldier, impatiently.

'Indeed. So we wait,' agreed the dwarf.

✳

The cart joggled along and I jiggled with it. The beautiful resistance fighter was seated next to me, to my left, and Alfie to my right. We had our legs dangling down over the end of the cart and were looking backwards, the way we had come. Red was stood further forward on the structure, looking up the road and occasionally barking with glee.

I must confess that for a moment I was taken back to more idyllic moments of my youth when I had sat in a hayloft with a girl or two. My mind was wandering and I initially did not notice that Kristiana de Morgaine had moved closer to me and her right leg was touching my left thigh.

'When this is over, Jiggles, perhaps you will have time to show me why you have such a strange nickname,' she whispered to me breathlessly, endearingly pouting as she did so.

'Er, yes, maybe,' I agreed hesitantly. 'I am a married man, you know, old bean.'

'That's never stopped you before,' barked Red but luckily Morgaine could not understand. Alfie made no comment.

'When will we reach this secret installation?' I asked, trying desperately to change the subject. Kristy was definitely fanciable but now did not seem the right time for such a dalliance. I did not even know whether I was Jiggles or James Scott so starting a romance was out of the question.

'Soon,' replied Morgaine. 'Just a couple more miles and we shall be there. Then the fun begins. It is heavily guarded but you must get inside.'

For a moment I thought she had used a double entendre but I shook my head and concentrated.

'Do you have a plan?' I asked

'A plan of the installation?' queried Kristiana.

'No. I meant a modus operandi.'

'Oui,' she replied. 'We shall create a diversion and slip in whilst the guards are busy.'

'And who will organise the diversion?' I inquired.

'Your talking dog, Red, with the help of Alfie and our cart-driver, Michel,' answered Morgaine. 'I am sure that they will be sufficient.'

The cart continued to jiggle and joggle over the old cobbled path and I braced myself by holding under the cart's edge with both hands firmly gripped on the rough metal lip. I was loathe to split up from Red and Alfie but I could see the logic in Morgaine's plan. If the installation was as important as the young resistance leader believed then it was essential that I had a good look at whatever the Nazis were up to. That way I would be able to report back to the Air Commodore and we could forestall the efforts of the evil Axis.

✶

I have left the mariner's ship to its fate and have flown hundreds of miles on currents of air that keep me soaring above the clouds. I have fed occasionally but something is pushing me onwards. I have almost crossed the ocean and I have no idea what compulsion pushes me this way but I do know that I must obey. I must obey.

✶

I landed with all four hooves on a beach of dry sand. The ocean is behind me, a forest in front and it is night. There is but one moon in the sky and the stars have a different configuration from those seen in Faerie. I have no idea where I am. I have moved in space and very probably in time also. I do not believe that this was due to usual magical spells....rather it seems to have been due to a mechanical device. As Jimmy Scott I can understand that I have been teleported but where, why and how? What next?

✶

'Joshua and Samuel!'

'Yes Mum,' they chorussed in reply.

'Have you had any dreams that you haven't told me about?'

The boys looked at each other and nodded.

'Dad as the centaur was teleported to a beach,' said Joshua. 'We both dreamt the same thing but I thought it was a daft dream so I didn't tell you.'

Sienna looked nervous and then took a piece of paper out of her handbag and passed it to Joshua. He read what his mother had written on the paper and passed it to Sam.

'Yep,' Sienna decided with a rather fixed grin. 'It's the dream that I had when I dropped off to sleep in the chair just now. So I have started to have the same dreams as you two. It just cannot be coincidence. It must mean something.'

'Did you have the feeling that Dad was trying to work out what has happened to him?' asked Sam.

'I did,' replied Sienna. 'I believe that he is lost somewhere and can't find his way home.'

✱

'Yet forty days and Nineveh will be overcome.'

I have not found a sensible opening in the forest so I have been practising my exhortation for the people of Nineveh whilst I wander up and down this beach. That sounds a bit weak.

'Nineveh, your days are numbered!'

That's a bit better.

'Repent and be saved!'

That's ok.

Hello? Something has appeared in the distance. It looks like a man on horseback. No, not quite. Is it half-man, half-horse? A centaur?

I'm Jimmy Jonah Scott and that is Jimmy Chiron Scott. We're all Jimmy Scott.

But how has he got here?

I'm confused. Jimmy Scott looking at Jimmy Scott.

My head is spinning.

I am
Holmes,
Watson,
Churchill,
Stone,
Hadrosaur,
Slug,
Robin Hood
Alfie
Red
Jiggles
Adolf Hitler
Mrs Coggins drinking tea
Freddo Bulgings
A different Mayfly

Hydra
Saint
Three-headed Drak
Einstein
Me
You
Everyone
Stop, stop, stop! My mind is spinning round and round.
Whose mind? My mind. Jimmy Scott. I am an archangel. No, that
sounds ridiculous. How can I be an angel? I am a man, a former
physicist, an electrician. I now work for the Government of the
United Kingdom.

Stone
Tree
Drak, Drak, Drak
Me
Sunshine
Sunshine?

I want out. This is too difficult.
I feel that I am going to explode.

✳

'Hello Lord James. This is Merlin. Keep up the good work. I
believe you are winning. We are getting closer to finding you and
you are getting closer to finding yourself. This is good news. Can't
stop, awfully busy.'

Chapter 10

I am Polkan, Chiron's brother, and we have arrived too late. The Spartans have left and Chiron, that great teacher and physician, is nowhere to be seen. I am privy to the secret of the hidden basement and wondered whether he may be down there. I found his miscegenated lover, Peggy, lying dead next to the famous magical mirror. I asked the mirror whether it knew where Chiron had gone and it reluctantly told me.

'Chiron knew that Peggy had died and he has taken the Path of the Dead,' the mirror grudgingly admitted. 'But I'm stuck down here in the dark and a cobweb, yes, a cobweb has formed over my top left corner. I can't believe it.'

'Will he return from the Path?' I asked

'No idea. Are you going to take me out of here and do you want to kiss me?'

If the mirror was not so valuable I would have smashed it, there and then, seven years bad luck or not. I left it in the basement and closed the door. Chiron may return and if he does he will find a gravestone next to Peggy's grave and the mirror in the basement. If he does not return maybe no-one will find the mirror. Few would miss it.

★

The cart jiggled and joggled for a couple more miles until it reached an even smaller lane. At that point it stopped and Kristiana de Morgaine beckoned for us to leap down from the cart. We then walked quietly down the small path keeping in the shadow of the overhanging trees. We were climbing a steep hill and it took some time to reach the summit. Over the ridge we were able to look down on the next valley. Nestled amongst the trees was the secret

Nazi installation. Covering several acres the site was completely surrounded by two concentric fences of razor wire and then a high wall. There was only one gate and this opened into a tunnel of curly barbed wire leading directly to a door in the wall. The wall was surrounding a camp which contained two ramps, one rocket launch site and several very modern buildings.

'I've seen the ramps and the rocket,' I said. 'Can we go home now. I need to report on this to the boss.'

'Non monsieur,' whispered Kristy de Morgaine. 'No you cannot go home. Not yet. Ce n'est pas possible.'

'Why not?' I asked, raising my eyebrows in an arch manner.

'Because the V1 and V2 planes are not the only things I wish you to see,' replied the resistance leader. 'We need to get you inside in order for you to view the most worrying development.'

'That's going to be almost impossible even if we do create a diversion,' I answered. 'The place is heavily guarded and looks to be locked.'

I stared a bit longer using my excellent miniature binoculars of pre-war German manufacture. 'Yes,' I continued. 'The guards are definitely locked out and must have to unlock the gate even to get in themselves. Or have the right password. We can't just lure them off then walk in ourselves. It won't be possible.'

Kristiana de Morgaine smiled with the slight quiver to her lips that Monroe had perfected...halfway to a laugh. She pulled up her skirt and from the stocking top of her left leg retrieved a piece of metal.

'It might just help that I have the key,' she remarked, winking at me wickedly and holding the item up for inspection.

✱

'The gnome seer has been found,' stated the dwarf Arch-Chancellor as he came into the room where the werewolf and the soldier were waiting.

'Good,' replied Peter Mingan, the werewolf. 'Now we are

getting somewhere.'

'Unfortunately not,' answered the venerable dwarf. 'He is dead.'

'How did he die?' asked the soldier, pragmatic as ever.

'We think hc was strangled. There is bruising around his neck and his face is a bright shade of purple.'

'Where was he found?' enquired the soldier.

'He was stuffed into a niche in Parsifal X's old throne,' replied the Arch Chancellor.

'You've kept that relic?' asked Mingan. 'I thought you had destroyed it when it was brought back to Faerie from Stonehenge.'

'We kept it,' replied the old dwarf, stroking his long white beard. 'We thought to make a museum warning people of the danger of hubris. The pride that cometh before a fall.'

'And instead it has become the tomb of the little seer,' said Peter the werewolf.

'That is so,' stated the old dwarf, shaking his head sadly.

'How long has he been dead?' asked the soldier, sticking to the point of his investigation.

'Some considerable time, I'm afraid,' the dwarf was still shaking his head. 'It's a nasty business and his body is very decayed.'

'But not his head?' asked the soldier, surprised.

'No, not his head. That is well preserved,' agreed the Arch Chancellor.

'So he did not successfully predict his own future,' commented Peter.

'Perhaps he did but could not avoid it,' remarked the soldier. 'And if that is so he may have left an indication of what was going to happen to him.'

'He was sitting on a disk made of vulcanized rubber,' replied the venerable dwarf. 'But we have no idea what it is.'

'The hole in the throne was where the gnome lived when X was in charge,' stated Mingan.

'That's right,' agreed the dwarf.

'So maybe the seer put the rubber disk in the hole knowing that his body would be stowed there,' concluded Mingan.

'Perhaps. But we still don't know what it signifies,' answered the aged dwarf. 'We have thaumaturgically examined its history and all we determined was that the disc had been hit by a lot of people wielding L-shaped sticks.... and that it was frequently very cold.'

'Perhaps the people in the physical world could help us with this puzzle,' suggested Peter Mingan. 'I could return and ask Chief Constable Devonport.'

'That may be helpful,' agreed the Arch Chancellor. 'Take the disk. Please let us know what you find out. This development is very disturbing. It may mean that there is a murderer loose in Faerie.'

*

"This is the BBC News Service. There is still no further news regarding the whereabouts of Jimmy Scott, the archangel. Our correspondent on superhuman phenomena, Aphrodite Jenkins, has been looking into the implications.

Thank you Donald. I am standing at the bridge on the Isle of Man where Jimmy Scott, who is reputedly also the Archangel Michael, was last seen. Ten days ago he was here on a mission to the Faerie reality and walked down this very slope which I am walking down right now. In full view of the security team manning the gateway to the Farie reality he stepped under the arch and, as many have done before, he disappeared. What was different in his case was that he did not arrive in the Faerie kingdom.

The Archangel Michael is the most powerful angel from the whole of the heavens and, as you will undoubtedly be aware, he has bested the devil in combat twice within the last few years. His disappearance will rock all three realities. What could possibly threaten such an entity as an archangel, especially when the devil is already subdued? Who will protect Earth from supernatural interference if our main

guardian angel is missing? These are all questions that need answers. I'm Aphrodite Jenkins for the BBC at the Fairy Bridge on the Isle of Man.

Thank you Aphrodite. In other news the stock market has made a surprisingly good recovery which has been sustained. We asked the Government's financial czar, Sir Robert Goodfellow, to comment on the recovery ....."

*

Robin Hood, Robin Hood, riding through the Glen... The strains of the old television theme tune rattled through my brain as the robotic trap worked its mechanical wizardry. The robot rose up out of the pit taking me with it inside the green glow. The merry men were all left behind as stationary as a carnival tableaux. *Where to now?* I wondered.

*

The sand is soft and as I gallop up and down the shore looking for an opening in the long forest I am leaving deep hoof prints. I have passed a bewildered hermit, or perhaps prophet, on the beach, muttering to himself. There is nobody else to be seen.

Wait.

Another person has arrived. A person clad all in green and carrying a bow and arrow

And now someone in a lab coat and with an unruly shock of grey-white hair.

Now another person

And another.

*

Aaah, aaah

The cry of an albatross

It's me

Jimmy Scott

Flying down onto a sandy beach.

*

'Bristol 2484597,'

'Hello Sienna. It's Maxwell here.'

'Yes, Maxwell, do you have news of Jimmy?'

'Not exactly.'

'Then how can I help?'

'They've found their best soothsayer, the gnome seer, in Faerie.'

'That's good. He'll be able to help us.'

'It's not good. The gnome is dead. Murdered.'

'Oh dear.'

'It appears that Jimmy had an appointment to meet the gnome on the day that he, Jimmy, disappeared. Do you know anything about that?'

'Not at all. I saw the gnome at Stonehenge but haven't seen or heard of him since. Why would Jimmy have arranged to see him?'

'We were hoping that you might be able to tell us that.'

'Sorry, I don't know a thing about it. Have you tried SIS or MI6, or whatever they are called? He went as one of their agents.'

'I did and I was referred to Sir Robert Goodfellow.'

'Does he advise MI6 as well as the Treasury?'

'Supposedly so. I did contact him and he was of the opinion that Lord James Michael Scott was only going to Faerie to talk to the Kingdom about access to Fairy gold. There was no scheduled meeting with the gnome.'

'Strange.'

'Indeed. And the Faerie realm would like me to visit them to investigate the murder. Apparently they have very few puzzling murders since it is usually possible to interrogate the dead subject. Something about the face of the murderer being magically etched on the dead person's retina.'

'Does that really happen? I've heard of that before now but thought that it was a myth?'

'No. It does not happen on Earth. It only happens in Faerie.'

Chapter 11

The triple headed dragon, Drak, has flown onwards through the night and clean over a continent. We are now reaching an unknown beach in the middle of the Great Southern Ocean.

I can see quite a few folk on the beach and I am sure that our presence will cause a stir. Saint George riding the dragon rather than stabbing it to death. Could only be more strange if I was "chasing the dragon" using my hubble bubble pipe. Which is something I don't normally do.

⋆

'Even with the key it is going to be difficult to get into an establishment like that,' I remarked, looking at the Nazi installation with my field glasses.

'The diversion has to be a good one, mon petit chou, or it will not work' remarked Kristiana de Morgaine.

'What did you have in mind?' asked Alfie.

'You've been riding on a cart loaded with explosives,' replied Morgaine. 'We shall plant them all around the perimeter du Nord of the installation.'

I did a quick direction check in my mind. The northern perimeter was the opposite side to the main entrance so that did seem sensible. The diversion could easily draw the majority of the guards away from the only direct means of access.

'But how will Alfie and Red get away?' I asked. 'That's presuming your intention is for the two of them to set off the explosives.'

'With the help of our horse handler, Michel, yes,' replied Morgaine. 'Alfie and Michel will set off the explosives then escape on the motorbike.'

'Motorbike?' I queried.

In reply Morgaine climbed on to the back of the cart and moved to the front where a tarpaulin was loosely draped over an irregularly shaped mass. She swiftly pulled the tarpaulin to one side revealing a pile of explosives and a small, rusty brown motorbike.

'And Red... what will she do?'

'The dog can chase after the bike,' replied Morgaine. 'Nobody will suspect a dog.'

✶

More and more creatures are appearing out of nowhere onto this beach. A black cat tried to scratch my eyes out, startled when a large stone just dropped out of the sky. Someone suspiciously like Sherlock Holmes is examining the stone right now using a magnifying glass. I shall go and speak to him in a minute.

None of this is possible in my understanding of the world. If objects can be instantly transported across space with no time in between it contravenes my rule that nothing moves faster than the speed of light. Unless, of course, they are being bent through another dimension. In which case almost anything is possible.

Hello, this old fellow scraping something on the beach looks very interesting. He has drawn something in the sand. It looks much like a section through a screw.

This surely can't be Archimedes or can it?

✶

'Sienna, sorry to bother you again, so quickly.'

'How can I help you, Maxwell?'

'I have obtained permission for you to travel to Faerie with me. I could do with your help in unravelling the mystery of the gnome's death and we could further investigate the disappearance of your husband, Jimmy.'

'I'd be delighted to come. We are not using the Manx portal, are we? That would be a little worrying.'

'No. We shall go via the fairy bridge in Skye. I've booked two seats on the flight to Inverness tonight and there will be a police car with escorts meeting us at the airport and taking us over to Skye.'

'And in Faerie?'

'Peter Mingan has agreed to meet us and take us to the site where the body was found. We will also be able to see the little mite's remains although I understand that they are badly decayed.'

'Sounds gruesome, Maxwell. Will you mind if I miss that bit out?'

'Not at all. I'd prefer to do the same but I'm sure that they will insist.'

'Will you pick me up?'

'I'll send a squad car to your house in one hour's time.'

'OK. See you soon.'

✶

'Achtung,' I found myself shouting in German and pointing to the sky. 'Himmel!'

I was trying to get the attention of other people on the beach and I was indicating a dot in the blue that was rapidly getting larger. Now it was clear to all that a three headed dragon was arriving with a knight in armour on the neck of the middle head.

My upper lip was itching and I felt it with my right hand. It had a slightly fuzzy texture. I had a small moustache. I had lank dark hair. I was Adolf Jimmy Scott.

✶

'Ok,' I acquiesced. 'Explosives to the North. That's if Red and Alfie agree.'

They nodded their assent.

'We will meet up at the field where we parked the plane after I have seen what is inside,' I told my two trusty companions. 'Let's say in four hours time.'

We all checked our watches.

'It will be dark by then,' remarked Alfie. 'So it will be a good time to fly out.'

Kristiana de Morgaine handed out some food and a canteen of water and then Red and Alfie disappeared off in the cart with Michel driving the two large horses. They had a fairly long journey in order to approach the installation quietly from the opposite side. The plan was to set off the explosives in exactly one hour's time and we had to be in position to take advantage of the diversion. The horses could pull the cart back home of their own volition whilst Michel and Alfie rode the motorbike in the opposite direction. Exactly how I was to get to the aeroplane I was not sure. If I did not arrive on time Alfie and Red were under strict instructions to fly out and leave me. It was important that they got home to Blighty with news of the V1 and V2 installations even if they had no idea about the other, more secret research.

I was inwardly rather concerned that indeed I might not get out of the Nazi encampment. It was one thing getting in but completely another getting out.

*

The police car was speeding towards Bristol International Airport. The traffic in the city centre had been dire, partly because a number of roads were closed for repairs on the mains water systems but also because of a major stoppage on the M5 southbound. Eventually the police driver decided that enough was enough and turned on all the lights and sirens.

It would be ironic if a 20th century type of traffic snarl-up prevented me from flying to Inverness and hence from investigating my husband's absence, thought Sienna. *The disappearance is very much 21st century with its overtones of the supernatural but so much of what we do is still rooted in the materialism of the 19th and 20th century.*

She sat back and tried to relax. Immediately she was dreaming about Jimmy Scott as an ace fighter pilot named Jiggles, fighting with the Resistance in occupied France.

*

'You're doing just fine, Jimmy.'

Merlin's voice came into my myriad heads reassuring me that things were getting better. I was certainly coming to terms with the situation but every time I thought I had a handle on it two new personalities would spring up. The beach was filling with living creatures that all thought they were me and meantime I was still battling away in occupied France. Which one was me or were they all me?

'Merlin?'

There was no reply.

*

The plane touched down at Inverness airport exactly on time and the Chief Constable with Sienna were whisked off immediately, before any of the rest of the passengers. Sienna thought that it was as if the Easyjet staff were worried that she and Maxwell might contaminate the airline's customers.

They were led straight through the terminal building by a police sergeant and to a large Range Rover. A uniformed driver climbed out of the driving seat of the police car and opened the offside back door of the vehicle and Maxwell climbed in. The sergeant had opened the near side door and Sienna tucked herself in and fastened her seatbelt.

'You wish to reach the fairy bridge in Skye as quickly as possible?' indicated the driver, twisting round in his seat and speaking to the Chief Constable in a broad Scottish accent.

'That's right,' agreed Maxwell. 'It's a matter of some urgency.'

'We wouldna be chauffeuring you if it weren't,' said the man adding a belated 'Sir' after a long pause.

Maxwell did not reply. In his experience it was best not to antagonise local policemen and the Scots were notorious for their dislike of Sassenach colleagues.

The car was silent as they set off then the sergeant twisted round in his seat to speak to Maxwell.

'Have you been in this part of the country, before, sir?' he inquired politely.

'Not this far north, sergeant,' answered Maxwell. 'Just to Edinburgh and Glasgow.'

'You'll find it's very different in the Highlands and Islands,' the policeman chuckled.

'We'll be taking the more northern route,' stated the driver a little gruffly as the car accelerated away from a roundabout.

The haven't asked me if I've been here before, thought Sienna. *It's almost as if I don't exist. Is that because I'm a civilian or because I'm a woman? Or both?*

*

The explosives created an enormous noise exactly on cue. Most of the guards disappeared in the direction of the sound leaving just one jack-booted thug guarding the entrance. It was the work of a moment to bash him on the back of his neck and then drag his unconscious body into the undergrowth. Kristiana was all for cutting his wrists, arguing that he was an evil man that she had previously had trouble with and deserved all he got. I disagreed and we compromised by tying him securely and gagging him tightly. It would be some time before he was found but if I managed to get away safely I resolved to leave a note detailing where the man was.

Then we tried Morgaine's key. It worked like a dream and we were into the establishment. We walked through the metal cage-work and the key also opened the door in the wall. We were now in the inner sanctum. Electric lights were blazing and the entire interior was painted white and fitted with chrome. The effect was dazzling giving me a sensation of snow blindness such that I had to squint. Through glass panels I could see a couple of clean, white-clad scientists working on a control panel to a further large structure which was centrally placed. I could still not work out what it was. Were they working on a bomb? Some kind of nuclear weapon? I had no idea.

'We need to go right in,' whispered Kristy de Morgaine.

'OK,' I agreed. 'But first we shall need to put on some of the protective gear as a disguise.'

Hanging on a couple of pegs were several of the white overalls, masks and white headgear. I selected a small one for Morgaine and a larger overall for myself. In moments we were costumed exactly like the scientists within.

I crept over to the glass door in the glass-panelled wall. The door was locked. Kristy tried her key but it did not work. I waved to the scientists working within.

One came slowly over, reluctant to leave his work.

'Wo ist dein elektronischen pass?' he asked in an accented German, perhaps the man was Austrian.

Where is my electronic pass? I translated the Hun's question in my mind.

'Es verloren,' I replied with a shrug telling him that it was lost.

'Das ist sehr leichtsinnig,' he scolded me for carelessness as he opened the door.

'Not really,' I replied in English as I chopped him on the back of his neck. 'You are the careless one to open a door to a stranger.'

The other scientist stood stock-still, speechless in amazement and Morgaine quickly bound him up and taped his mouth.

'Make a noise even as loud as a mouse and I will kill you,' she told him in fluent German.

We dragged the bound scientists into a large, white-doored cupboard and dumped them amongst racks upon racks of printed circuit boards.

More anachronism I thought to myself, remembering as Jimmy Scott that such things did not exist in 1944.

Chapter 12

'It is elementary,' I expounded, waving the magnifying glass to add expression. 'Once you have eliminated all the possible causes only the impossible remain.'

'So what is that supposed to mean?' I disagreed furiously. I was Lord Kelvin Scott. Pragmatic scientist. 'Are you trying to invoke the supernatural? Because if you are that is quite ridiculous.'

'If we don't do something about the sanitation we shall have problems whether this is natural or supernatural,' I said this in a rather demure voice as I held the lamp in my hand. I was dressed as a Victorian nurse. I was Jimmy Florence Nightingale ....

*

'Quickly,' commanded Morgaine. 'You must take a look inside the central installation.'

My attention was drawn to the Nazi secret experiment.

'Is it safe?' I asked, looking in amazement at the huge electro-magnetic coils around the structure. 'It looks a little like a torus, a magnetic bottle, for a fusion reactor.'

'No, no,' she disagreed. 'It is nothing like that. One of us must stay outside and I have been inside already so it is your turn.'

She took my arm and guided a reluctant Jiggles towards a small door in the central equipment. She grabbed the door, opened it and pushed me forcefully inside.

The interior was like a small round tubular room, approximately six foot in diameter but eight foot high. The walls were as smooth as glass. There was nothing at all in the room.

I turned, fearing some form of treachery. *Why did I need to be inside something that was completely empty?* Morgaine had closed the door and there was no handle on the inside.

✷

This isn't the way to Skye, thought Sienna as the police car took another wrong turn, leading further away from any route she had used on her frequent trips with Jimmy. She took her diary out of her pocket and scribbled a note to Maxwell. He read the message and nodded.

Sienna took the diary and placed it back in her pocket. What were these Scottish policemen doing and why?

✷

More and more entities were converging on the beach.

I landed, still in control of Drak.

'Oh toss,' said the central head of the dragon.

'What is it boss?' asked the two lateral heads.

'Down the other end of the beach, look.'

We all looked and could now see that a large lizard-like creature had appeared on the sand.

'Is it another dragon?' I asked as I watched the large creature rear up on its hind legs, huge jaws clashing.

'It's a dinosaur, can't you tell?' said Drak.

As Saint George I had no idea about dinosaurs but as Jimmy Scott I knew that the creature was an example of Tyrannosaurus Rex. One of the largest and fiercest of the carnivorous dinosaurs and much to be feared.

Oh toss, I now thought echoing the sentiments of Drak's middle head. *Toss indeed!*

✷

'I'd like you to stop the car right now,' said Maxwell Devonport, firmly. His right hand was in his jacket pocket but he was otherwise sitting in a completely normal position.

Will they obey him? wondered Sienna.

'Now why should we be doing that?' asked the driver with a bit of a sneer.

'I have reason to believe that we are going in completely the wrong direction,' replied the chief constable.

'I thought you had never been here before,' answered the Sergeant. 'And now you are telling us which way to go.'

'It is not your position to question my orders,' replied Devonport, somewhat annoyed. 'I am a higher ranking officer and you have been seconded to help us.'

'New orders came in just before we left,' said the driver clicking a switch that locked the car. 'We are taking you in for questioning.'

'New orders from whom?' asked Maxwell, irritated. 'Show them to me.'

'Orders from Whitehall and reiterated and confirmed by Holyrood,' replied the sergeant.

'Fascinating,' snarled Maxwell. 'I am countermanding them. Turn the car round and take us to Skye as originally planned.'

'Can't do that,' said the driver.

'Then I may have to shoot you,' said Maxwell, pulling his gun from his jacket pocket. 'Now do what I say or I shall get very angry.'

∗

What are these strange creatures on this yellow soil? They are food. That is what they are. I am the king. I am Jimmy Rex. I shall eat them.

∗

There was a loud whirring sound and a shimmering vibration of the walls. Was it going to explode? What was the machine doing?

'OK, Morgaine,' I said calmly. 'What is your game. Why did I have to climb inside this empty tube?'

To my surprise she answered immediately over a tannoy system and I could see her face projected onto a curved screen. 'Don't be annoyed Jiggles. I could not tell you exactly what was happening because there were other people listening.'

'Such as?' I asked in rather petulant tones. I did not like being manoeuvred into situations which were not of my doing.

'Such as Merlin,' she replied.

'Merlin!' I exclaimed. How could she possibly know about the voice in my head of Merlin, the wizard? 'What do you know about Merlin?'

'Firstly that he is not Merlin. Or at least that may be his name but he is not the ancient wizard Merlin.'

'You know that for a fact?'

'I do.'

'How do you know this and who is he?'

'I will explain more in a moment but I must tell you the second point.'

She paused and I could see that she was trying to decide how to phrase the information.

'Go on,' I demanded. 'Just tell me your second point.'

'The voice that calls itself Merlin is not your friend.'

'Oh really?' I was incredulous. Merlin was the only person who had given me hope as Jimmy Scott. He was the only one who was making sense of this farrago of nonsense, this chaos of clashing personalities, this schizophrenia of horror. 'So are you saying that you are my friend?'

'Yes, that is so.'

'And yet you have trapped me inside a vibrating tube of glass and wire.'

'That was the only way we could talk sensibly.'

'So now explain the background. What is happening. I'm a simple fighter pilot. Why am I trapped in this science fiction world.'

'Don't lose it, Jimmy,' she shouted at me. 'You are not just Jiggles, you are Jimmy Scott the Archangel Michael.'

Jimmy Scott? I was Jiggles the Ace Fighter Pilot, hero of the First World War and secret agent in the Second. Was I also Jimmy Scott? I must have had a surname but I could not remember it.

Was it Scott?

'You've got to remember that you are also Jimmy Scott,' reiterated Morgaine. 'You are our only hope.'

Jimmy, was I also Jimmy?

*

The police car pulled into the side of the road.

'I don't know whether your orders are real or false,' said Maxwell angrily. 'But my orders are definitely genuine. I don't like being kidnapped and I don't like people issuing orders over my head. So open the car door locks and let me get out.'

There was a resounding metallic clunk as the locks were released. Maxwell got out of the car, all the time keeping his gun levelled at the driver.

'Now the two of you, out of there,' he demanded to the Scottish policemen. 'I'm not going to hurt you because you may just be following orders from your superiors. But I can't afford to let you raise a hue and cry. We are on an important inter-reality mission that must not be held up.'

The two policemen reluctantly climbed out of the Range Rover. Maxwell indicated that they should move off the road into the trees. He took out two pairs of handcuffs from his pocket and locked the policemen to each other with their arms around a small tree.

'I shall let the authorities know where you are as soon as we reach the Fairy Bridge and just before we make the crossing,' announced the chief constable. 'So you may just as well sit down and make yourselves comfortable. It will be a bit of a wait.'

Sienna had climbed out of the car and now climbed back into the sergeant's front passenger seat. Maxwell positioned himself behind the wheel.

'Now we go to Skye,' he said. 'I presume that you do know the way because I really do have not a clue.'

'Certainly,' answered Sienna. 'Like the back of my hand.'

*

'The Tyrannosaurus is charging,' warned Einstein Scott, 'And that is no illusion.'

I, Robyn Jimmy Hood was standing right in its path. I was not intending to let the creature past. Many of the people behind me, men and women, were completely defenceless and Saint George, who looked equipped to help, was at the far end of the beach. This Tyrannosaurus was the worst dragon I had ever seen, more disturbing in its sheer ferocity than the three-headed monster being ridden by Saint George. At least that could be reasoned with whilst the creature running straight at me was pure savagery. It had its gaping mouth wide open and the enormous teeth were already soaked in blood.

I took two arrows from my quiver, notched them both at once and let fly at the creature. For some reason, maybe the influence of Herne the Hunter, I had never missed my target.

The arrows diverged slightly and flew straight into the monster's eyes. The creature let out a huge bellow and fell to one side in great pain.

I could feel the pain as if I had the arrows in my own eyes.

We could all feel the pain until Saint George arrived and finished the monster with one blow of his sword. That hurt badly but the pain then swiftly ebbed.

I felt generally weaker after the monster had passed away as if some of my strength had gone with it. Einstein Scott visibly staggered and Jimmy Florence Nightingale almost dropped her lamp due to the shock and the accompanying numbness. All around were people fainting with the horror of the pain.

*

'Morgaine. How is it that you are happy to talk to me whilst I am in here but not when I was outside?' I was feeling angry with her for trapping me inside this contraption.

'This machine will hide your thoughts from Merlin,' Morgaine replied.

'They're hiding my thoughts from myself,' I countered.

'Yes, that can be a problem especially when your consciousness is spread so thinly.'

'What do you know about that?' I asked.

'All I know is that you are experiencing life via multiple living souls. Is that not so?'

'Yes, it is so. Or at least it was until you turned the machine on.'

'So the machine is working. Good,' answered Morgaine.

'Look, I want out of here so you better finish what you have to say and tell me all that you know,' I demanded.

'Merlin is your enemy but I am your friend. He has you in his power and he has scattered your mind throughout a thousand or more subjects.'

'So who is this Merlin character and how do you know that he is not the real Merlin?'

The questions seemed perfectly reasonable to me and I was not going to be happy until the resistance fighter gave me some answers.

'I know he is not the real Merlin because I saw him die one and a half millennia ago. Merlin has been dead for over fifteen hundred years.'

'So you are not simply a resistance fighter. You can't be!' I interjected.

'How astute of you,' she replied sarcastically. 'No. I am not a little French girl who has decided to fight the invaders.'

'Then who are you?' I asked. 'Who am I dealing with and how do I know that you are really on my side?'

And who am I? I asked myself. *Am I Jimmy Scott or Jiggles? Does it matter who I am? Should I trust Merlin or this Kristiana de Morgaine who has trapped me in this machine?*

Chapter 13

Maxwell drove the car as fast as he safely could, directed by Sienna.

'The most obvious route is the A82 alongside Loch Ness but the more northern route is spectacular,' she announced as they headed back the way they had erroneously come.

'Which is likely to be the quickest?' asked the chief constable.

'Probably the Loch Ness route,' Sienna replied. 'The roads are better.'

'Then that is the route we shall take.'

✱

'You are Jimmy Scott, or part of him,' replied Kristiana de Morgaine. 'And I am Morgaine.'

'You told me that before,' I said with a measure of irritability. I prided myself on being unflappable but being trapped in a tubular machine inside a Nazi installation controlled by a fifteen hundred year-old girl was a predicament that was disturbing me. 'But who are you really?'

'Sorry,' she replied. 'I thought that you would have realised. I am Morgan le Fay. Arthur's half-sister.'

'King Arthur?'

'Indeed.'

I groaned. This just got worse. First Merlin and now Morgan le Fay. Of course I had heard of her. She was the sorceress who fought against Arthur. I had read stories about her when I was a child but how in the heck did she think that I would have guessed her identity?

'Forgive me if I've got this wrong but weren't you the evil sorceress who was always fighting her brother?' I asked this in as innocent a tone as I could muster. There was no point just insulting people, especially when they had you trapped. In a tube. In the heart of a Nazi installation.

*

Sienna was concerned as they drove along the edge of Loch Ness. She was worried that something strange might happen. It was nighttime now and the road was very quiet. Maxwell Devonport kept the car going at a steady eighty wherever possible but there was a feeling of foreboding in the air. The dark waters of the deep loch next to the road could hide many mysteries and Sienna worried that some ancient creature might be conjured from the depths.

At Drumnadrochit they both had a slight fright when they viewed a monster rising from the mist but it was only a plastic replica of the famous mythical creature. The rest of the trip was uneventful. Sienna felt she was reaching home territory when they passed Eilean Donan Castle and then over the bridge and onto the island.

The Cuillans loomed up out of the dark and Maxwell remarked on their ruggedness then added. 'Almost there, I imagine.'

'It's further than you'd expect,' Sienna replied. 'We're making good time but I expect it to take at least forty minutes before we get to the fairy bridge.'

Maxwell turned on the sirens to pass a slow car in Broadford but the road was pretty deserted from then on. Within thirty-five minutes they had reached the minor road between Waternish and Dunvegan which led close to the abandoned bridge. They parked the car and jumped out.

Since the collision between Faerie and Earth the fairy bridges had become very important as border crossings between the realities. There was now a row of small buildings beside the road and the site of the bridge itself was surrounded with chain-link fencing. The place was being controlled in the manner of a national boundary and passports had to be shown and crossings booked in advance.

A number of uniformed police stood at the entrance to the site. Sienna Scott and Maxwell Devonport strode up to the entrance and the chief constable asked to see the officer in charge. A sergeant came forward and the West Country policeman presented his credentials.

'We heard you were coming but expected that the Inverness police would be courteous enough to drive you here,' said the sergeant.

'Have you heard any new orders or information from Inverness?' asked Maxwell.

'No,' replied the sergeant. 'Should we have done?'

'Not at all,' answered Maxwell. 'So the crossing is booked and they are expecting us on the other side.'

'As far as we know the answer to that is yes,' replied the sergeant, eyeing Maxwell suspiciously in the way that policemen always seem to do.

'Before we cross over I need to make a quick phone call to Inverness to tell them that we have arrived,' said Maxwell.

'We've already done that and they asked us where their drivers were,' countered the sergeant.

'All the more reason for me to make the call,' answered Maxwell, taking his mobile out of his pocket and flicking onto the Inverness number.

Sienna only listened with half an ear as Maxwell had a tense conversation with his Inverness counterpart. Finally the chief constable turned to Sienna.

'They weren't too pleased that we have their car but I promised to bring it back tomorrow when we return,' he explained.

'Had they received any new orders from Government?' she asked.

'Not that they owned up to,' replied the West Country police chief. 'They're going to fetch the driver and his companion from where we left them and question them carefully.'

The sergeant in charge of the fairy bridge crossing was listening intently to the conversation.

'If you are intending leaving the car overnight you'll have to move it into the car park,' he announced. 'You can't leave it out on the road. It might get damaged.'

'Certainly,' replied Maxwell in his most urbane voice. He immediately walked back to the police car and drove it into the parking space indicated by the sergeant and then returned to Sienna and the sergeant.

'You can look after the keys until we get back,' Maxwell chuckled, lobbing them over to the Skye policeman who caught them awkwardly. 'The car is one of yours after all.'

They walked down a small flight of temporary, metal steps that had been erected on the bank leading to the stream which flowed under the fairy bridge. From the steps they then walked gingerly along a boardwalk immediately under the bridge and crossed into Faerie.

✴

On the beach there was still consternation after the death of the dinosaur.

'Ve must all vork together under my direction,' stated Adolf Jimmy Scott. 'Otherwise we shall all die, one by one.'

I agree that we must work together, I thought in myriad forms. *But I'm pretty certain that I don't want the Führer as the leader.*

'Let's keep the leadership question flexible at the moment,' I suggested as Robyn Jimmy Hood. I knew that people would listen to me as I had proven myself by bringing down the reptile monster. 'But we all agree that we should work together.'

'I believe ve haf to go into the forest,' I, the Führer, stated.

'Possibly so but we don't know the best place to do so yet,' Saint Jimmy George replied.

'Zat may be immaterial,' said the Führer. 'Speed is of the

essence. I haf been watching the sea and it is imperative that ve make for higher ground.'

We all looked out to sea and could see that the water had receded far into the distance. A whale, Moby Dick, was stranded about a mile out. We all realised together that the returning water would come as a huge tidal wave. There was going to be a tsunami and it was not long since I had witnessed one of those in Scotland. The results would be devastating.

'I'll lead the way into the forest,' cried Saint Jimmy George and Robyn Jimmy Hood simultaneously. We marched into the nearest part of the close packed thicket, slashing our way in as we went.

The trees were some of the oddest I have ever seen. Most were spindly with long whippy branches that swept against us as we walked. Every third or fourth tree was much larger and had hollow trunks with big gaping holes at the base. Out of the corner of my Robin Hood eye I was pretty certain that I could see one of these holes close up. I warned Saint Jimmy George who was leading the trek and we passed the message round. At the back of our column the message had not reached the tail-enders when a cry went up...

'Help, help. The tree has got me.'

Jimmy Florence Nightingale was caught by her left leg in one of the thick trees. As Saint Jimmy George I ran over and used my saintly sword to slash at a few whipping branches that were trying to entwine around her body.

'Tree,' I said in firm tones. 'Florence always carries a lamp with her and she will set fire to you if you do not let her go.'

A sigh went up from the wood and the pressure on my left leg lessened.

'Thank you, Saint George,' I said in a high voice to the Saint.

'You're welcome,' I replied, putting my sword back into its scabbard. I then addressed the tree. 'And, whispering tree, you can warn the rest of your wooden-top friends that they must leave us alone or we will not react kindly. We have swords, knives, flame and saw. You will let us through or you will suffer.'

There was a consternation amongst the tree branches and an impression of a breeze passing through the enchanted wood.

That's where we are, I suddenly realised. *We are in the enchanted wood.*

*

'Vat do we have here?'

I could see a Gestapo face on the screen and Morgan le Fay was struggling against the Nazi.

'So ve haf captured every person,' continued the Hun. 'Your friend Alfie was very helpful.'

'Don't be stupid,' I replied from iside the machine. 'You can't fool me with that old trick. Alfie is my most loyal friend, apart from my dog.'

'Yes, ve lost your dog but zat is not a problem,' the Gestapo agent was talking again. 'Alfie vas a double agent for the last three years.'

'Do you think I'm daft?' I countered. 'There is no reason for him to have been a double agent.'

'He is an Italian Jew,' replied the Nazi. 'His name is Alfredo and ve had his wife and children in a concentration camp. He vould do anything to help them.'

'You say you had his family in a camp,' I asked. 'Where are they now?'

'Ve killed them two years ago but of course ve did not tell your friend Alfie.'

'And Alfie?'

'His usefulness has expired so ve haf executed him,' replied the German officer, grinning into the camera.

'When I escape from here you must watch every step you take,' I said in a menacing tone. 'You don't really know who I am. I am Alfie and his family's avenging angel and I will come for you. You will never have another easy night's sleep.'

'Very dramatic Mister Jiggles, ace fighter pilot. But you are completely wrong. You are in no position to threaten us,' said the Nazi, slowly and determinedly. 'We do know exactly who you are and we know who this is.'

He shook Morgaine as he said this and then opened the door and thrust her in with me and before I could move the door was slammed shut again.

'You are James Michael Scott and she is Kristiana de Morgaine le Fay,' said the Gestapo man. 'We haf been trying to capture both of you for some considerable time and at last ve haf been successful.'

'What do you intend doing with us?' I asked this, not expecting to get a reply but believing that keeping the dialogue going might just prove useful.

'That is up to the master,' replied the Gestapo agent.

'Hitler? Heinrich Müller? Goering? Himmler?' I queried.

The Nazi laughed and spat.

'None of those. They vill lose the war but the person ve vork for vill rule the world.'

'So who is it?' I asked

'You know him as Merlin,' grinned the evil man, his face right up to the camera and appearing huge on the screen. 'And you vill never know him as anythink else!'

✳

'Sir Robert!'

'Yes Prime Minister,' Sir Robert Goodfellow replied to the insistent call from Darcy Macaroon, the British Prime Minister. He looked up from his desk at number ten Downing Street.

'Are you sure that we are doing the right thing?' asked Macaroon.

'Certainly Prime Minister,' replied Goodfellow smoothly. 'You only have to look at the opinion polls and at the financial news.'

'I can see that but it doesn't feel right to me. This fairy gold and the other matter.'

'We obtained the fairy gold at a thousand to one discount,'

sighed Goodfellow, twiddling his pen as he spoke. 'We've been over this again and again. Something had to be done to stabilise the pound. Our gold reserves had all gone and our bonds were valueless. Now our policies are working.'

'I know that but it is a very unfair reward for all the loyal work.'

'Our public servants risked working until they dropped on pay that was being rapidly devalued by inflation. No pensions, no welfare state, no votes and no Macaroon in Downing Street.'

'But we could have found another way.'

'There was no other way and we have to live with it. On the plus side the pound has regained value, inflation is down to single figures for the first time in months and is still dropping and your popularity has risen to an all time high. What's wrong with that.'

'It sits uneasily on my conscience,' groaned Macaroon.

'Politicians cannot afford the indulgence of a conscience,' replied Sir Robert with a sardonic smile, pouring some liquid as he spoke. 'Here, have a glass of wine. It is a very fine claret. It will make you feel a lot better.'

Chapter 14

Maxwell and Sienna stepped out into bright daylight. Sienna looked round at her first glimpse of Faerie. The Skye fairy bridge gateway opened adjacent to a fairy castle deep in the heart of the fairy kingdom.

The castle dominated the scene. It was made of a pale pink stone and had multiple castellations and a central green dome that reflected and refracted the sunlight with an iridescence that reminded Sienna of the body of a dragonfly.

Sienna tore her eyes away from the fairy castle and studied the rest of the surroundings. The bridge on this side of the reality gateway looked almost new, as if it had been completed for just a few months rather than hundreds of years. Running up to the castle and then down and over the fairy bridge was the yellow brick road. To one side of the road Sienna could see a woodchopper's house, easily identified by the piles of wood neatly stacked outside and the man busy chopping more wood with a very large and very sharp axe.

Sienna looked up. The sky was like a great dome, very blue with the occasional fluffy white cotton-wool cloud held in place as if on a wire. In the distance she could just make out a huge beanstalk winding up into one of the clouds. A small lad was climbing up the huge plant and about to disappear into the mist. Violets were growing profusely in brightly coloured pots alongside the yellow brick road and there was a heady scent of roses in the air.

Yes, this is the fairy kingdom, thought Sienna. *So where are the people who should be meeting us?*

*

Slam. The robot landed on the sea shore with Friar Tuck in tow.

'Not my best landing but adequate. Within two standard deviations of predicted landing so therefore just satisfactory,' I told the Friar who was quaking in my force field grasp.

'That hurt, you old tin can,' I replied, lifting my habit, a brown tunic, and rubbing my left knee which had just been jarred onto a stony part of the beach. 'You said that Robin would be here. I can't see him.'

I raised a periscope from my steel body and viewed the scene in infra-red.

'There's a heat trail running straight into the woods over there,' I indicated the direction with one of my extendible appendages.

'Maybe we should follow them,' Friar Jimmy replied.

'Hurry, hurry, hurry,' I, the albatross, cried as I flew high above the beach.

I looked round again with my general purpose camera. The sea, which had been at low tide when we arrived, was racing towards us. I computed the velocity of the approaching wave. It was slowing as it rose up the shore and was now at about forty-five miles per hour. I saw a beached whale lifted up about a mile out. It was undoubtedly a tsunami. The progress of the water would slow further as it came towards us due to wave shoaling causing compression. I calculated that we had just under ninety seconds to get to safety. I turned on my anti-gravity facility but there was no response. I would have to use my ground-based caterpillar treads.

'Seat yourself on the top of my head,' I instructed the good Friar. 'We have to move quickly.'

'Can't you just whisk me through time and space like you did before?' I asked, incredulous that the mechanical man wanted me to sit on its head.

'Do it now or drown,' I replied in a monotone and the reluctant cleric climbed onto my dome. I started to run up the beach and reached my top terrestrial speed of one hundred and twenty kilometres per hour. The fat monk was hanging on grimly and screaming with terror which I found highly amusing. We ran into the wood followed by the flying albatross and had to reduce speed due to the density of the forest. The path that had been cleared by Robin Hood and the people from the beach was already growing over. Some plants were up to six feet in height where, less than an hour before, they had been chopped down to ground level. I had to use my laser cutters to allow progress and the fat monk's screams increased hilariously when I accidentally cut off part of his dirty brown clothing. The one advantage of the forest's phenomenal growth and repair, for it was already closing up behind me, was that it would absorb much of the shock of the tidal wave. But the ground was rather flat, the gradient was less than one in a hundred, and it would be fifty/fifty odds whether we would reach safety in time.

✷

'Now listen very carefully. I shall say this only once,' Morgaine was whispering to me, Jiggles, imprisoned next to her in the tubular structure, the Nazi soldiers having disappeared temporarily. 'Time is very limited. I am Morgan le Fay, the sorcerer but I am not evil. The person who says he is Merlin is evil. I need your help to find out who or what that person is. He, she or it has split your personality and reduced your strength. You can no longer see reality correctly. You are Saint Michael the Archangel. You are the most powerful of the angels. You lead the cohorts of heaven's army and you have thrice defeated and subdued that greatest of adversaries, Satan. But at the moment you cannot access your power because.....'

'How can we do anything imprisoned, as we are, in this featureless tube?' I interrupted Morgan's flow.

'I escaped from this fake Merlin's clutches previously and we can escape again,' she replied confidently. 'He overestimates his own power and underestimates ours.'

'So how shall we escape?' I queried.

'That I don't know as yet,' replied Morgan le Fay. 'But I'm working on it.'

*

'So sorry to be late,' gasped Peter Mingan, the werewolf and ambassador to Faerie. 'We were told by British Government officials that you had postponed the meeting so we were on our way home.'

'Who exactly told you we were not coming?' asked Maxwell Devonport.

'It came from the highest level. The very highest level,' replied Peter. 'That I managed to ascertain. All the right codes were used. But I don't know the name of the person who called.'

'Who are you taking us to see?' asked Sienna.

'The Arch Chancellor,' replied Peter. 'The dwarf you met in Bristol. He is the leader of the Western alliance in the absence of Lady Aradel, the Queen of the Elves and Dragons.'

'And Lady Aradel is still absent?' asked Devonport.

'That is one of the things we need to talk about in addition to the death of the gnome seer,' answered the werewolf. 'Her continued absence is puzzling us.'

*

'Tuck!' I shouted at the friar who was perched precariously on top of the robot. 'What are you doing on that contraption. Is that really you?'

'Yo, Robin,' I replied. 'The sea is almost here!'

We all put on as much turn of speed as we could. The ocean could be heard crashing through the trees but we reached a rocky promontory and climbed up onto it just in time. Perched on the rock was a large, diamond-studded chair.

Another megalomaniac with a throne, we thought to ourselves as we peered at the chair. A hazy mist was forming into the shape of a man.

'So pleased that you made it,' came the voice of Merlin from the ghostly figure. 'Your tribulations are almost over and you will be troubled no more. Well done Jimmy Scott.'

✶

'Welcome to Faerie,' the Arch Chancellor stood up as Peter Mingan led the chief constable and Sienna Scott into a brightly lit room in the fairy castle. 'It is an honour to have such a famous policeman and equally famous wife of Lord James in our midst. Welcome.'

The ancient dwarf executed a very exaggerated bow and his long white beard scraped the floor. Sienna had to stifle a laugh and cover it with a cough. The small figure was comical despite his formal manners .... or perhaps because of them.

'This is the space we have set up as the incident room,' explained Peter as the two visitors from the normal physical realm looked around them. There were photographs of the gnome seer on the wall and next to this were rows of mirrors. The image of a hard rubber disk was pinned in several places and the offending object was displayed on a velvet cushion. The last picture was that of the dead seer crouched inside Parsifal X's old throne.

'Did you take fingerprints from the throne?' asked Maxwell Devonport.

'We did and they all belonged to the gnome. Not even a single print from X was found,' answered Peter. 'Mind you, the chair has been on display for a year, cleaned each day. It's a museum piece.'

'And were their any prints on the puck?' asked Sienna.

'On the what?' simultaneously asked the dwarf Arch Chancellor and Peter the werewolf.

'The puck,' repeated Sienna and pointed to the object on the velvet cushion. 'The ice hockey puck. You know what I'm talking about .... a game with sticks played at an ice rink.'

'Like field hockey but on ice?' asked Peter.

'That's right,' agreed Sienna.

'And that's what the object is? Like a ball but for ice?' queried the werewolf.

'Correct,' affirmed Sienna.

'No, there were no fingerprints on it,' replied Peter, looking confused.

'That leads to an obvious question. Who has played ice hockey who lives or visits Faerie?' suggested Maxwell Devonport. 'If the seer was trying to give a clue to his attacker that could be very significant.'

'Nobody in Faerie that I know of,' answered Peter. He turned to the Arch Chancellor.

'Nor me. I know nothing of the game and it is never played here. The weather is too mild for ice skating,' added the dwarf.

'Jimmy played ice hockey,' admitted Sienna. 'When he was at college.'

'You are saying that your husband was an ice hockey player?' asked Maxwell for confirmation.

'Yes,' agreed Sienna. She looked round at the staring faces. 'It's not particularly strange. He spent a sabbatical year in Seattle and, because he was good at ice skating, was invited to play. He enjoyed the game and joined an amateur team. He played a couple of times for the Bristol Pitbulls when he returned to England but his work made it difficult for him. He couldn't put in the commitment.'

'I imagine that there are other people who have visited Faerie who could have been ice hockey players,' suggested Maxwell. 'We mustn't jump to conclusions.'

'I have a list of all the visitors in the past six months,' stated the Arch Chancellor. 'There have not been all that many.'

Maxwell and Sienna looked down the list. It was not very extensive and most of the people could be eliminated because of lack of opportunity or they were obviously not sporting in nature. Finally they concluded that only Sir Robert and Darcy Macaroon, who had come over on a trade mission, were possible candidates.

'Sir Robert is far too old and far too fat to be a current player,' Peter remarked.

'He could have played when he was young, I suppose,' said Sienna, disturbed that she had pointed the finger of suspicion at her absent husband.

'Unlikely to be the thing to single him out, isn't it?' countered Maxwell. 'Surely the seer could have thought of something which more related to Sir Robert if he wanted to tell us who was going to kill him.....'

'If that was really what he was doing,' Sienna parried. 'We don't know the reason for the puck being in the throne. Maybe Parsifal X put it there or maybe the seer used it as a chair.'

'It was too big and too uncomfortable for the gnome to use as a chair and only his fingerprints were on it,' argued Peter. 'Moreover it was not there when the chair was last cleaned.'

'We did also ask the mirrors,' added the dwarf Arch Chancellor.

'The mirrors?' queried Maxwell with a quizzical look. 'You asked the mirrors?'

'Yes indeed,' affirmed the dwarf. 'We have the finest set of magical truth mirrors in the whole of Faerie and they are right here, in this castle, in this very room.'

'It was one of the reasons we set up the incident room here,' said Peter Mingan.

'And what did the mirrors have to say?' asked Maxwell Devonport, feeling that the investigation was taking a very strange turn. Magic mirrors indeed!

'They told us that the gnome put the disk there in order to tell us who killed him,' answered the werewolf.

'Why didn't you simply ask the mirrors who did the dirty deed?' asked Maxwell.

'That's what we normally do if there are problems of this nature,' beamed the dwarf Arch Chancellor. 'And the answer has always been forthcoming. So you can understand why we do not normally need your style of investigative detection.'

'And this time?' prompted the chief constable.

'This time the mirrors said that the perpetrator was obscured from them. They could not tell us,' replied the dwarf, crestfallen.

'Can I ask them?' inquired Maxwell.

'Yes, of course,' agreed the dwarf. 'They are up there on the wall right behind you.'

Chapter 15

"This is the BBC news service. The fourteenth day of Jimmy Scott's disappearance and there is still no further news of his whereabouts. The police, dragging the river downstream from the fairy bridge, are working on the theory that he may have fallen in and drowned. It was noted that there was a small earth tremor at the time he was passing under the bridge and this could have dislodged Lord Scott from the temporary planking. The river, usually very small, was in spate at the time due to heavy rains. A police spokesperson has pointed out that his body could have been washed down the heavily swollen river and into the sea, in which case it may never be found. Questions are being asked as to why the connections with Faerie are so unsafe that even someone as important as Jimmy Scott could be harmed in this way.... Questions that need answering. A special programme on Faerie, past, present and future can be viewed on Channel 1050 immediately after this broadcast.

Sport... Dwayne Rumour has been sold to Chelsea FC for a record two hundred million pounds. The player will be paid a million pounds a week plus half a million bonus for each goal he scores. As long as it is against the opposition, I expect!

Financial news. Another good day on the stock market, futures and bonds are looking good. The world economy is back on target and both the pound and the euro are doing well. The Yuan has faired less well but the Chinese Government are arguing that a correction in the value of their currency was long overdue and that this will strengthen their export drive. Emily Factworthy, our correspondent in China, will takes us through the complex thought processes involved here. Emily...

Thank you Justin. It is exactly as you say. The economy is on target and the......"

'There you are Darcy, I told you that there was nothing to worry about,' murmured Sir Robert, putting the sound to mute.

'Thank you, Rob,' replied the Prime Minister. 'You've been a great help, a great help. You are right. It is all working out well.'

Darcy Macaroon sat back and sipped another glass of the perfect claret that Sir Robert seemed to have on tap. Sir Robert, known to his friends as either Bunny or Robin, was a bit of an enigma to Darcy. Goodfellow had worked under the previous administration and had been dismissed from office on no less than three occasions due to alleged improprieties. Each time he had claimed innocence despite overwhelming evidence against him. And each time he had finally been vindicated. It had been an embarrassment to the establishment and in recompense they had given him a very well paid sinecure post in the European Commission but now he was back helping a government of a different colour. His policies, though disturbing to Darcy with his conservative and staid way of thinking, had proved successful and the economy was out of recession and well into recovery if not yet quite into a boom period.

But still Macaroon found Goodfellow disturbing. The man could be too pompous and too condescending to the other politicians including Darcy himself and this attitude might have been the reason for his previous repeated downfalls. Moreover the man was Machiavellian and you could never quite tell what he was thinking.

The business of the fairy gold grated on Darcy. Surely you couldn't build an economy on money that disappeared overnight, or could you?

It seemed that you could.

*

'Mirror,' said Maxwell Devonport self-consciously addressing one of the large wall mirrors in the fairy castle. 'Mirror, I wish to ask you a question.'

'Certainly Chief Constable Devonport,' replied the mirror in a pleasant female voice. 'How can I help you.'

'I am investigating the death of the gnome soothsayer of no known name,' said the policeman. *How do you interrogate a mirror as a witness*, he thought to himself. *This is seriously weird.*

'I know that,' replied the mirror.

'Do you know the seer's name?' asked Devonport.

'No. No-one knew his name,' replied the mirror.

'Do you know who killed him?'

'No. But I saw it happen,' said the mirror.

'So why didn't you see who killed him?' asked the policeman. 'If you saw it happen you must have seen who did it.'

'The gnome was on his own when it happened,' said the mirror.

'So how did he die?'

'He was strangled.'

'But there was nobody there. Who strangled him?'

'He strangled himself.'

'So you are saying it was suicide.'

'No. Someone made him strangle himself.'

'Someone who wasn't there?'

'Yes. That's right. Someone who wasn't there made him strangle himself.'

Maxwell Devonport went and sat down again. This needed thinking about. It was very odd indeed.

✳

'You are all wondering why you are here,' said the swirling figure on the large chair. 'So I am going to tell you. Settle down for a moment. You are safe from the wave and you all need a few minutes of rest.'

We all sat down, a large group of very disparate Jimmy Scotts, on a rocky outcrop in the middle of an enchanted forest.

'Firstly I would like to introduce myself. I am the ancient wizard Merlin.'

There was an inspiratory gasp from some of us who had not

heard Merlin's voice before. We all listened intently.

'I have managed to save you from the grasp of the evil Lords of Chaos,' said the ghostly figure. 'In order for you to be fully integrated you will need to accomplish a quest together. This will not be very difficult for a group like you with such talents but you will need to work together as a team. Finally, it will be important for you to determine which of you is actually Jimmy Scott.'

I am Jimmy Scott, we all thought and looked at one another. *How do we deal with this situation?*

∗

The Gestapo chief had been gone from the room for some considerable time.

We could see on the screen the empty laboratory and that the scientists in the cupboard had not yet been found.

Suddenly I could hear a barking noise. Red! My talking dog! The dog appeared on the screen, a big doggy grin all over her face.

'Thatta girl, Red,' I cried as the dog barked into the microphone.

'We've got to get you out of there,' barked Red. 'Tell me how to open this machine.'

'Don't do that,' cried Morgan le Fay. 'Don't open the door. It will only expose us to the evil spells of the fake Merlin. Press the green button and randomly select a destination. That will keep us safe.'

'Stop,' I cried. 'Before Red does anything I want an explanation of what is going on. What exactly is this machine? What do you mean by selecting a destination? Can this machine move? And Red …'

'Yes Jimmy,' smiled the dog, tail wagging vigorously, pleased to be able to see and hear her master.

'How the hell did you get in here?'

∗

'What can make someone strangle himself when no-one is

there?' pondered Maxwell Devonport, out loud.

'A spell,' replied three mirrors, the dwarf Arch Chancellor and Peter the werewolf, simultaneously.

'Are there spells of that nature?' asked Sienna.

'They are forbidden but the answer is yes, unfortunately so,' replied the Arch Chancellor sorrowfully. 'It requires a powerful mage to set such a spell.'

'Then Jimmy is off the hook,' Sienna riposted. 'He doesn't know a single spell and he is not a wizard or mage.'

'Maybe not,' countered the Arch Chancellor. 'But he has had the opportunity to learn and he is the possessor of extremely powerful innate magical force.'

'Possibly the most powerful supernatural being directly known to us, unless, of course, there is a God,' added Peter the werewolf.

'It would be interesting to know where the gnome obtained the ice hockey puck,' suggested Maxwell.

'Ask the mirrors,' replied the venerable dwarf.

The chief constable stood up and went over to the row of three mirrors. Addressing the reflective surfaces made him feel just a little silly but he was overcoming his prejudices. After all it was much like addressing a computer using Skype.

'Mirror, mirror on the wall,' he started to say and all three mirrors groaned.

'Boring start,' explained the one he had addressed previously in a rather cross female voice. 'I was relieved that you didn't start that way when you asked the last question. But what do you wish to ask us?'

Devonport coughed. This was not quite as easy as he had hoped.

'Are you able to tell me where the gnome seer obtained the ice hockey puck?' he asked politely, ignoring the fractious nature of the mirrors.

'Yes,' replied the mirror.

The chief constable waited but no further answer was

forthcoming.

'What is the answer?' he finally asked.

'To which question?' queried the mirror.

'I asked whether you were able to tell me where the gnome seer obtained the ice hockey puck,' explained the policeman as patiently as he could.

'And I answered yes!' said the mirror in an exasperated tone. 'Didn't you hear me?'

'Yes, I did,' replied Maxwell, silently chuckling. 'Please tell me where the gnome seer obtained the puck.'

'He was given it by Lord James Scott on one of the Lord's visits to Faerie,' replied the mirror.

'Why?' asked Maxwell.

'Because the gnome asked him for it,' replied the mirror.

Maxwell sat down again. Sienna had a sinking feeling in her stomach. Had her husband purposely disappeared because he had murdered someone using supernatural means? Certainly Jimmy had been aware of the gnome soothsayer's work for Parsifal X but he had never mentioned any angry feelings towards the diminutive fellow. Had something else happened that had made Jimmy kill the seer?

'We must not jump to conclusions,' said Maxwell. 'There is no obvious motive leading Jimmy Scott to murder the seer.'

'Maybe he was not acting under his own volition,' suggested the Arch Chancellor. 'The dreams that his sons were having did lead me to consider whether Lord James might be suffering from an Allegorical Cave spell and that could explain both an attack on the seer and the disappearance of Lord James.'

'And there is the absence of Lady Aradel,' added Peter the werewolf. 'She was due back some time ago.'

'And the near-comatose state of her husband,' said the Arch Chancellor. 'We must not forget that. When our last representative went to ask the dragon king for help the dragon was deeply asleep.'

Chapter 16

Joshua woke up in a sweat and ran through to see Samuel. They were staying at a friend's house but each had the luxury of their own bedroom. The friend had three brothers but they had all grown up and were either at college or away working so their friend rattled around in a huge Redland Victorian house with just his mother and father.

'Sam, did you have that horrible dream in which Dad had his eyes shot out with arrows?' asked Joshua.

'Yes, Josh. He was about to eat Robin Hood so I suppose Robin couldn't do anything else.'

'And now he is Jiggles the pilot...'

'Trapped in a strange machine in occupied France,' added Sam. 'Do you think there is anything we can do?'

'Not yet,' replied Joshua. 'But we might need to warn Mum if the dreams get even weirder. I know she had one or two dreams like ours but she has not been getting them all.'

'We might have to do more than just warn Mum. I've got a feeling that Dad is about to make a big mistake,' said Sam.

'I've got the same feeling. He has to make a decision and I think he is going to make the wrong choice.'

✳

'Woof, woof,' barked Red and I could immediately understand that she was telling me how she had entered the building. She had befriended a guard who was part German and part French. The guard had talked to her in French and Red had responded by rolling over on her back.

'You are a tart!' I complained.

'I know,' barked Red. 'But you wouldn't have it any other way, would you?'

I laughed.

'So he befriended you. What happened next?' asked Morgan le Fay.

'He looked at my collar and called me La Read,' woofed Red.

'La Read?' I queried. 'Not chien rouge or just Red?'

'La Read,' replied my talking dog and then spelt out the letters. 'LAREAD.'

'Why are you telling us all this?' asked Morgan, who now seemed to understand everything Red was saying. 'There is very little time and we need help.'

'But how can I help?' woofed Red. 'You told me not to open the door!'

'Finish the explanation of how you got in here,' I commanded Red. 'Ignore Morgan. I need to know all the details and I will then make a decision about what you should do.'

Morgan le Fay could hardly contain her irritation. 'There is no time for all this. Just press the buttons randomly and it will send us away.'

'Don't do that!' I countermanded her order. 'Tell me what happened first.'

'I whined and pretended I was hungry,' explained Red. 'Well, I really was hungry. He fetched me a biscuit which I scoffed down in one gulp. He then went to find me a nice juicy bone and I simply followed him inside. Simple really. The place is almost deserted. Most of the guards are still looking for Michel.'

'Is it true that they caught Alfie?' I asked.

'I'm afraid that it is,' woofed Red. 'Shot him and didn't even use a humane killer.'

'Drat!' I said. 'Double drat! I was hoping it was a lie.'

I turned to Morgan le Fay.

'Now I want to hear more of your side of the story, Morgan

le Fay. What is this machine? What does it do and how come you are here in Occupied France claiming to be one thousand and five hundred years old?'

✶

'The King of the Dragons is in a coma?' queried Sienna.

'Yes. That is true,' replied Peter Mingan, the werewolf. 'We finally plucked up courage again and sent another representative, a brave volunteer, to wake him and ask for his help. The dragon was asleep in his lair, lying on a pile of gold coins. But our man could not wake him up. The dragon did not move even when the courageous fellow picked up some gold coins and rattled them together. The dragon just continued sleeping, snoring occasionally.'

'So we have two missing people, one person in a coma and one dead gnome,' summarised Maxwell. 'That's if we classify dragons as people.'

'And archangels,' added Peter Mingan.

'Quite,' said Maxwell and turned to the Arch Chancellor. 'But please explain about the Allegorical Cave spell.'

'Certainly,' replied the venerable dwarf. 'You have read Plato?'

'A little,' answered Maxwell. 'Something about Atlantis if I remember correctly.'

'There is more to Plato than just his brief mention of Atlantis,' the Arch Chancellor tutted. 'This is to do with his teaching of philosophy.'

'Then I confess to ignorance,' replied Maxwell.

'The allegory of the cave, or it could be called a parable or analogy, is this. Imagine a group of people who have lived their lives chained in a cave. The only aspect of the outside world that they can see is the flickering of shadows on the otherwise blank wall of the cave. That is the nearest they get to seeing reality and they believe it to be all that reality possesses,' the Arch Chancellor paused and then continued. 'Do you understand the analogy.'

'I think I get the drift,' replied Maxwell. 'Presumably Plato was implying that we all see only aspects of reality and never see the full picture.'

'There is that, indeed,' agreed the venerable dwarf. 'And that freeing your mind via philosophy allows one to see more of reality. But the spell is different.'

'Ah yes. The spell,' prompted Maxwell. 'What is the Allegorical Cave Spell?'

'The spell puts people into an Allegorical Cave. The wielder of the spell can then alter the information going to the subject in such a way that they perceive only the desired aspects of reality. The flickering of the shadows. It is a very strong perception-filter spell and the subject has no idea that they are under the enchantment so they do not try to break out. If wielded with skill it can keep the most powerful adversary in subjugation. It can even be used to make the subject fight himself with his own strength since he does not know that he is doing it.'

'Rather like the bull in the bull pen?' suggested Sienna.

'Explain,' said Maxwell bluntly.

'The bull pulls on a ring which is attached to a large curved piece of wood. The wood is arranged such that it continues under the floor which the bull is standing on,' Sienna expanded the analogy. 'When the bull pulls he is trying to lift his own weight like a man trying to pull himself up by his bootlaces. He can't do it.'

'Yes,' agreed the Arch Chancellor. 'Nicely put. Bootlaces and bulls. I like it.'

'Would the Allegorical Cave spell explain everything?' asked Maxwell. 'Who is able to cast such a spell?'

'I could,' said the Arch Chancellor. 'But not very well. I've not used such a spell for several centuries. Of course Lady Aradel and the Dragon King could do it. Parsifal X could but he is far too busy in his Atlas role. Lucifer has the power but is chained in hell. Oberon and Titania could easily cast such spells, the fairies are masters of deception as are the sprites. But Oberon and Titania are still missing.'

'Lord James would have the power if he was taught how to cast the spell,' added Peter the Werewolf.

'But it is more likely that he is under such a spell?' suggested Sienna.

'That's what we think,' agreed the venerable dwarf.

✶

'The task that you must all do is to rescue a maiden from captivity,' said the shadowy figure on the throne.

We all looked on wondering who this maiden might be.

'The maiden is held by constraints physical and metaphysical. Here is a picture of her.'

The ethereal figure projected an enormous image onto a cloud in front of the throne. The image showed a beautiful, sleeping, naked girl, held in place on a bed by wrist and ankle chains. There was something about the girl that was familiar. Then we realised what it was. It was a picture of Lady Aradel.... just as she had been when I, Jimmy Scott, had first seen her change from a rat into an elf. She had, of course, been naked then, as well.

As we looked the focus shifted and drew away from the bed and out of the adjacent chained window. We were now looking at the window from a distance and it was in the top floor of a castle. A dirty grey, solid-looking castle not at all like the fairy constructions in the alternative reality. The focus now swooped down to the ground and we could see the moat around the castle and in it were alligators snapping at imaginary targets in the air above the moat.

The drawbridge was raised and positioned outside the castle wall were griffins, snakes and sabre-toothed tigers.

The overall effect was one of total impregnability.

The focus swept back up to the window and into the room. The naked girl, Lady Aradel, was still lying on the bed. She moved, woke up and looked at us.

'Help me Jimmy,' she said plaintively. 'You are the only one who can help. I'm trapped and need help. Help me Jimmy, please help me!'

A tear rolled down the left cheek of the imprisoned girl and we all shuddered with the horror of her situation.

'So your task,' said the shadowy figure. 'Is to free the lady. I shall give you clues on how to start on this mission, if you care to accept it.'

The shadowy figure on the throne paused and then continued. 'As I know you will!'

✶

'Morgan le Fay,' I addressed the resistance fighter. 'I need to know what this machine is and what it does before I can agree for Red to press the buttons.'

'This is a matter transmitter,' replied Kristiana de Morgaine la Fay.

'Matter transmitter?' as Jiggles I could only just about recall my life as Jimmy Scott. The isolation in the machine seemed to have severed some connection and I was remembering my former life as if I had read it in a book some time ago, not as if I had experienced it myself. I knew that I should be conversant with theories of quantum tunnelling and entangled pairs but could only recall the vaguest outline. Was matter transmission even possible?

'Can that actually be done?' I asked bemused.

'With the help of dark energy, yes,' replied Morgaine.

'And dark energy is what, exactly?' I enquired.

'You would probably call it magic,' replied Morgaine. 'It is what I wield and it is what the so-called Merlin used to activate this machine.'

'So who invented this contraption?' I asked.

'This is the prototype and it was invented by Nazi scientists. It would not, however, have functioned except in a very small local way involving just a few molecules if it were not for this Merlin character who channelled dark energy into the cryogenic circuits and fundamentally altered its nature.'

'So what does it do now?' I asked.

'This machine can take people from one space-time continuum and dump them into another.'

'Meaning ..?'

'It can take a person from 1920 in one reality and, par example, drop them in 2019 in another,' expounded Morgaine. 'It is an amalgamation of hard science and loose magic. It can possibly capture the quantum events of thought processes also and make them into solid reality.'

'And I needed to see it?'

'You have to stop this machine and the diabolical force behind it. This Merlin has bigger things on his mind than just capturing Jimmy Scott. He is using you for a purpose but I have not yet discerned what.'

'And Merlin can read my thoughts?'

'Not when you are in the machine ... it shields the occupants. But Merlin can read the thoughts, daydreams and nightmares of anybody by focussing the output of the machine on the subject. He can then whip them out of their reality and put them into one of his choosing.'

'But that would make the person who wielded this machine virtually omnipotent,' I protested.

'Only point by point, person by person. But allowing for those constraints, nearly omnipotent, yes,' agreed Kristy Morgan le Fay.

'So where do I come into it?' I asked. 'And how did you escape his clutches, whoever he is?'

'Mon dieu! You are a powerful archangel and Merlin wishes to use your power,' answered Morgan le Fay. 'I am a sorceress and this fake Merlin was surprised by my response when I was captured and he tried to place me under an enchantment. I had a built in defence spell, ready primed. The machine or machines aborted their program and dumped me in 1944, presumably because this is the default setting on the original machine.'

'I can see how this machine could help Hitler win the war,' I remarked.

'I'm not worried about the Second World War or about Hitler,' replied Morgan. 'I am worried that this Merlin could control the whole of the real world and beyond. So does Red hit the buttons or not?'

Chapter 17

'You are all doing very well, but it's not an easy task' Sir Rupert was talking into his mobile phone and hammering on his computer as Darcy Macaroon popped his head into Goodfellow's office at 10 Downing Street.

'Just sorting out the economy,' Sir Rupert explained as he put the cellphone down on the desk. Then he added with a chuckle. 'Saving the World just like Gordon Brown.'

The office was spacious and well laid out. It had the best view of the house out of the back into the beautiful half-acre garden and was undoubtedly the principal office in number 10. The building had around one hundred rooms but this had been Darcy's favourite and the room he used himself until Goodfellow had commandeered it.

Sir Rupert had originally been given a small office that was not much bigger than a broom cupboard but had soon complained that his increased work required more space. Macaroon had obsequiously swapped offices accepting Goodfellow's reasoning that he, Sir Rupert, was taking on much of the Prime Minister's graft work and that Darcy would not need so much space.

This was true but Macaroon wistfully considered the view. He had enjoyed sitting at the desk staring out at the flowers in the garden, hearing the birds sing and experiencing the day go by. Undoubtedly Sir Rupert's efforts had sorted out the financial crisis and Macaroon's party were riding high in the polls. Moreover it was true that Goodfellow kept himself busy, had a stream of visitors and was constantly on the phone and computer. But the chap was overreaching himself just like he had done before. Darcy considered this and was just resolving to tell Goodfellow that he would have to take one of the slightly smaller offices and relinquish some of the responsibilities he had accrued to other members of staff when the chap looked up and gave Darcy a truly beaming smile.

'It is all going swimmingly well, old bean,' said Sir Robert. 'Let's celebrate with a little Port!'

If there was one thing that beat Goodfellow's claret it was his Port. As Sir Robert poured a glass for Darcy the prime Minister tried to catch a glimpse of the label. Was that Taylor Scion? Surely that cost over two thousand pounds a bottle! The size of glass Goodfellow had just given him made that four or five hundred pounds just for one snifter!

Darcy swallowed the nectar gratefully. Every time he came in to see Sir Rupert he received a gift of some sort .... a wonderful glass of claret, a malt whisky, vintage port. The list was endless. The man was truly generous ... why, just yesterday Darcy had admired Goodfellow's fountain pen. Sir Rupert had waved his hand and told the PM to take it if he liked it. It was a Mont Blanc! Darcy searched his pockets fruitlessly. Where had the pen gone? It would be embarrassing if he had lost it so quickly.... he might even have to buy another.

The conversation about the office and the responsibilities would have to wait for another opportunity.

I've lost the desire to pursue it today, thought Macaroon. *But I must bring it up soon. I would like the office back and some of the foreign visitors should be seeing me, not just Sir Robert Goodfellow. But there's time enough tomorrow. Plenty of time.*

And, after all, the less he, Darcy Macaroon, seemed to do the better the opinion polls liked him and the higher the ratings of his party. He might even get back in for a third term and have a chance of rivalling his great mentor, Maggie, or his arch rival, Tony.

*

We had all set out on the task allotted to us by Merlin. The ghostly figure had presented us with a map which showed the path to the castle where Lady Aradel was held prisoner. The initial route was easy to follow but involved a long hike along a rocky path with occasional steep sections that made Einstein Scott pant a little but there were no true hazards. The first challenge would be crossing a gorge... a great rift in the landscape which had no bridge spanning it. We would have to decide whether to climb down sheer cliffs into the valley, cross a river in torrent and then climb up the other side or to put a temporary bridge across. Merlin had made it clear that there was no way round the obstruction by going up or down the river and gorge without making a detour of several hundred miles. In his opinion that would take far too long and the prisoner would die from starvation before we reached her.

As we walked we discussed various ways, given the shortage of materials. I quickly went through as many personalities as I could adding my knowledge gleaned as Jimmy Scott to that already possessed by the personality. I vaguely recalled having several other avatars, a second world war pilot being one of them. It was clear to me that not all had made the transition safely and that any loss weakened the whole. I did a resumé of characters and it gave me vertigo. Was I one person at all? Did Jimmy Scott still exist?

Stone
Robot
Centaur
Mayfly
Tree
Hydra
Saint
Cat
Pilot
Albatross
Dinosaur
Frog

Fish
Whale
Archer
Dragon
Nurse
Einstein
Hitler
Friar Tuck
Heinrich Gestapo Müller
Isambard Kingdom Brunel
Archimedes
Lord Kelvin
And a good few others

The pilot had not arrived, the stone was left on the beach, the whale and fish were still in the sea, the frog had not kept up with the route march and nobody had thought to carry it. The albatross was still flying along above us, the dinosaur and the mayfly were both dead. Hitler kept trying to take charge, assisted by Müller.

The most useful characters were:
Robin Hood, the archer,
Brunel, the engineer,
George, the saint,
Archimedes, the philosopher
Chiron, the centaur

Einstein was very entertaining but was old and spent all his time trying to flirt with Florence Nightingale, the nurse. Now there was another useful person.... she seemed so frail but was very clever and practical. She had sorted out the rota for cleaning and preparing meals. She had sterilised the water supplies and arranged for long drops to be dug for toilet facilities. Lord Kelvin, the scientist, had refused to believe that any of it was real. "I'm dreaming and there is no more to be said," had been what he had concluded and Kelvin had then gone off into a long sulk. Hood and George had arranged shifts for guard duty and taken the brunt of it with the centaur. There was no knowing what could happen. The tree trying to swallow Nightingale in the enchanted wood was one example and the attack by the dinosaur quite another. Any of our own party might turn rogue and attack the others. The large three-headed dragon was a worry but we had reassured ourselves that we were all friends.... the agony from the death of the dinosaur had persuaded many that pain to any individual was pain to all.

We had been here for two days and two nights having stayed on the rock overnight before setting off on the quest. After a march of more than twenty miles, in which Chiron had to carry Einstein, we reached the gorge. It reminded me of the Avon Gorge in Bristol. I knew, as Brunel, that the gorge had not been bridged in my lifetime but as Jimmy Scott I could reassure myself that it had been completed after my death, as a memorial.

Isambard Kingdom Scott stood observing the gorge for some time, accompanied by Archimedes.

'If we could get a rope across, somehow, I believe we could rig up a temporary bridge that would permit most of us to cross the chasm,' I concluded, adjusting my top hat and stroking my beard as I said it.

'Does the mechanical man have a means of getting across?' I pondered as Archimedes.

'Normally I could use my anti-gravity facility,' I replied. 'I could then ferry everybody across with no problem. Unfortunately it was damaged when we landed so I have to use my terrestrial locomotion.'

'Do you have anything else that might help us?' we asked.

'I do,' I replied. 'I have a very light, monomolecular rope. It is almost invisible but as strong as steel cable. I have been assessing the width of the gorge. It is almost exactly one thousand feet wide and five hundred feet deep. The rope is easily long enough.'

'About fifty percent wider and sixty percent deeper than the Avon Gorge,' I stroked my beard again as I replied. 'But it is not impassable.'

'I could shoot a loose arrow across the gorge,' said Robin Hood Scott. 'I could probably send an arrow twice that distance but it would have to pull the rope so whether it would reach the target I cannot tell.'

I've never missed yet but they say that there is always a first time.

*

I was still trying hard to sort out who was telling the truth and who wasn't. Why had the Gestapo leader told me that he was working for Merlin? Had he told me that to confuse me? Was Morgan le Fay telling me the truth or was le Fay my enemy?

How could I let the rest of my gestalt know that Merlin was the enemy, if indeed that was the case?

Should I agree to Red pushing the buttons?

The decision was taken out of my hands for the Gestapo chief marched into the laboratory and I saw him grab at Red's collar.

'I have your precious bitch in my grasp now, Jimmy Scott. I shall kill her if you do not do what I say,' menaced the Gestapo officer.

'Hit the buttons, Red!' I shouted.

'Come back for your mixed up La Read,' woofed Red. 'I know I'm not what I seem but I cannot say more.'

She then jumped at the panel and pressed a few random switches with her paws. The vibration of the walls increased in intensity, the tone rose to a sickening screech and then   disappeared into the ultrasonic levels. The screen went blank. Seconds later the sound returned in a decrescendo of reducing pitch, the walls stopped vibrating and a pleasant study appeared on the screen, replete with a large mahogany desk, leather chair and walls lined with full book shelves. The door opened automatically but the outside was mysteriously dark. We clambered out of the machine and groped around until we found a switch. A dim electric light revealed a tiny cupboard-sized room containing a replica of the Nazi machine. The apparatus was abutting a wall on one side and a thin pencil beam of light was seen through a hole in that wall. I affixed my eye to the hole and looked out on the study that had appeared on the screen.

'There's a study beyond this wall,' I told Morgan le Fay. 'Take a look.'

She peered through at the room.

'It is empty,' she announced. 'There must be a way out of this room. I expect the door is hidden by a magical spell.'

So saying she muttered a few words under her breath and made a complex pattern in the air with her hands. I felt a rush of air and a section of the wall flew back revealing the study. Morgan had been right. The door in the wall concealing the machine had been kept closed by some thaumaturgical enchantment and Kristiana de Morgaine le Fay's "open sesame" spell had successfully countered it. We stepped out into the study belonging to someone who could wield such spells and was presumably a wizard or magician. But where were we, what year was it and who was that wizard?

✶

'We have just received a message that the British Government wishes us to detain both of you,' reported Peter the werewolf. 'They say that you stole a police car.'

'Almost right,' growled Maxwell Devonport. 'Except that someone in power did not want us to visit you in Faerie and we managed to outwit them.'

'Someone in Government is trying to shut down the investigation into Jimmy's disappearance and the murder of the gnome soothsayer,' explained Sienna.

'We can't let them do that,' responded the Arch Chancellor. 'But nor do we want to antagonise our friendly neighbours in the real world. It could easily prove to be counterproductive.'

'I could meet them and deny that you ever arrived,' suggested Peter Mingan. 'Whilst you are taken to a different access point, a different gateway.'

'The British Government will be watching the fairy bridges in Sky and the Isle of Man,' mused Devonport. 'And it is highly likely that they have asked the US authorities to watch the gateway in the Bronx.'

'Which really just leaves the newly discovered fairy bridge in China,' concluded the dwarf. 'That was what you were thinking, wasn't it, Peter?'

'Yes indeed Arch Chancellor,' agreed the werewolf with a deep growling consent. 'The Captain of the Armies of the East could probably accompany them. He is still here on the Western Continent of Faerie. I'm sure he would enjoy another trip to the real world.'

The Arch Chancellor sat back on his little chair, put his fingers together for a moment and then spoke again.

'I'd like to go with them, I believe. There is someone I have heard of in China who is an expert on dragons. He may explain what has happened to the Dragon King,' the dwarf looked pensive. 'I would also like to meet Sienna's two sons again. I would like to question them about the dreams with nobody interrupting and trying to prevent us from talking. There are aspects of their nightmares that fascinate me and I would like to learn more. Yes, I would indeed like to learn more.'

'Are you in agreement with that idea?' Peter asked Maxwell and Sienna.

'Certainly,' Maxwell replied.

'I want to get back as soon as possible,' affirmed Sienna. 'And that sounds like the best plan.'

Chapter 18

I selected my second best arrow, notched it into the bowstring and pulled hard. The arrow flew across the chasm and smacked into the tree of my choice on the other side. So much for the scout arrow and so far, so good. Its movement through the air had given me food for thought and I was ready to send my best arrow over the gorge tied to the monomolecular rope.

Saint Jimmy George had been busy unreeling the rope and laying it out in a zig-zag fashion on the ground in front of me. I knew intuitively that I would not be able to get even this gossamer thin fibre over the yawning gap if it had to be pulled off the spool by the arrow so George was doing the right thing.

I took my arrow and used my knife to fashion a small hole near the three feathers fletched to the base of the arrow. I then carefully pulled the fibre through the hole and tied it tightly. This was easier said than done due to the amazing fineness of the cord. This might be as strong as rope but it was thinner than a spider's thread. Eventually satisfied that the knot was secure I fitted the base onto the string and took aim.

With the extra weight of the fibre and increased air resistance I had to aim considerably higher with this second arrow. I pulled back much harder than before, waited for the crosswind to die down and let fly.

Initially the arrow was exactly where I wanted it, arching up over the gorge but as the fibre stretched out, lifting off from the zig-zags on the cliff edge, the resistance started to make the shaft drop and I could tell that the trajectory was wrong.

'Come on Herne', I muttered sub-vocally. 'Don't let me down now.'

Were my worries right? Would this be my first failure?

Then, just as it looked as if the arrow would fall well short the wind picked up again and lifted the arrow and fibre back on course. Ker-thunk. I could almost hear the arrow as it thumped into the tree right next to the first arrow.

I pulled on the fibre. It stayed firm.

I tied my end to an adjacent tree.

We now had a monomolecular rope across the gorge. The only problem was that it was amazingly thin and somehow we had to use it to cross over.

✳

'Robin,' said Darcy Macaroon as he strode into the best office in Number 10. He had decided that he would tackle Robert Goodfellow on the business of the office. He was fed up with the broom cupboard and wanted the best office back.

'Ah yes, Prime Minister,' replied the political adviser, who Macaroon had recently elevated to the house of Lords and had given a place on the cabinet. 'I'm glad that you were able to come.'

Able to come! thought Darcy. *Had Robin Goodfellow asked him to come? He thought he had gone to see the man of his own volition.*

'Darcy, old fellow,' continued Goodfellow. 'I will need to take over the next office as well. I am bringing in a few extra assistants. Only a temporary measure. I really hope you don't mind.'

'But, but...' started Macaroon but Lord Robert interrupted.

'Someone sent me this,' he picked up a Fabergé egg. 'It's perfectly genuine but I'm sure that they meant you to have it. Here, take it. Oh yes.' He riffled through the top drawer of the desk and pulled out a Rolex watch. 'And this.'

'Thank you, Robin,' spluttered Macaroon. 'Are you sure?'

'Of course,' said Lord Robert. 'They were meant for you anyway. Just take them.'

I'll have to acknowledge these on the gift list, thought Macaroon. *but they're worth a small fortune.*

★

'So whose study is it?' I asked as I gingerly stepped into the room, removing my flying goggles and helmet as I did so and depositing them in the pocket of my leather jacket.

Why didn't I do that before, I idly wondered, smoothing the leather.

'Jiggles, I really have no idea,' replied Kristiana de Morgaine le Fay and for a moment I thought she was reading my mind.

'Hey!,' I cried noticing some correspondence on the desk. 'I don't normally read other people's mail but this is an emergency.'

I picked up the letters which had been carefully opened and placed in a correspondence tray. There were a dozen letters, six addressed to Sir Robert Goodfellow, five to Lord Goodfellow of Hampstead and one, a personal letter to Robin Goodfellow.

'We're in the twenty-first century and it looks like the place belongs to a Robert or Robin Goodfellow. Sir or Lord,' I told Morgan le Fay.

She started. 'Did you say Robert or Robin?' she asked alarmed.

'Both in fact,' I answered. 'But then Robin is simply the diminutive of Robert. Isn't it?'

She sat down heavily and stared at me blankly.

I continued. 'Robin is a nickname for someone called Robert.'

'I know what a diminutive is,' she replied. 'But I don't think you know who Robin Goodfellow is.'

'There must be dozens if not hundreds of people called Robin Goodfellow,' I replied. 'What makes this one so special?'

Morgan le Fay stared at me as if I was an idiot.

★

'Jiggles has arrived in London!' Samuel shouted, jumping out of bed and running through to see Joshua.

'I got that dream too,' replied the elder brother. 'We must see if we can contact him somehow.'

'Josh, he's in Sir Robert Goodfellow's study right at this moment at Sir Robert's home in Hampstead. If we could find the number we could give him a ring.'

'Jiggles wouldn't answer the phone,' replied Joshua.

'He might,' protested Samuel. 'He's very bold. He laughed right in the face of the Nazis.'

'We can't lose anything by trying, I suppose,' replied Joshua. 'We'll have to run home and find Dad's address book. He's got all the phone numbers of the politicians in his book.'

'He can't have all of them.'

'You know what I mean and stop being a drongo.'

*

Sienna and Maxwell Devonport felt very uneasy. They were both mounted on tame wyverns, small dragons that were used as transport. Sienna was sat behind the Arch Chancellor on one and Maxwell behind the Captain of the Eastern Continent was on the other. They were perched on the castellations of a turret of the fairy castle.

'I'm sorry to inconvenience you in this way,' said the Arch Chancellor before they set off. 'Unfortunately your internal combustion engines don't work properly in Faerie so long distance travel is best conducted on horseback or by wyvern.'

'Jimmy told me that wyverns were small dragons that could barely fly,' replied Sienna. 'But these are three times bigger than human beings and we are just about to take off.'

'I suspect he was quoting Lady Aradel's view of wyverns,' explained the venerable dwarf. 'The golden dragons don't have much respect for the wyverns but I can assure you that a well trained wyvern is very useful.'

He patted the side of the one that he and Sienna were sitting upon.

'We've had this one in the family for eighty-five years,' the dwarf was becoming lachrymose with nostalgia. 'She's extremely dependable and particularly friendly. Not a cross bone in her body.

Loves to be stroked.'

'Eighty-five years!' exclaimed Sienna.

'Oh yes. They're very long lived and she is barely more than a child. Just about adult, I would say.'

'So where are we going?' enquired Maxwell. 'Whereabouts is the fairy bridge that opens in China?'

'It is on the southern most tip of the Eastern Mainland,' answered the Captain. 'We will be flying over the straits between the Western and Eastern continents and then flying down the spine of the Eastern mainland.'

'How long will it take to get there?' asked Maxwell.

'About ten hours total flying time but we will stop on a couple of occasions to stretch our legs and have a break,' the captain smiled and looked over to Sienna. 'Does that suit you ma'am?'

'You're in charge,' replied Sienna. 'We're sorry to put you to all this trouble.'

'You're welcome,' replied the Captain. 'I like a little adventure now and again. Up, Jocelyn.'

The Captain's wyvern rose into the air followed by the venerable dwarf's mount and they flew off in an opposite direction to the setting sun. The flight would be mainly overnight but already the twin moons and the millions of stars were lighting the scene below sufficiently for Sienna to make out all the details. The fairy castle soon dwindled away and became a speck in the distance and the Straits of Thaumaturgy between the continents could be seen ahead.

I'm on a dragon flying over Faerie, thought Sienna. *I never imagined that the alternative reality was quite like this. When Lady Aradel took us to the USA and back the flight was almost instantaneous. This is much more exciting.*

They suddenly hit an air pocket and dropped tens of feet before the wyvern managed to break the fall.

And more frightening, Sienna concluded, gripping hard onto a rope attached to the wyvern's back.

✶

We stood staring at the void and the gossamer thin thread that extended out over it, visible only for a short distance due to its thinness.

'Now how do we cross that?' asked Jimmy Saint George.

'If we had a pulley system we could put it over the rope and pull ourselves across,' suggested Isambard Scott.

'I have no pulleys,' I robotically answered.

'We could use a stone with a hole in it, thread it on the fibre and dangle a piece of rope and a strong branch from it,' suggested Einstein Scott. 'If there was another rope tied to the branch a person on it could be pulled across from the other side.'

'Once someone has reached the other side, that is,' protested Jimmy Saint George. I just could not see how that person was going to get there.

'The first person could sit on the branch and if Robin sent another rope over the chap on the branch could pull himself all the way over using that second rope,' suggested Isambard Scott.

'There's not sufficient monomolecular fibre left,' interjected Scotty Robot. 'I have a much heavier rope but I do not believe that even Robin Hood could send that over with an arrow.'

'What we need is Chevalier Blondin, or someone like him,' I said demurely, clutching my lamp.

'Who is he, ma'am?' I asked, putting my bow back over my shoulder and adjusting my green hat.

'A very good tightrope walker,' I replied, fluttering my eyes demurely. Robin Hood was rather attractive.

'Quite the best there has ever been,' agreed Isambard Scott.

'Or if not him someone who is an action hero,' suggested Saint George. 'Someone who can walk tightropes, scale rock faces and knows no fear. I'd do it but I suffer from vertigo and my balance is shocking.'

'Yes, an action hero. That's what we need,' agreed Jimmy Florence Nightingale

Suddenly a voice came from behind us.

'At your service ma'am.'

We looked at the man, dressed exceedingly smartly in a perfectly tailored dinner jacket, immaculately pressed white shirt and a bow tie. We had not noticed him before but he must have been quietly amongst the "good few others" when I had made my mental list. The fellow spoke again in his soft but powerful voice with a hint of a Scottish accent.

'The name's Scott. James Scott.'

For some reason that I could not fathom I felt obliged to pick up the cat and stroke it before replying.

'Ah, Mister Scott. We have been expecting you.'

Chapter 19

I was standing at the beginning of the tightrope. The fibre was barely visible for more than a few yards in front of me and initially plunged quite steeply into the void. I was carrying a long rod horizontally, fashioned from a tall, ash sapling. This I needed to help my balance. I tried my shoes on the first part and almost slipped straight into the void.

'It would be better to go barefoot, Mister Scott' stated the robot.

'Why?' I asked. 'The fibre is very thin. Won't it cut into my flesh?'

'Not whilst it is dry,' replied the robot. 'It has an amplified electrostatic field and modified size differential. In dry conditions it can be walked on with no problems and your bare feet will give you a better grip.'

'And in the wet?' I queried.

'Not so good,' admitted the robot. 'There is between a sixty and eighty percent chance that it would cut your feet and it would also become very slippery.'

'So you just have to hope it doesn't rain,' said Jimmy Saint George cheerfully.

Thanks a bunch, I thought to myself. *But I could do with a vodka martini, shaken or stirred, either would be fine to steady my nerves. It's not as easy being an action hero as it appears in the book or on the screen. There is a belief that in fiction the hero always wins but that it is not true in real life. It's not actually the case in fiction either when you examine the genre. Holmes died at the Reichenbach Falls but was only resurrected by Conan Doyle due to popular demand. There have been many very varied heroes who have died from Captain Ahab to King Kong. And the death of heroes in real life is simply expected. Perhaps today would be my day? Would I die a glorious death another day or would I simply slip off a tightrope into a chasm?*

I'm getting too old for this. Just add up the years that I have been around. I should have been pensioned off years ago. I'm getting a paunch. I can only just see this blessed fibre and I'm too vain to wear my glasses. I really don't know why I volunteered for this task. For Queen and Country I suppose......

We watched Scott, James Scott, walking out onto the gossamer thin tightrope. It was amazing that the man could do it at all and he seemed so calm about it, so confident, so beautifully dressed. As he descended slightly into the gorge it appeared to us, the onlookers as if he was walking on air. Deep below we could see a river flowing through in a torrent, breaking with white spume over a series of jagged rocks and plunging onwards downstream. A fall from the height would definitely be fatal. He had the heavier rope from the robot attached to his belt but that would give no protection and there was the danger that the heavy rope could unbalance him.

None of us envied the tightrope walker. None of us at all.

✳

'Don't answer that phone,' ordered Morgan le Fay.

I was in a good mind to disobey the girl who had introduced herself to me as a resistance fighter and then had turned out to be an ancient sorceress but I stood still, the phone rang and rang.

'This is Lord Robert Goodfellow,' came a voice which startled me until I realised that it was a recording.

'See, I told you that he wouldn't answer,' a boy's voice came over the phone, the tone breaking as if the owner of the voice was in his teens and entering adolescence.

Vaguely, as if reading a script, I could just recall that it was Joshua speaking. I grabbed the phone and spoke.

'Jiggles here. Can I help you?'

'Dad?' queried the voice. 'I mean Jiggles. Is that really you?'

'Yes it is me,' I replied. 'But who did you think it was?'

'You sound just like my Dad, James Scott,' explained Joshua.

'I am James Scott,' I replied. 'I am Jimmy "Jiggles" Scott. I ..'

'You're a First World War fighter pilot who is now fighting the Nazis in the Second World War,' interjected Joshua.

'Ask him if Kristiana de Morgaine le Fay is with him,' came the higher pitched voice of Samuel.

'I heard Sam's question,' I replied before Joshua could speak. 'Yes. Morgaine le Fay is with us. How did you two know?'

'We've been dreaming about you,' replied Joshua. 'But there is more happening than just you, Jiggles. And all the people are Dad.'

'It's really peculiar,' Sam's piping voice could be heard in the background.

'Yes,' I replied. 'There is something really strange going on and we need to find out what it is. Can you tell me what led up to this?'

'Sir Robert Goodfellow sent Dad on a trade mission to Faerie and he never arrived,' replied Joshua. 'Then we started dreaming and in every dream Dad is in dangerous situations and he is lots of different people. You have one of the most important roles.'

I felt flattered to think that I was one of the important characters but I couldn't help wondering what was happening elsewhere.

'So what is going on with the others?' I queried.

'Robin Hood, Saint George, Sherlock Holmes, Florence Nightingale. There's loads of them even a stone and a robot.'

'Yes,' I said patiently. 'But what are they doing?'

Before I had stepped into the machine I had perceived an outline of what was happening to all my other multiple personalities as my consciousness shifted from one to the other but from the moment the machine started working I had become an island. I was part Jiggles and part modern-day Jimmy Scott.

The conversation with the boys was bringing back my working knowledge of Jimmy Scott the physicist, electrician and part-time archangel. I now desperately needed to know how the other characters fared and what they were doing. Yes, most definitely I needed to know what they were doing.

'They're on a quest to save Lady Aradel,' replied Joshua. 'She's tied up in a castle and they are all working together, first of all to get to her and then to free her.'

I listened in some trepidation. There was something wrong with that story but I could not fathom what it was. For some reason I knew that Red, my faithful navigator and talking dog, could have sorted it out. She had a nose for peculiarities like that. She had saved us from the Gestapo in Berlin and then again in occupied France.

'Who is sending them on the quest?' interrupted le Fay.

'Some shadowy guy called Merlin,' replied Joshua.

'Merlin!' exclaimed Kristiana de Morgaine le Fay. 'Merlin again. I tell you he is dangerous.'

'Yes, but who is he?' I asked.

'I have no idea,' replied Kristy. 'But I do know where we should be and that is down with Joshua and Samuel in Bristol and then, whenever they dream, they can tell us what is happening. We will also be able to question them further about the dreams they have had.'

'So where are you, kids?' I asked Joshua. 'We should come and meet you.'

'Yes, yes,' replied Joshua excitedly. 'Even if you are only half Dad it will be better than none.'

Half Dad? I didn't like the sound of that.

'But where?' I continued.

'We're in Bristol and at the moment we are at home in your study,' replied Josh.

'If you stay there we will be with you as quickly as possible,' I answered. 'We'll catch the steam train from Paddington and be with you in about two hours.'

'It won't be a steam train, Jiggles,' replied Joshua. 'It will be a diesel. A 125.'

'OK,' I accepted what Josh had said and knew somehow that he was right. 'I've retained the address. I'll see you very soon.'

'By the way,' said Joshua. 'You really do sound exactly like Dad.'

'But I'm only half Dad?'

'He's a difficult act to copy,' replied Joshua.

*

The wyverns flew above the mountainous central ridge of the Eastern Mainland. They were following the range south and, in the bright moonlight, Sienna could see the valleys to either side of the ridge. Isolated farms were dotted into the hillside and occasionally there was a larger village or small town.

Despite the interesting nature of the terrain the undulating motion, as the wyverns flapped their huge wings, was very soporific. Sienna found herself drifting off to sleep. She awoke with a start. What had she just been dreaming? It was something about Jiggles, the ace fighter pilot version of Jimmy. Was he on a quest? No, he was with a sorcerer and they were on their way to Bristol.... to meet the boys!

Quickly she tapped the Arch Chancellor on the shoulder. The venerable dwarf was deeply asleep, sleeping the sleep of the just. He woke up rather slowly and looked around at his surroundings.

'For a moment then I thought that Caroline, here,' he patted the wyvern. 'Was taking me on holiday with my parents. Foolish thought really, she's much too young. 'Twas a long time ago, a long time ago.'

The Arch Chancellor then realised that Sienna had woken him.

'Sorry my dear,' he mumbled to her. 'Just an old dwarf's ramblings. Nothing more. How can I help you?'

'I've just had another of the dreams,' she explained. 'And in this one Jiggles, the fighter pilot, had crossed into our reality with someone called Kristiana de Morgaine le Fay and they were on their way to meet my two lads, Joshua and Samuel.'

'Oh dear,' said the dwarf. 'That's quite disturbing. When

avatars cross realities they can cause dilemmas and in the company of Morgan le Fay, of all people.'

'So you know Morgan le Fay?' asked Sienna.

'Rather too well,' said the Arch Chancellor. 'She was King Arthur's half-sister and at one time an adversary of Arthur and his Round Table. She is also a very powerful sorceress. Some would call her a witch.'

'So she's not necessarily good news,' suggested Sienna.

'I think that may be an understatement,' replied the dwarf. 'And she has no great love for me.'

'Why is that?' asked Sienna and she imagined that she could see the venerable Arch Chancellor squirm slightly in his seat and blush.

'I must say she was rather keen on me, or so I am led to believe,' he replied quietly after a slight pause. 'And I spurned her advances.'

'But you're a dwarf!' blurted Sienna, before she could stop herself.

'I was considered quite dashing when I was younger,' retorted the Arch Chancellor, somewhat offended. 'Quite a few gigantic ladies were interested in me. She was just one of them.'

'So she's big?' asked Sienna.

'Tall. Huge, really,' replied the dwarf. 'Only slightly smaller than you.'

✶

'Thank you for agreeing that I take over the entire floor,' said Lord Robert Goodfellow to Darcy Macaroon, who stood speechless in front of him. 'You will have no reason to regret it. But for now I have to dash back up to my humble pad in Hampstead. My alarm system is going off and I received an alert on my cellphone.'

Humble! thought Macaroon. Robin Goodfellow's pad in Hampstead was anything but humble. On Bishop's Avenue, it was reputed to have fourteen bedrooms, six reception rooms, two studies, home cinema, two swimming pools and a sauna. He,

Macaroon, in comparison had a small house, which he owned, in his constituency and he could use Chequers and the flat at Number 10. Genuinely humble compared with Goodfellow. He'd heard tell that Robin had several other houses as well. Now the man was taking over the whole of 10 Downing Street. But there was not much he could really do despite being Prime Minister... he was beholden to the man for getting him out of an economic downward spiral. How could he rein him back and get him under control? Was it even possible?

Chapter 20

I have never really liked heights, I thought this as I stopped for a rest, balanced on a gossamer thin rope five hundred feet above a rocky torrent. I never told my superiors that fact. Never told M. It's a weakness I had fought all my life. Successfully really given that I had scaled buildings, jumped from helicopters, fought on cable cars, balanced on the wing of a plane, dived off dams etcetera. *Still don't like them.*

We all looked at Scott, James Scott, when he stopped in the middle, the heavier rope trailing down behind him and back up to our side. Why had he stopped? It was a relief when he set off again. Presumably he was just having a rest. He was now doing very well but the only problem on the horizon was the weather. Sherlock Jimmy Holmes, having taken off his deerstalker for a few moments, reported a slight spitting sensation on his head. We looked up at the sky and noted dark clouds forming. The weather could break at any moment and the heavens open.

That would not auger well for the ascent of the other half of the monomolecular tightrope.

⋆

Morgan le Fay convinced the ticket seller to give us two tickets for Bristol without receiving any money in return. Despite having seen the "open sesame" spell work in Robin Goodfellow's study, I had difficulty in really accepting that this slip of a girl was a powerful sorceress. The trick with the ticket vendor convinced me... that was real magic. I knew what the railway staff were like... jobsworth to a man. They would not give tickets out freely unless under very powerful enchantment.

The trip down in the train was fun. As Jimmy Scott I must

have travelled that way many times but those memories were not uppermost. Jiggles recalled rail travel as dirty, uncomfortable and reliant on coal-powered steam engines. In comparison this was clean, quiet, efficient and air-conditioned.

We reached Bristol Parkway Station about one hour and thirty minutes after starting out. Since the distance was about one hundred and twenty-five miles this did not seem particularly fast. I seemed to remember a steam train that ran at one hundred and twenty miles per hour. *Was it the Flying Scotsman?*

✱

The wyverns landed for the second rest period and a chance for their riders to stretch their legs.

'We need to discuss your latest dream,' remarked the Arch Chancellor as they sat having a cup of warm honey mead.

Having never tasted mead before, Sienna was impressed with the drink. She liked honey and that was exactly what the mead tasted like... alcoholic honey. What was there to dislike? She sipped her drink and prompted the Arch Chancellor to continue by nodding her head.

'We need to decide what to do after we have spoken to the Chinese dragon expert,' stated the venerable dwarf. 'Now you, Sienna, have had a disturbing dream in which one of the Jimmy Scott avatars has appeared in the real world with the sorcerer, Morgan le Fay.'

'And we think that the dream is really happening?' asked the Captain.

'Oh yes. There's little or no doubt about that,' replied the dwarf.

'What is more they are on their way to meet my two young lads in Bristol,' explained Sienna. 'We've no idea what will happen when they are together.'

'We should certainly try to get there as soon as possible,' suggested Maxwell Devonport. 'Do you have any ideas on that?'

'We were going to leave the wyverns in Faerie,' answered the dwarf. 'But I propose that we take them through the gateway between realities and use them as our transport in the real world. Any other method will take too much time as we arrange air flights, tickets, permits ectetera.'

'And we may all be arrested,' said the Captain, sardonically.

'I've no objections,' said the chief constable.

'I certainly don't,' added Sienna. 'I'd like to get back to my sons as soon as possible.'

✷

So far so good. It has started to rain but as yet the monomolecular fibre is still walkable with bare feet. I've only got a couple of hundred feet left so I'm eighty percent there. If the rain can just hold off from totally pouring down I might just make it. I had a bad moment a little while ago when I missed my footing. Basically, in the poor light due to the dense clouds I completely lost sight of the thread but the balancing rod and my inherent sense of balance saved the day. I have the worst bit yet to come. I shall be walking up a slope with a gradient that is steepening as I go but lady luck is on my side. She always has been, so far.

Sherlock Holmes lent his field glasses to me, Saint George.

'I don't trust everybody with my binoculars,' he told me as he did so. 'But if you can't trust your nation's patron saint, who can you trust? Elementary, really.'

I decided not to tell him that I was the patron saint of nineteen different countries and as many cities.

Through the glasses I saw the tightrope walker almost fall to his doom. He caught his balance at the last minute but it was touch and go. He is now coming to the worst bit and the weather is decidedly worse. It has been raining lightly but now it is chucking it down. Scott, James Scott, is continuing to walk but I've noticed blood dripping from his feet.

Why couldn't Drak have flown across the chasm? The three headed dragon had been walking behind me and I had quite forgotten that he should be able to fly straight across. I asked him why he hadn't volunteered. Very reluctantly he replied.

'Can't,' the middle head had answered monsyllabically.

'Why not?' I pursued the question.

'Something's preventing me from flying over the gorge,' replied Drak's leading head. 'Some spell or hex I expect.'

'And what about the albatross?' I asked. 'Surely he can fly across the chasm.'

'If you notice,' replied the insolent Drak head. 'And are not completely unobservant, the albatross has also touched down and is not flying. The spell appears to prevent any air flight whatsoever.'

✶

'Hello Prime Minister, Robin Goodfellow here,' said Lord Robert on his mobile. 'There's been a break-in at my house. Nothing taken but I will have to pursue it, I'm afraid..... No, I've not involved the police but a message was recorded on my telephone so I know where the perpetrators have gone..... I'll see you tomorrow. Toodle pip.'

✶

Damn! It really is pouring down. The thought was dominant in my head but I tried hard to ignore it. I also tried hard to ignore the pain from my feet which were both being cut into shreds by the monomolecular thread. I inched upwards towards my goal, the rope cutting into my skin and the way becoming steeper and more slippery as I went.

✶

'Peter Mingan, the werewolf, told me that in the dreams Lord James was told by Merlin that the Lords of Chaos had captured him,' queried the Arch Chancellor, as they got ready to remount the wyverns. 'Have I got that right?'

'Yes, that is the case,' agreed Sienna. 'That was in Joshua and Samuel's dreams. I haven't had exactly those dreams.'

'And that sometimes the Lords of Chaos were called the Gods of Confusion, or something similar. Is that also correct?' asked the venerable dwarf.

'I think so. Perhaps the Captain or Maxwell can remember. They were there when we were discussing the dreams,' replied Sienna.

'It is correct,' replied the Captain. 'Lords of Chaos and God of Confusion were both discussed.'

'Although we are aware that there is a world of confusion nearer to the primordial chaos,' pontificated the dwarf. 'We have never had any evidence or information which would lead us to believe that it is ruled by gods or lords. In fact no evidence that there is life there at all.'

'So where could Jimmy be?' asked Sienna.

'That is the question,' nodded the wise old dwarf. 'And where is Lady Aradel?'

✶

I've almost reached the other side of the gorge but the thin wet fibre is killing my tootsies. Luckily the soles of my feet are hardened from running with naked feet whilst recovering from my last mission or I would not be able to do this at all. Just a few more yards but becoming very steep and slippery. The rain has stopped and the sun is shining on the gossamer thread. With the water on it I have to say that it looks rather spectacular. A thin band of rainbow colours. Oh sherbet, I've slipped......

'Looks as if he has slipped and fallen,' cried Saint George, handing the binoculars back to Holmes.

I took them and focussed on the scene. Scott, James Scott, was dangling from one arm and had somehow attached himself to the rock face.

'He's hanging on with one arm but he is not moving' I announced. 'I think that he has some sort of wire from his wrist to the rock.'

'Can he get up the side of the gorge?' asked Florence Jimmy Nightingale in a concerned voice.

'I'm not at all sure,' I replied, looking closely with my field glasses. 'I think he is unconscious.'

Heinrich Gestapo Müller Scott laughed, rather unpleasantly.

'Zat must be a novel experience for him,' commented Müller Scott.

'What on earth do you mean?' demanded Florence Jimmy Nightingale primly.

'This is the perfect example of a cliff hanger,' replied Müller.

Only Hitler laughed.

We all tried to distance ourselves from the two Nazis.

Chapter 21

Good Lord what is that pain in my shoulder? Hell's bells I'm hanging from the rocks. OK. I've got it. I slipped off the tightrope and reflexly pointed my watch at the rock face as I was taught to do by HQ, bless them. I flexed my left wrist thus setting off the small charge that sent the wire from my watch out at the cliff. The barb buried itself into the rock. I then swung and smashed against the cliff knocking myself out. I've now woken up and I'm hanging from my left arm and my left shoulder feels like it is dislocated. So I've got about fifteen feet to climb up this cliff with a dislocated shoulder and aching head. No problem. I've felt worse after too long a night at the casino. I hope I haven't damaged my DJ.

✳

'Dad!' shouted Joshua and Sam when they met us at the station. 'We got Steve to drive us out here.'

Was I their Dad? I wasn't sure. Most of my memories were of Jiggles the fighter pilot and proof of the reality of that experience was the beautiful girl by my side, Kristy Morgan le Fay.

But then what sort of proof was that? She claimed to be a sorceress one and a half millennia in age. One thousand five hundred years old! None of it made sense to me but then I was just a simple fighter pilot. Or possibly an electrician acting as an agent for the government. Or somewhere a stone, an albatross, Saint George, Sherlock Holmes, Robin Hood, secret agent number double 0 ....

My head was spinning as I sat down in the car that was taking us home. To a house I could only remember as a place in a book.

Was it just that I had lost my memory and all the other experiences were imaginary? It had to be more than that. I was sure that there was more meaning to this than a simple head injury and a bit of amnesia...

*

The wyverns flew on through the night, over a small shire town where the houses were tiny and had round doors, over a forest of trees that chorussed greetings to us as the light of the false dawn showed our presence above them. Finally the party of Sienna, Maxwell, the Arch Chancellor and the Captain arrived at a far valley where deep in the shadow the twinkling of a few candles was the only indication of habitation.

The wyverns landed less than gracefully, tired after their long flight. The Captain led them off to be fed and watered and the Arch Chancellor took Sienna and Maxwell to a low, roughly built timber building.

'I'm sorry about the makeshift nature of the accommodation,' the venerable dwarf apologised. 'This area was unexplored until recently. The population round here is very sparse and the doorway to your reality was only discovered a matter of months ago.'

'What about the gateway in our world,' asked Maxwell Devonport. 'What is it like?'

'I understand that it is a very beautiful natural arch in a remote part of China,' replied the dwarf. 'I have not been through yet but I'm looking forward to the experience. But first we must have a little food and a short rest before we cross the boundary between realities.'

*

Lord Robert Goodfellow sat back in the passenger seat of his Rolls Royce Hyperion Pinifarina. His driver was smoothly taking him down the motorway towards Bristol where he confidently expected to meet the people who had broken into his house. Quite how they had done it he was not sure but he had a suspicion that it was via the matter transmitter hidden behind his study. If so this could be a problem but nothing that he could not sort out.

Certainly not with the support he could conjure up. He took out his smart phone and chose a number to call. A few brief sentences.

That's sorted it, he thought, smiling with satisfaction.

✷

We approached the house in Redland, Bristol, and it was just exactly as described in a book of my life. Not that there has been one but that was how I remembered it, page after page wafting through like the sheets of a calendar in an old movie....and the house featured in most of the pages. A large detached Victorian house in a leafy suburb.

Probably cost at least a thousand pounds I thought and then corrected myself. This was the Twenty-First Century, not 1944! I could vaguely remember that houses in Redland cost between half and three-quarters of a million pounds. Some were over a million!

'Do I look like your Dad?' I asked Samuel as he sat next to me.

'Of course you do,' he replied. 'You're a bit thinner and you've grown an RAF moustache but otherwise you are just like him because you are him'

'Did your father have a scar on his left knee?' I pulled up my trouser leg and showed him where the bullet from the Red Baron had ripped through my leg in early1918. I'd caught up with him and finished him off at Amiens.

'You've shown me that scar lots of times, Dad,' replied Sam. 'It's where they operated on your cartilage.'

Was my Jiggles career all a lie? Had I been in occupied France with poor Alfie and Red? If not who was Morgan le Fay and where had I met her? Confusion reigned in my head.

✷

Not so bad that last bit. I've often practised climbing with just one arm. You never know when it might come in useful. Now to put my shoulder back. Turn the lower arm out, pull the whole arm across my front and, plop, its in place. Now to pull someone across on the improvised pulley. This heavier rope is long enough to go across and back so they'll be able to pull the contraption back over once the person is safely here. It's going to take quite a time but we should be able to get everybody across safely. Fingers crossed.

✳

'He's made it,' pronounced Holmes. We all gave a little cheer. 'Who is to go first?' added Conan Doyle's detective.

'I shall go first,' said Hitler Scott and, in order to defuse any argument, we all agreed.

Hauling the Nazi leader across the chasm took several long minutes but soon we were pulling the pulley device back across the gorge.

The second person to be hauled across was Florence Jimmy Nightingale. It took just as long because we could see through the binoculars that Hitler was refusing to help pull. Nightingale did her bit when she was over there and Robin Hood was soon over safely. The entire operation was going smoothly until I, Saint George, shouted in alarm. Marching in a column towards us was a cohort of Spartan soldiers.

'Stop where you are,' I cried, standing in their path, sword drawn. 'State your business or we will not allow you to proceed.'

'We shall stop you crossing the gorge,' stated the leader of the troop. 'You do not know what you are doing and it will result in disastrous consequences.'

'We're crossing a chasm and on our way to save a maiden in distress,' I replied, my sword held defiantly in front of me. 'And we don't intend letting you stop us.'

I made no further word of defiance for a small throwing knife appeared in the hand of the Spartan captain and was instantly thrown at me. The knife pierced my throat in the exposed section above my armour. I looked at it bemused as I sank to my knees. the pain was indescribable and I realised that I was dying.....

We all felt the pain of Saint George as he lay dying and were momentarily weakened. The first to recover was Drak, the three headed dragon.

'I liked that saint,' said the middle head.

'I agree,' said both lateral heads simultaneously.

Drak launched himself at the Spartans assisted by Chiron the Centaur, Holmes, Friar Tuck and Müller. Despite the Spartans' disciplined prowess the sheer ferocity of the dragon and the agonised attack by the rest of the company put the soldiers to flight. We could see them regrouping some distance away and were sure that they would be back soon.

'They'll attack us again when we are reduced in number,' remarked Holmes. 'Spartans are a determined bunch and they won't let us all get over the gorge.'

'I cannot cross over on the small pulley and piece of wood,' said the leading head of the dragon. 'And I cannot fly across. So I shall stay here and protect our rear.'

'Good idea, boss,' chorussed the other two heads.

'I shall stay with you,' I said, sadly, examining my four horse-like legs as I said it and swatting an errant fly from my flank with my right hand. 'It is my fault they are here.'

'Why is it your fault?' asked Holmes.

'They followed me along the Path of the Dead,' I replied. 'That is how I got here and I can be pretty certain that they did the same.' I continued to stare sorrowfully at my handsome horse body. No more would I miscegenate with Peggy, the Pegasus. No more would I gallop along the beaches of Hellas, heal the sick, tend the dying, teach heroes compassion and write beautiful poetry. The odds of the talking mirror would be fulfilled and the Spartans would have their day.

'Anyway,' I added, brightening up. 'The pulley was too weak to take my weight either, so I have to stay.'

✻

I must do something about Robin Goodfellow, thought Darcy

Macaroon as he sat in his small cubbyhole at Number 10. He felt like Henry II after he had spoken the immortal words *"Will no one rid me of this turbulent priest?"* If, of course, Henry had actually uttered such a sentence.

*It was not that Goodfellow was Thomas à Becket. No, no, no. Goodfellow was Reginald fitzUrse or Hugh de Morville or one of the other two knights who killed Becket. And maybe, just maybe, James Scott was Beck*et.

Chapter 22

The Spartans did not attack again immediately so the passage of the party over the gorge had gone ahead fairly smoothly. I, Friar Tuck, was the next across with the albatross perched on my shoulder. When we reached the other side the bird squawked with relief and was able to fly again, no longer under some witch or wizard's spell. The last of our company to attach itself to the pulley was the robot who had donated the two ropes. When it was half way across the gorge the dragon and the centaur were attacked and overwhelmed by the Spartans who had been fortified by a group of Nazi stormtroopers. The stormtroopers cut the monomolecular rope and the robot plunged into the chasm and smashed to pieces on the rocks and was swept away by the current.

Crossing the gorge has been costly and I am both saddened and weakened by the loss of our companions. The two Germans, Hitler and Müller, were clearly expecting the intervention of the stormtroopers. They waved to them and marched off from our party. We do not know where they are now.

I've written a short passage to be left as a memorial by the gorge. We have lost the cat, it did not want to climb on with Archimedes, who tried very hard to persuade it to do so.

So departed from the company at the gorge, due to death,
Saint George
Drak, the three-headed dragon
Chiron, the centaur
and the Robot.
For whom I say the psalm
"De profundis clamavi ad te, Domine

From the depths, I have cried out to you, O Lord"
Deserted!
Hitler
Müller
The cat

Lord Kelvin never returned when he went off in a sulk much earlier so he can probably be included amongst the deserted but he could have been killed. Lord knows this place is hostile enough to have done for a sulking scientist who did not want to believe in its reality. I have no idea where Jonah is and have not seen him since some time before we reached the gorge.

Our group now consists of the following:
Robin Hood
Einstein
Isambard Kingdom Brunel
Archimedes
Florence Nightingale
Sherlock Holmes
Scott, James Scott
Myself, Friar Tuck
and the Albatross, to which I have become rather fond.

Merlin was in touch with all of us in the group, voice only, telling us that we had done very well to cross the chasm but also urging us onwards, saying that time was pressing.

Robin Hood is leading us. Einstein, Archimedes and Brunel are not at all healthy. The nurse is bearing up very well and reminds me of Robin's bride. Sherlock Holmes is twitchy and I believe that he may normally have a drug problem. Scott, James Scott, is not complaining but he is clearly in trouble with his shoulder. The only fit men are Robin Hood and myself and I am overweight and not used to so much walking.

The next hazard that we now must face is the Clashing Rocks, which are also known as the Symplegades or Cyanean Rocks. Archimedes is the only one amongst us now who has heard of anything like this. Chiron and Archimedes apparently discussed them on the trek to the gorge and remembered them from the tale of Jason and the Argonauts. They could not work out how the rocks, which were supposed to be in the Bosphorus, could be on a plateau of dry land. We shall, presumably, find out.

★

'I do remember this,' I said to the kids as I looked around the house. 'But not as if I really lived here. It's as if I read about your house in a magazine article, the sort of thing they write about John D. Rockefeller. So I know every room but not in detail.'

'Jimmy this is disturbing,' said Steve. 'I can't really leave you with the kids when you are in this strange pyschological state. Sienna would never forgive me.'

'You're right, of course,' I agreed. 'It's a jolly poor show. I'm really frightfully sorry.'

'It's not your fault. We.....'

Steve was interrupted by an insistent ringing at the doorbell. We were upstairs and able to look out at the front without disturbing the curtains. Two burly policemen were at the door.

'They are not our friends,' said Morgan le Fay with no hesitation.

'They may go away if we ignore them,' suggested Steve.

'Unlikely with your car out there,' said Joshua. 'They look very persistent.'

'You folk hide and I'll answer the door,' proposed Steve. 'I might be able to persuade them to leave.'

Morgan le Fay looked very reluctant to accept the idea but I persuaded her that the British policemen were the salt of the Earth. As a compromise the boys quickly hid themselves upstairs whilst Steve walked downstairs to answer the ringing, to which had now been added loud knocking. Morgan and I sauntered down behind Steve and hid in the front hall such that we could view the proceedings and be ready to partake if need be.

'Hello,' said Steve amiably as he opened the portal. 'Can I be of assistance?'

'And who might you be?' asked the larger of the two uniformed men. 'Are you the owner of this house?'

'I'm Steve Clarkson, a friend of the Scotts,' replied Steve in a gentle tone. 'How can I help you?'

'We have been sent to find the Scotts' two sons and take them to the police station,' replied the other policeman and then, in a suspicious tone, added. 'But first tell me why you are in their house.'

'The Scotts are away at the moment,' replied Steve. 'And I am looking after their house. I come round periodically to see if everything is OK.'

'So where are the Scott boys?' asked the burlier policeman.

'They are living with friends,' replied Steve. 'Not quite sure where but I have their mobile phone numbers if that helps.'

'It might do,' replied the burly man. 'But first we would like to come in and look around.'

'I'm not sure that I can agree to that unless you show me your warrant cards,' replied Steve in a friendly voice. 'After all, it is my duty to look after this place.'

The response was dramatic. The slight obstruction put up by Steve instantly annoyed the huge uniformed man and he punched Steve in the stomach. Steve fell to the floor gasping for breath and the two men stepped over him and started looking around the house.

'We don't have to put up with this,' I remarked to Morgan le Fay.

'Nor do we,' she replied. 'I'll take the bigger one, you take the smaller.'

I always liked to take on the larger opponent but with no time to argue I accepted the topsy-turvy arrangement. I was glad that I had done so.

I stepped out from behind my hiding place and shouted boo. The smaller man was close to me and turned round as I spoke. I let out a perfect straight left followed by a right uppercut that caught him on the chin. The man barely wobbled and came at me fists flying.

Morgan le Fay was having no trouble. She waved her hands around in front of the bemused monster of a man and the fellow stopped dead in his tracks. The smaller policeman kept coming for me and though I dodged his blows I could do nothing to stop him. Steve recovered his breath, regained his feet and picked up a wooden chair. This he brought crashing down on the policeman's head to no avail. The man turned round and grabbed at Steve but Steve feinted sideways with an excellent Tai Chi move. The policeman crashed to the ground but was up again very quickly and then froze in his tracks. Morgan le Fay had got both of them under control.

'What the hell are they?' I asked. 'I've never come across a man so strong.'

'That is because they are not men,' replied Kristiana de Morgaine also known as Morgan le Fay.

'Then what are they?' asked Steve, rubbing his stomach.

'I smelt wet clay when they answered the door,' replied Morgan. 'I waited to see if I was wrong but when one hit you I knew.'

'What did the smell of clay signify?' asked Steve, recovering from his ordeal.

'They were golems,' replied Morgan.

'What the heck are golems?' I asked.

'They were not the salt of the Earth. They literally were earth. Vivified clay brought to life by magic. Someone sent magical golems after Joshua and Samuel. Someone powerful who has important contacts.'

✳

A fat monk like myself should not be doing all this fast walking. The plateau on this side is far worse than on the other side of the gorge. The albatross is sitting on my shoulder as I walk. My sandals are wearing through as the ground is rough basalt with almost no top soil. Nothing is growing and there is no water. We have only half our supplies as the robot was carrying quite a proportion and we left some with our two largest members, the dragon and the centaur.

According to Merlin we should reach the clashing rocks within a few hours. I view this with foreboding.

The fat old monk keeps crossing himself and muttering and I really can't blame him. My shoulder is painful but my dinner jacket remains spotless. No idea how that can be the case since the cliff was wet and smeared with lichen. It doesn't feel like a purely synthetic fibre. Never really questioned it before but it is strange that I manage to look so perfect when I'm thrown through brick walls, dropped onto trains, shot in the chest, kicked off a satellite or dropped from a bridge.

Chapter 23

The Arch Chancellor woke Sienna from a deep sleep. She asked how long she had been semi-conscious and the dwarf replied that it was only just over two hours.

'It is important that we move on quickly,' he added. 'The time over here is very different from the passage of time in your reality. A week here can be three to five weeks in your timeframe although it does vary depending on where you are in Faerie.'

'So although I have only been here for one day I will have been away from my sons for three days?' she queried.

'Correct,' replied the venerable dwarf. 'Plus or minus a day or two. It can be difficult to tell. But we must not waste time talking. Let me show you to the boat.'

'We are going by boat?' Sienna was surprised. 'What sort of boat?'

'A bamboo raft' replied the Arch Chancellor. 'It will not look out of place when we reach the other side.'

✱

'Stop!' commanded the vision of an angel holding a golden sword. 'None shall pass.'

'Ignore the vision,' came the voice of Merlin. 'He has no power, only that of persuasion.'

The angel looked familiar to me and the voice was an educated one, much like my own. As a secret agent I have seen many things that would be strange to most people but this gig is something else. Dragon, robot, centaur and now an angel.

Presumably I am being held captive and fed with hallucinogenic drugs. I would then be interpreting things I see completely incorrectly. But what am I actually doing when I'm climbing a cliff or walking across this barren land? One thing is certain and that is that we are being followed. I can't see who is following us but it is certainly there. I have a niggling sensation between my shoulder blades, a sixth sense that I always get when I am a target. Something unseen is following us, something powerful.

✶

I looked closely at the policemen that appeared frozen in place by Morgan le Fay. What would happen now? Could they really be lumps of clay?

I touched one on its hand. Although it looked like flesh it felt completely solid and quite warm.

'They're too hot to be frozen solid,' I remarked. 'What the heck did you do to them?'

'As I said they are not men,' replied Morgan. 'They are made from clay and I used a simple spell that heated then from inside thus baking them in place. They are now solid brick.'

'You can't just go round turning policemen into brick however heavy-handed they are!' protested Steve, who had now completely recovered from the blow they had landed in his stomach. 'We'll be arrested for murder!'

'Zut alors!' exclaimed Morgan le Fay in reply. 'Will you not listen? These creatures were never men. They are not even really living they are more like a machine than a person.'

'They look like people,' said Steve.

'Mon dieu! Of course they do,' said Morgan. 'That's what they are supposed to look like.'

As she spoke she pulled the clothes of the torso of one of the golem policemen.

'See,' she stated. 'The golem is only poorly formed. There is no umbilicus, there are no nipples and, voila!' She ripped off his trousers. 'No sexual organs!'

'Seems that I have a pair of ceramic statues,' I remarked. 'To go in this garden that I can barely remember.'

✷

The two wyverns, Sienna, the Captain of the Armies of the East, the Arch Chancellor and Maxwell Devonport were squashed together in the small raft which was being steered from the back by a large yellow-skinned individual who looked as if he could be Chinese. The man professed to be from Faerie but added that many of the people from that part of the Eastern Mainland did look Mongolian or Chinese in origin.

'The theory,' he expounded. 'Is that there was a connection between the two realities in the past centred on this area. The opening of this fairy bridge may therefore be a re-opening rather than something completely new.'

'Would that explain why the Chinese are so interested in dragons?' asked Maxwell, who had been listening intently to the conversation.

'It might,' agreed the steersman. 'But I am no expert on dragons so do not quote me.'

'We are hoping to see an expert,' replied Sienna.

'That would be Fu Chang Wo,' replied the steersman. 'He is exceedingly knowledgable on all things dragon.'

The boat was moving lazily along the slowly moving river towards a huge natural arch. As the raft swung under the arch the boat was caught up in a counter current for a moment and the steersman had to fight to control it. Sienna noted with amazement the change in the scenery but more alarming still was the way that the sun seemed to jump in the sky from one quadrant to another... from early morning it switched to late afternoon.

'This is the largest natural arch in the entire real world,' said the steersman proudly. 'It is four hundred feet in length and its name in Chinese is Xian Ren Qiao, which roughly translates to Fairy Bridge.'

The raft moved slowly up the Buliu River to the village of Buliu.

*

Isambard Kingdom Brunel has died of a heart attack. I'm surprised he perished before me...I'm the fat one. An overweight monk. The pain of Brunel's going was not as agonising as when the others died. Perhaps we are becoming immune to the death of our company? Perhaps we are all slowly dying? I said Ave Maria over his dead body. We could not bury him as the ground is too hard and we have no tools. The best we could do was build a cairn of stones over the last mortal remains of a man that I have been told was a great engineer.

Robin Hood leads us with a spring in his step. He is really the only one who is untroubled by this frame of existence. Scott, James Scott, marches resolutely forwards but has the look of a man who is haunted by his past. On the surface he is smooth, suave and saturnine but I can see in his eyes the echoes of his history.

Einstein and Archimedes have been walking along muttering and they just pronounced that this world is not the Earth. They based this on observations of the length of time stones took to fall to the bottom of the gorge compared with their heart-beats or some such complex process.

I already knew this was not Earth. If they had looked up at the sky they would have noticed that there are three moons starting to appear even though it is only early evening.

Or is it? Time moves in a very peculiar way here. I have taken to thinking of this place as purgatory.

*

I looked at Kristiana de Morgaine le Fay, also known simply as Kristy Morgan. How could this beautiful girl who looked so much like Brigitte Bardot be so old? How could she know how to defeat clay monsters that my best straight left could not shift? My knuckles were still painful from thumping the creature and there was a broken chair as testimony to its invulnerability. But I had more pressing questions in my mind. Why had Morgan le

Fay been so startled when I told her that the house we had arrived at in London belonged to a Lord Robert Goodfellow? Why was I constantly plagued by thoughts that I must go back for my dog, Red? Why did the dog insist the the guard was right, she was a mixed-up La Read? Was I the true Jimmy Scott and where were the others?

Even that question paled into one that was forming. What should we do now?

✶

Sienna had worried that the appearance of the Arch Chancellor might make a stir in an out of the way spot such as Buliu but when Fu Chang Wo appeared from inside a small pagoda her mind was put at rest. Wo was also a dwarf with a long white beard and the local people barely gave him a second glance.

'My old friend,' exclaimed Fu Chang Wo when he saw the Arch Chancellor. 'Such an unexpected pleasure to see you. I knew someone was coming under the fairy arch but I did not expect to see you. You don't normally travel more than ten miles from your home.'

'You exaggerate old pal,' protested the venerable dwarf. 'But I certainly could not turn down the opportunity of seeing you again. Besides, I need your advice.'

'And I shall give it freely,' replied the dragon expert. 'In return for a few jars of Faerie ale.'

'That is easily arranged and I will certainly get them for you. But they may have to wait,' agreed the Arch Chancellor. 'I must first tell you a story that includes an angel, a gnome and at least two golden dragons. Plus a good many very interesting dreams.'

'I'm all ears,' replied Fu Chang Wo.

Sienna looked over at him and had to agree. Dwarves all had very long beards and very large ears. Fu Chang Wo's ears were, indeed, particularly prominent.

Chapter 24

'That was very interesting,' said the Chinese-domiciled dwarf. 'A very interesting story indeed. I can see why you have come to me and I can help you with one part immediately.'

'Which is?' asked the Arch Chancellor eagerly.

'There is no power in the land of Faerie that is stronger than the mind of a golden dragon,' pronounced Fu Chang Wo.

'So there is nothing that could put one into a trance?' asked the Arch Chancellor.

'Only another golden dragon,' answered Wo.

'Do you have any other thoughts on our predicament?' asked Maxwell Devonport.

'I agree that you should return as soon as possible to Sienna's home,' replied the dwarf. 'I am most suspicious about this meeting between Jiggles and Sienna's sons. What shade or avatar of Jimmy Scott is he? Is he a copy set up to strike at the children?'

'I'm worried stiff about the kids,' agreed Sienna. 'Any other thoughts?'

'Morgan le Fay is an infamous sorcerer of legend,' answered Wo. 'But not one that I understood was still alive. Did you think she was alive, Arch Chancellor?'

'No,' replied the venerable dwarf. 'No inkling of that at all. I thought that she died more than a thousand years ago, real time.'

'Maybe she is Morgan or Morgaine le Fay and maybe she isn't. The question is, if she is not Morgan le Fay, who is she?'

*

We've reached the clashing rocks and they are worse than I, Robin Hood, expected. Archimedes described the Symplegades or

Cyanean Rocks as being cliffs on either side of a narrow stretch of sea....something like the Straits of Gibraltar with a will and movement of their own.

This is nothing like that. We are standing on dry land looking down at the area we have to cross. The clashing rocks are powered by a pair of volcanoes and the land between them is riven with earthquakes and the lava streams down to a sea of molten rock. As we look we can see solid rock being pushed up and down in this ocean of magma. If we could work out the sequence of the rocks we could, just perhaps, jump from one rock to the next before they sink beneath the surface. As yet I certainly can perceive no sequence. I have asked Einstein and Archimedes to bend their powerful minds to the task.

✷

I crouched down and ran my fingers through the pockets of the golem policemen's uniforms. Nothing. No warrant cards, no wallets, no keys. The uniforms were very flimsy and the hats made of card. They were certainly not real police uniforms so we did not need to worry too much about where the clothes had come from. I had worried that somewhere there may be some of our fine constabulary lying dead in their underwear. These uniforms, I felt their lack of quality, came from a joke shop or carnival store.

Morgan le Fay was looking at me with a sardonically bemused expression on her face.

'The golems were already made and waiting,' she explained. 'Somebody had them ready primed.'

'So they are like robots,' said Steve, who was shaking a little from his ordeal. 'And someone set them off to capture the Scott boys.'

'That's about right,' agreed Morgan. 'But robots are powered by mechanical means. These are powered entirely by magic.'

'Magic!' Steve looked horrified. 'We've had nothing but trouble since the two worlds collided. Magic will be the downfall of everybody.'

'Let's hope not,' I said, trying to dispel the gloom that had settled on us. 'We had better tell the boys that the coast is clear and then we should move out. We are sitting ducks here. These ceramic statues are proof that our enemy knows where we are.'

'Shouldn't we hide the robot policemen first?' asked Steve.

'We'll put them in the back garden,' I chuckled. 'They'll make good statues and the pigeons can perch on them and do their worst.'

✶

The Arch Chancellor jumped into his place on the wyvern in a motion that belied his extreme age. Sienna more carefully climbed behind him onto the dragon. The Captain signalled that he and Maxwell Devonport were ready to take off on the other wyvern.

'Just one thing before you go,' said Fu Chang Wo. 'You said that ice hockey is a clue but when I listened to the story it appeared to me that the clue was the puck, not necessarily ice hockey.'

'But it was an ice hockey puck,' protested Sienna. 'And Jimmy gave the puck to the gnome.'

'Nevertheless,' replied the dragon expert enigmatically. 'The clue is that which you see not that which you surmise. Thus the clue is the puck.'

They took off with a flurry of flapping reptile wings and were soon flying West over the northern part of China. Sienna had been told that they would be moving thence via Kazakhstan into the Ukraine.

'We are touching down at Kiev,' the Arch Chancellor informed Sienna.

'Won't two large dragons and a dwarf be rather obvious in Kiev?' she asked bemusedly.

'We will be resting for a couple of hours with a group of people amongst whom dwarves and dragons are considered normal,' replied the venerable dwarf.

Who could that possibly be in the real world? wondered Sienna without saying it out loud. The dwarf continued as if hearing her unspoken question.

'We will be joining the circus,' he said. 'The Chinese State Circus is visiting Kiev and we shall be visiting them.'

✶

I was listening to the conversation that our scientists were having with Robin Hood but only paying partial attention. I was also looking back along the trail. I could still not discern what manner of creature was following us. Something was there but despite my secret service training I could not make out what it was. I had picked up just a flicker of movement, a glint of light but little else.

'We can perceive no pattern in the clashing rocks,' Einstein was saying. 'But that does not mean that there is not one.'

'Looking back at a problem once it has been solved one can often discern that there was a pattern all along,' added Archimedes.

'Once you have the solution hindsight is twenty-twenty,' smiled Einstein in an avuncular manner.

'And sometimes the answer arrives unexpectedly,' added Florence Nightingale. 'I remember serving a pie to wounded soldiers in the Crimea and realising that I had an answer to how I should display the statistics I was collecting.'

With a jolt I recalled being told that Florence Nightingale was not just a very brave nurse who tended to soldiers in terrible circumstances but also an astonishingly accomplished mathematician.

'Perhaps there is a way that we can look back on the puzzle,' suggested Friar Tuck.

'I don't see that,' asked Archimedes. 'We are here now without the answer to the puzzle. How can we look back on the answer?'

'Maybe my pet albatross can help,' replied Friar Tuck.

I looked at the huge bird perched on Tuck's shoulder. The bird understood everything that was being said. It stood up taller then hopped onto Tuck's bald pate, stretched its enormously long wings out fully and then pulled them back in again.

'If the bird was willing to fly over the sea of lava and clashing rocks it might discern a different pattern looking back,' suggested Tuck.

'That would surely depend on whether it was prepared to do so in the first place,' replied Holmes sardonically. 'Whether there was indeed a solution after looking back and then whether we understood the bird when it returned. If it returned.'

'There are many imponderables,' agreed Robin Hood. 'But I agree with the idea if the bird does.'

The giant sea bird nodded its head in reply then, giving out a loud "Aaaah" lifted off from Tuck's suffering head and wheeled out towards the great sea of red bubbling rock.

'Good luck,' cried Tuck and we all joined in saying the same.

*

'There is a particular magician at the circus who I need to consult,' said the venerable gnome as they glided in over Kiev and landed at the football stadium where the circus was housed.

'Can a circus magician help you?' asked Sienna, amazed. 'I assumed they were all flim-flam. Phoney conjuring tricks.'

'That's what they let people think,' replied the gnome. 'It's a double bluff. The true magicians pretend that they are phoney prestidigitators fooling the public with speed of the hand that deceives the eye. In reality they are doing simple spells.'

'Is this only since the clashing of the two realities?' asked Sienna, astonished by the revelation.

'No, no. Not all,' the old dwarf contradicted. 'No. They've been crossing over into this reality from faerie for millennia. They can make a good living as long as people don't really believe in it.'

'What happens if people do believe?' inquired Sienna.

'The public become frightened and they burn the magicians as witches or put them in psychiatric hospitals,' replied the dwarf as they dismounted from the wyvern.

'So this is a real magician that we are going to see?' said Sienna.

'As real as I am,' answered the dwarf. 'And in many ways a more rounded ability. Greater depth.'

Chapter 25

The venerable dwarf is right, thought Sienna. *This magician is definitely more rounded!*

The magician was billed on the circus billboard as the world's largest wizard.

COME AND SEE THE GREAT WIZARD ZHANG! MARVEL AT THE HEAVIEST MAGICIAN OF THE CENTURY! SEE THE FATTEST, TALLEST WIZARD'S WACKY WHEEZES! HOW CAN SOMEONE SO BIG MOVE SO QUICKLY?

The magician was huge, a giant of a man. Standing over two metres tall the wizard looked almost as wide. He had long black hair pulled backwards into a pigtail, sallow complexion and long straggling Fu Manchu moustache and beard. He was wearing a huge cloak of dark blue velvet on which were embroidered stars, planets and moons. This he flung off with a groan revealing a track suit underneath and a very large body which he flung into an oversize chair by a solid oak table.

To Sienna's surprise Zhang's accent was American.

'Gee,' the magician gasped. 'That was a long show. Carrying all this extra weight is a bind but it is part of the act. Now, Arch Chancellor, who is this gorgeous female you have brought with you?'

'Now stop that, Zhang, you old rascal,' laughed the Arch Chancellor, his venerable body shaking with his amusement. 'You never change do you? This is Sienna, the lovely wife of Lord James Scott.'

'Wow!' exclaimed the huge Chinese American wizard. 'Not *the* James Scott, James Michael Scott?'

'One and the same,' agreed the venerable dwarf.

'At your service madam,' cried Wizard Zhang. 'I am honoured to meet the wife of so famous a man.' The great Wizard Zhang bowed deeply and then subvocalized. 'Not just famous but, of course, also so powerful.'

'Except that he is presently missing,' the dwarf said pointedly. 'We thought you might give us a clue as to what type of magic could affect Lord James.'

'Magic that might affect an archangel?' queried Zhang. 'And not just any archangel but the most powerful angel of them all? Now that takes some thinking about.'

The enormous magician looked crestfallen and worried for a minute and then brightened up.

'I will give this thought but lets eat first. I'm famished. Then we'll look at all the possibilities. There must be something that could be used against an archangel.'

The magician waved his hands and huge plates of food were brought to the table.

'Not that we want you to use magic against Lord James,' added the dwarf. 'Just tell us what you think might have been used against him.'

'That's OK then,' said the vastly fat man as he started to eat from a plate piled high with food. 'I can certainly suggest some ideas just as long as you don't want to involve me. I'm too old and fat to get involved in battles with Archangels. This gig suits me fine.'

The magician waved his hands at the varied plates on the table and added.

'Lady Sienna, do tuck into the food, the chicken is particularly good and so are the burgers.'

✳

We all piled into Steve's battered old Citroen. Steve drove and I sat next to him.

The two boys climbed into the back with Morgan le Fay. I still did not know what to think of the young-looking female sorcerer and sometime resistance leader but I suddenly remembered what I wanted to ask her. As we were driven away from the house I turned round and looked straight at her.

'Kristy,' I asked. 'You almost said something about Lord Robert Goodfellow when we were in his house. You jumped when I mentioned his name. Can you tell me now and what was it?'

Morgan le Fay looked worried as she spoke.

'If you are looking for trickery you do not need to look further than that man. He has the machine in his study and he has the ability,' she replied.

'Who is he?' asked Joshua. 'Who is Lord Robert Goodfellow and why is he so important?'

'He is Robin Goodfellow,' replied Morgan le Fay. 'He is the *original* Robin Goodfellow.'

✷

They ate from the groaning table as more and more dishes were added to those already piled up. Sienna, the Captain, the Arch Chancellor and Maxwell Devonport made little impression on the feast despite eating hard but Wizard Zhang, the magician, managed to reduce the table's contents prodigiously. He kept up with the conversation despite eating so much and was introduced to the other companions.

'And my guys will be looking after your wyverns,' Zhang announced. 'It's so good to see real dragons again, if only the lesser sort.'

The Arch Chancellor summarised, for Zhang, the dreams, the death of the soothsayer gnome, the absence of Lord James and Lady Aradel, the coma of the Dragon King and the conclusions of the dragon expert who lived near the fairy bridge in China. When the story was finished Zhang had almost completed his phenomenal repast. He then sat back and belched loudly then put his hand across his mouth and apologised to Sienna.

'Sorry ma'am,' he remarked. 'I normally eat alone. Few people can stand to see me eating so much food.'

'Why do you eat so much?' asked Sienna, puzzled, for the man was clearly very intelligent. 'Doesn't being fat put you in a high risk group?'

'Shorten my life, you mean?' asked the magician. 'Maybe. But then again I am already exceedingly old like the dear Arch Chancellor here.' The magician prodded the dwarf in the belly. 'And I spent many of those years very skinny indeed. I'm happier fat and, besides, it's part of my act.'

'Tell us what you've decided about dragons and archangels,' prompted the Arch Chancellor.

The gigantic, fat magician stretched his arms out and put his hands behind his head.

'I believe that you are right,' he pontificated. 'The best way to capture an archangel would be to use his strength against himself and I believe the Allegorical Cave could be used in that way. But it does not explain everything.'

'What doesn't it explain?' asked the dwarf.

'Why he has been gone so long,' explained the magician. 'Couldn't it simply be that Lady Aradel had an argument with her husband and just went off with Lord James?'

'That wouldn't explain the dreams,' countered Sienna. 'And I don't believe that Jimmy would leave me and the kids.'

'And there is the death of the gnome,' added Maxwell Devonport.

'That's an easy one,' replied the magician.

'Easy?' queried Devonport and the Arch Chancellor simultaneously.

'Yes. Easy,' said the magician calling for more drink as he did so. 'Of course, that is down to Puck.'

'Puck?' queried Devonport. 'Is that a person or is it the object used in a game of Ice Hockey?'

'Both,' replied the magician. 'And that it is the reason for the soothsayer, who had predicted his own death and was unable to avoid it, asking Lord James to bring him the object. It's a very strange memento otherwise.'

'Puck?' queried Devonport again.

'Certainly,' said the giant magician. 'You know who I mean. Come on Arch Chancellor tell them his other name, it escapes me for a minute. It's on the tip of my tongue.'

'The sprite!' exclaimed the dwarf. 'Of course. Puck the sprite. Robin Goodfellow.'

'But that's the nickname of the fellow in Government who joined us in my office,' protested Devonport. 'Are you suggesting that Sir Robert Goodfellow is a sprite called Puck.'

'Obviously so,' answered the gigantic magician, mopping his brow. 'He's your man. Puck is the person who killed the gnome. Not James Scott.'

*

I'm more at home with the calculable odds of the Bridge table or playing Backgammon scientifically. This is a strange existence for a lounge lizard like me.

I adjusted the collars of my tuxedo for the twentieth time as I watched the albatross fly off. The huge bird did not give us a second glance. It glided out over the clashing rocks and disappeared into the murky, smoke-filled distance.

'What do we do now?' Archimedes asked.

'We wait,' replied Robin Hood.

'And if it doesn't return?' asked the Greek philosopher.

'Then we die,' concluded Hood.

'We're probably dead already and in purgatory,' suggested the fat monk, Friar Tuck.

Charming, I thought fiddling with my sleeve yet again. Just what we need, a pessimist. Give me an optimist any day.

✱

'What are you doing?' I asked Kristiana de Morgaine le Fay
as she leant out of the window waving her arms around and then
sprinkling salt over he shoulder and muttering.

'Ce n'est pas possible!' she exclaimed. 'It is impossible that you
don't understand!'

'Don't understand what?' asked Joshua.

'That Robin Goodfellow will follow us, of course,' replied
Morgan le Fay. 'He will be round shortly after his golems.'

'So you reckon he sent those weird policemen,' asked Sam.

'Who else?' asked the girl sorcerer, still sprinkling salt.

'So what are you doing?' I repeated.

'I am hexing our trail so that it cannot be found and I suggest
that we go further than just round to Steve's house,' she answered.
'He'll find us there by a simple mind sweep.'

'Where do you suggest?' asked Steve, timidly.

The whole thing was a bit much for him, I could tell by the way
he was responding, nothing like his normal bouncy self.

Hey, I thought. *Proximity with the family and friends is making
you remember.*

'Somewhere over water and beyond would be good,' Kristy
Morgan replied.

'Wales?' I queried. 'Would that do? We could take the ferry
from Aust.'

'Ferry from Aust?' the boys said together and then Joshua
continued. 'We can take the Second Severn Crossing. That would
be quickest.'

As he said that I could vaguely remember going over the
Second Severn Crossing on the very day that it opened. All four of
us, Sienna, Joshua, Samuel and I, had taken a trip there and back
in our battered Morris Minor Convertible. It had been a lovely day,
the sun had shone and the bridge had been a marvel.

'Yes,' I agreed. 'The Second Severn Crossing. Like we did the day it opened.'

The boys visibly relaxed when I said that but I knew that it was a memory in my book section rather than in my living recollection.

✳

The Rolls Royce Hyperion rolled to a halt outside the Scotts' large detached Redland house. Lord Robert Goodfellow climbed out and looked around. He sniffed the air and then spoke to his driver.

'I'm going inside but you stay here. I believe they have left but I must make sure. If they are not here we will have to follow them right away.'

✳

'Tell us about Puck,' demanded the Chief Constable, Maxwell Devonport. 'What do you know about the fellow.'

'Fellow he ain't. That's the number one thing,' replied the magician. 'He is a kind of half-tamed wood spirit who delights in leading people astray. He has many names but Robin Goodfellow is one that he uses a lot. He is also known as the hobgoblin and pixie is a diminutive of Puck. He's a little pixie, a sprite.'

'But Sir Robert Goodfellow works for the Government,' argued Sienna. 'He's not a pixie. He's a rather fat, middle-aged man.'

'But he also sent your husband on the mission to Faerie when he went missing,' added Maxwell, rubbing his chin. 'If I'm not very much mistaken.'

'So he had all the opportunity in the world for attacking Lord James,' replied the magician. 'And don't worry about his appearance. He can make himself resemble anything he likes, so a middle-aged man is easy. I can, of course, do the same.'

The magician waved his hands and suddenly sitting next to Sienna at the table was a beautiful girl, then a pig and then a large, fierce-looking bear before the figure turned back into that of the over-large magician.

'So a spell such as the Allegorical Cave that the Arch Chancellor suggested, could be used by him,' queried the chief constable.

'I expect so but to hold an Archangel for so long is the problem,' replied the magician. 'Usually the illusion created by the spell breaks up after a short time and the subject discovers the subterfuge. It requires not just power but continuous invention and that's where the perpetrator of the spell falls short.'

'But what if it was combined with a Literati spell and power was added from another source?' asked the Arch Chancellor.

'Brilliant,' answered the magician. 'That is truly brilliant. It could work on almost any living creature. But how could Puck get the archangel in his power in the first place? Puck would have to bodily remove the archangel and then break-up his psyche by a powerful spell that continues to drain energy.'

'So there are other forces at play here as well as Puck,' agreed the Arch Chancellor.

'Wait a minute,' asked Maxwell Devonport. 'You lost me there. I understand about the Allegorical Cave because you explained it to us but what's a Literati spell?'

'That's the clever bit,' mused the huge magician as he called for yet more drink. 'The spell the Arch Chancellor is referring to uses the spare telepathic energy of the population.'

'What spare telepathic energy?' asked Devonport.

'That produced when people read books and magazines of course. The by-products of literature,' replied the magician.

'What sort of literature could do this?' asked Sienna.

'Any,' interjected the Arch Chancellor dwarf. 'Stories, fiction or non-fiction. Novels, biographies, historical romance, adventure stories.'

'Anything that stimulates the imagination such that the reader can believe they are leading a different life whilst they are reading the story,' added the magician.

'Am I getting you right?' said the policeman. 'You want me to believe that Lord James Scott is being held by a spell that makes him perceive reality through the eyes of a large number of different people who are reading books? It seems very far-fetched.'

'So does the fact that he is an archangel. Or that an electrician from Bristol could subdue and control the devil,' said the magician. 'And I wonder whether you noticed how much the pound rose after your husband went missing?'

'That was unrelated, wasn't it?' asked Sienna.

'Maybe or maybe not but whatever you think about these spells you had better get over to Bristol as soon as possible. Your sons are likely to get the attention of people who mean to do them harm and your boys need powerful support,' the magician raised his bulky form from the chair. 'I suppose I should come with you for a short while. The circus can function without me, temporarily, although I am considered a big draw. A very big one.'

Chapter 26

The albatross has returned and as it did so it pooped on my spotless tuxedo. It is no longer spotless.

The bird appears to want us to follow it. It does not look in a too good state.... its tail feathers are scorched as are the flight feathers at the end of its left wing but it is definite that we should follow.

According to Friar Tuck, the bird discovered a simple route through the rocks. Also, according to the good Friar, it is a maze and only one way reaches the other end thus making it easy to choose from that direction. Looking back as Archimedes had suggested.

★

'We'll have the soft top down, Jankers,' ordered Robin Goodfellow, otherwise known as Puck.

The sprite, who still had the resemblance of a portly middle-aged man, sniffed the air and then pointed.

'That way, Jankers.'

The chauffeur, used to his employer's strange behaviour, started off in the direction indicated. They had not gone very far before Puck stopped him.

'The trail's gone,' he announced and then opened the car door and examined the road. 'Not by accident either. There is salt on the road. Park here for a few minutes.'

The driver pulled in closer to the kerb and Puck got out. He looked wildly around for a moment or two and then ran straight up one of the larger street trees, a London Plane. He then sat on top of the tree and waved his arms around. He jumped straight down from the top and bounced back into the car.

'They've gone. I've lost them,' he growled and then howled with irritation before settling back in his seat.

'What now, Boss?' asked the chauffeur.

'We go back to the Scott's house and await developments,' answered the sprite, with an evil laugh. 'Sienna Scott will return soon and we can deal with her first. She will not know what hit her.'

*

The wyvern groaned with the extra weight of the magician until the huge wizard waved his hands. There was a flash of light temporarily blinding everyone and when they could see again Zhang was looking a shadow of his former self.

'I've lessened the load,' explained the skinny Zhang. 'But I will have to put the weight back on when I return to the circus.'

'Can't you just give the impression of obesity without actual being obese,' suggested Sienna.

'My dear!' exclaimed Zhang. 'It's a matter of integrity. I like my act to be completely genuine. Otherwise I find it hard to face the punters.'

The wyverns leapt into the air and Sienna was once again being flown over a continent on the back of a dragon.

As they flew the Arch Chancellor and the Wizard Zhang kept up a learned discussion about magic spells and the vulnerability of dragons, angels and saints.

'Regarding the dreams' said Zhang, finally turning to Sienna, who was half asleep. 'What was this bit about the Lords of Chaos and Confusion?'

'Apparently the Merlin character told Jimmy that he was being held by the Lords of Chaos, whoever they might be.'

'To make the Allegorical Spell work the wielder has to tell the subject the truth but in such a way that the subject does not understand it,' mused the magician, who was still tall but not anywhere near as fat as he had been.

'So what you are saying is that he is being held by the Lords of Chaos and Confusion. Is that it?' asked Sienna. 'Where does Puck or Robin Goodfellow come into this.'

'He is a past-master of confusion,' replied the magician. 'But that is only one Lord. You implied it was a number or at least two Lords of Chaos.'

'I can only think of one other,' murmured the Arch Chancellor. 'And Lord James has already defeated him.'

'Parsifal X?' suggested Sienna.

'No. Not the elemental,' replied the venerable dwarf, shaking his ancient bearded head. 'I'm referring to Lucifer. The Prince of Darkness and Lord of Mischief.'

'Satan!' exclaimed the magician. 'But he is chained in hell!'

'One and the same,' replied the dwarf. 'I reckon that the power Puck lacks is being supplied by the devil. Satan himself.'

Wizard Zhang shifted uneasily in his seat.

He is disturbed by the thought of Satan's involvement, pondered Sienna as they flew ever westwards.

✱

The old citroen motored over the Severn on the Second Crossing and Steve paid the toll at the Welsh end.

'We must take the offensive,' said the resistance fighter who called herself Kristiana de Morgaine le Fay, or Kristy Morgan for short. 'We have lost Robin Goodfellow but we should circle back and find out what he is up to.'

'What do you suggest we do?' I asked. 'I'm a simple fighter pilot. All I know about is Sopwith Camels, Spitfires, Hurricanes and a load of Fokkers.'

'And you only know about them because you helped me make the Airfix models,' said Joshua.

'And we made a Wellington bomber,' added Sam.

'I suggest we leave the boys over here in Wales, out of harm's way, and double back to Bristol,' said Morgan, ignoring the conversation about model making.

'No way,' said both boys together.

'I don't like that idea either,' I said. 'I want the boys to stay with me. They're helping to bring me back to sanity and I think they need me.'

'We do Jiggles. I mean Dad!' exclaimed Sam.

'I don't think we should go back at all,' argued Steve. 'We're safe over here so we should keep going.'

'Sorry Steve, I disagree,' I opposed his view. 'I think that Sienna will be coming back soon and that Robin Goodfellow will be waiting for her. He knows by now that we are on to him but he may gain the upper hand if he can capture my wife.'

Up until that moment I had barely mentioned Sienna, if at all. They all looked at me except Steve who kept his eyes firmly glued to the road and his hands rigid on the steering wheel.

'You are getting better, Dad,' said Joshua. 'And you are right. I've got a strong feeling that Mum is on her way back right now.'

'Is there a way of doubling back without going over the same bridge?' asked Morgan.

'Yes,' said both boys together. Steve said nothing and I had to stop myself from mentioning the Aust ferry again.

'Which is?' asked Morgan rather roughly. 'Quelle manière devrions-nous aller.'

'Back over the Severn Bridge, the one that was put there first,' explained Joshua. 'We have to get from the M4 and join the M48 to go back.'

'I'm absolutely against this course of action,' said Steve. 'But I'll go with the consensus.'

'M48 it is then,' I agreed.

✶

The hunch I had about my albatross friend has turned out to be correct. He is now leading us through the clashing rocks along a narrow path that I'm sure we would not have seen without his help. I've had to hitch my habit up as it kept catching alight when it swung out over the fiery rocks but otherwise this path is fine. I knelt down and touched the path with my hand and was surprised to find that it was perfectly cool so as long as we keep to the track we will be fine. The secret agent Scott keeps looking behind him. He's told me that we are being followed. I've seen no-one. He says that the two Germans are certainly following us along this path but that there is something else as well. He cannot say what but he is sure that it is there. I said a quick Pater Noster to ward off evil spirits.

✶

The wyverns landed in the back garden of the Scott's house in Bristol and furled their leathery wings. The dwarf jumped down followed by the magician who gallantly helped Sienna off the dragon. The Captain and Maxwell Devonport climbed off the other wyvern. Sienna led the party up the path towards the back door where she lifted up a flower pot and revealed a key.

'Naughty, naughty,' admonished Devonport. 'What sort of security is that?'

'If they really want to get in, they can,' replied Sienna. 'They can break windows or do whatever. I doubt if any of the bunch we have been talking about needed a key to get in here.'

'I certainly wouldn't' agreed the magician and waved his hands. The locks opened and closed to his command.

'Nor I,' added the dwarf but forbore from showing off his similar abilities.

Sienna led the company into the kitchen and sat them down at the kitchen table.

'Would anybody like a cup of tea or would you prefer something stronger?' she asked.

'I'll have a beer if you have one,' replied the Captain.

'I'll second that,' answered the magician.

'Tea please,' said the dwarf.

'Two teas and two beers,' counted Sienna. 'I'll put the kettle on and then go to the far fridge where we keep the beers.'

She filled the kettle and switched it on and walked into the hallway and thence to a small dark back room which served as the utility area. She opened the fridge door and stood selecting a couple of bottles from the eclectic collection in the spare fridge.

'I think they would enjoy Hobgoblin,' she suggested under her breath.

'Funny you should say that,' she heard a wheezing male voice whisper as she felt hands round her mouth and neck. 'That's just what you are getting. A taste of hobgoblin.'

Chapter 27

The path started off fine but for the last mile or so we have had to jump between rocks and this has not been easy. As a secret agent I am obliged to keep fit so I'm used to that sort of exercise and so are Robin Hood and Holmes, by the look of it. I was worried about Tuck but he is bearing up well.

The most worrying of all are Archimedes and Einstein. They are both old and unfit. Hood is assisting Einstein with the help of Holmes. I am supporting Archimedes. The albatross continues to guide us and the Germans continue to follow us. Behind them, at a distance, is some other presence that I cannot discern. It is, however, definitely there.

✶

The old Citroen whistled over the suspension bridge and along the motorway towards Bristol.

'Hurry,' I said to Steve. 'I've got a dreadful feeling that Puck has got there first.'

'I've got the same feeling,' said Joshua.

'So have I,' added Sam. 'But tell me Dad, is Puck the same as Robin Goodfellow and is Robin Goodfellow the same as Robin Hood?'

'Goodfellow is Puck but Robin Hood is a different person,' replied Morgan le Fay, answering for me. 'They are two different Robins. But there is no time for discussion. Hurry, driver, hurry!'

'Can't go any faster or I'd be breaking the law,' muttered Steve.

'A minor consideration, mon ami,' cried Morgan le Fay. 'Lives are at risk.'

Steve put his foot down and the car slowly accelerated, joined the M4 and onto the M32 into Bristol. Then through St Paul's at three times the twenty mile per hour limit, and up the A38, the Gloucester Road, and into Redland. We drew up at the house just in time to see a Rolls Royce disappear round the corner.

'That was Robin Goodfellow's car,' I said looking towards the disappearing super-car.

'How do you know?' asked le Fay.

'I saw a picture of it in his study,' I replied. 'I've always been fond of Rolls Royce cars. I love their aero engines too. The Merlins and the Griffons...great in the Spitfires.'

We ran into the house and found a dwarf and three men in the kitchen. They looked up as we entered.

'Where's Sienna?' I asked.

'We thought you were her. She was supposed to be bringing us some beers,' replied the tallest of the men, a guy dressed in a track suit.

'Then where is she?' I asked.

They stood up and ran round shouting for her and we joined them. The boys were shouting out..... 'Mum, where are you?' I was screaming ...'Sienna?' but she was nowhere to be seen.

'Goodfellow must have got her,' said the dwarf.

'He just disappeared round the corner in his car,' I shouted.

'We'll have to follow them,' demanded the chief constable, Maxwell Devonport, who I now began to recognise dimly.

'Can't do that in my car,' replied Steve. 'It couldn't get near the Rolls. That car is much too fast if it comes to a chase.'

'Then we'll have to take the wyverns,' said the chief constable. 'Come on Arch Chancellor, lead the way.'

I ran out after the dwarf and the policeman and saw them leap onto a dragon. I did the same followed by the tall track-suited man and a fellow I vaguely recognised as the Captain from Faerie. The two wyverns jumped into the air.

'You follow us in the car,' I shouted to Morgan le Fay, Steve, and my two boys. As we left I could hear Morgan arguing with Steve and demanding to drive, saying that she was a much faster driver.

'That's as might be,' replied Steve. 'But you're French and you drive on the wrong side of the road. You wouldn't be safe round here.'

I could faintly hear le Fay's reply.

'Mon dieu. Ce n'est pas possible!'

✶

We have had a disaster. Einstein slipped and the two helping him, Holmes and Hood, could not grab him in time. He disappeared into the bubbling magma. Archimedes seeing this, gave up completely. He sat down on the path and started scratching right-angled triangles in the dry, dusty surface. I threatened to knock him out and carry him over my shoulder but Tuck, Holmes and Hood thought better of my plan. Holmes has agreed to stay with Archimedes until he is ready to continue. I am worried that the Germans will do something dastardly .... I know what they are like having been in the Navy during the Second World War. And if they don't there is always the hidden follower .... something or someone that I do not trust at all.

The albatross is having to fly back periodically to check on Holmes and Archimedes and they have not started after us yet.

✶

'There's the car. Goodfellow's Rolls,' I pointed at the beautiful drophead coupé.

'A green Hyperion,' remarked the tall Chinese-looking man in the track suit. 'I thought that the Hyperion Pinifarina Rolls Royce was a one-off. That was a blue car.'

'Well there are two now, unless its been resprayed.'

'Doubt it,' said the man who now introduced himself as Wizard Zhang. 'I know the owner of the other car and he is most unlikely to have sold it.'

'Then how come there is a second Hyperion?' I asked.

'Puck has conjured it,' said Zhang. 'Which just goes to show how powerful he has become.'

'I can see two men in the car,' I said, peering with my excellent pilot's vision at the scene below me. 'The fat man is on a mobile phone. Can they see us and where is Sienna?'

'They can't see us because I have rendered both wyverns invisible,' replied Wizard Zhang. 'And Sienna is in the boot.'

'You really are a magician,' I said. 'The place is crawling with them.'

'You are a powerful mage too, Lord James,' said Zhang. 'But I understand that you have lost your memory.'

'It's not just that,' I replied. 'I'm only half here. Perhaps less than half.'

'Then we must try to get you back together with the rest of you,' replied the magician. 'Once we have saved Sienna.'

I nodded gratefully and Zhang continued.

'Once you are back whole again, Lord Scott, please remember that I have been very helpful.'

The man is almost obsequious, I thought. *Could it be that he is frightened of me? Surely not!*

✶

That ruddy hobgoblin Robin Goodfellow caught me unawares, thought Sienna as she lay bound in the boot of the Rolls. *These cars always have a toolkit in the boot. I'm going to find it and get free and when I do there will be hell to pay.*

I do not like being manhandled and even less do I like being hobgoblinned by a fat politician.

✶

No word from Robin Goodfellow, thought Darcy Macaroon. *Maybe now is the time to take back the space he has purloined.*

He walked into the office space. The rather faceless workers that Goodfellow had drafted in were still slaving away at their desks.

Good lord, thought Macaroon. *It's late at night and they are all still working. It's unbelievable. I can't face shifting this lot now. I'll have to do it tomorrow.*

✦

'Keep up the good work,' intoned Goodfellow in his best Merlin voice. 'I'm sorry about the losses but the quest must go on. Your lives and that of Lady Aradel depend on the success of this mission.'

He put his mobile back in his pocket and inclined his head towards his driver.

'Don't stop until we get to London,' he instructed the chauffeur. 'We will go straight to the place in Hampstead. I intend taking Sienna to the machine in my study. You can wait with the car.'

'Certainly, sir,' replied the driver. 'It will be a pleasure waiting for you.'

✦

I am fat and it is slowing me down. I'm having trouble keeping up with the others but I am trying not to show how difficult I am finding this unholy jaunt.

Archimedes has been shot by the Germans and we could feel his departure from this strange world. I said a quiet prayer for the dead. My friend the albatross told me that it was Heinrich Müller who did the deed although Hitler tried and missed.

Our cleverest scientific minds have gone. Holmes is the sole analytical brain left and his pet subjects are only related to detection... he appears to have ignored everything else. He is hurrying to catch up with us while we wait. Probably also trying to put some distance between himself and the Germans, I suspect.

'Where is the nurse?' I asked Holmes as he arrived. We were waiting at the end of the sea of magma, gratefully standing on solid, cool land and in front of us there stretched a pleasant looking orchard, heavy with fruit.

'You mean Florence Nightingale?' said Holmes. 'She was with you.'

'She did not join us,' retorted Robin Hood, our leader. 'So we assumed she had stayed with you to help look after Archimedes.'

'The elementary conclusion would be that the Germans have either killed her or have her captive,' replied Holmes. 'We should send the bird to look for her.'

'There vill be no need for that,' came a harsh German voice. The unpleasant German soldiers had also reached the end of the maze through the clashing rocks. 'The nurse is our hostage. You vill do what we say and take us through the next hazard or ve vill be forced to kill her.'

I looked back to the spot where the voice was coming from and from behind a solid mound stepped the Germans holding a bedraggled but unbowed female figure.

'The next hazard appears to be something no more dangerous than a fruit bush or two,' said James Scott, the secret agent, laconically. 'So there is no need for your Nazi hysterics.'

The shorter of the two Germans, the one who sported a small, black moustache, took a shot at Scott with what appeared to be a musket powered by air pressure. The German missed Scott but accidentally hit one of the trees. There was an instant response from the orchard with many of the adjacent trees whipping their branches in our direction and a grinding noise from older, more solid trunks.

'Not quite such a passive barrier as I thought,' remarked Scott, the secret agent. 'Rather like the enchanted forest.'

'Vise guy. Zis orchard is indeed hazardous,' said the taller German. 'Some of the fruit is poisonous but some is life sustaining. Ve haf to pass through the trees but they vill only give us passage if ve eat from the correct trees. The problem is this...which are the correct trees?'

The voice of Merlin could suddenly be heard addressing us all.

'Well done team. You have passed through the clashing rocks. Now you have to trek through the Garden of Delights. This garden is what remains of Eden after Adam and Eve were thrown out and contains many types of tree and numerous bushes. You have arrived via a route that is not normally used. In order that the angels guarding the front entrance of Eden do not become suspicious of you and throw you out into torment, it is important that you eat the fruit, tend the garden and drink of the waters of the river of life. Unfortunately if you eat the wrong fruit or drink the wrong water you incur heavenly wrath and die. It can be decided on the toss of a coin. That is all I have managed to learn about this ancient place.'

'Not such a passive barrier, at all,' repeated the tuxedo-clad secret agent.

'Let us not despair,' said Robin Hood. 'There has to be a way through this and we will find it.'

'That is no problem,' remarked the short, harsh German. 'You will sample the fruit as our food taster or the lady wiz the lamp dies. Very simple.'

Robin Hood, my companion of old who led his merry men on so many an amusing rollick through Nottingham and beyond, looked levelly at the evil German.

'I'm not afraid to face my maker,' he said, tossing a coin and picking a large plum from a tree that was groaning with fruit. 'If it is determined by a toss of the coin then I have a 50% chance of being right.'

I watched my friend Robin as he put the plum into his mouth and bit into the soft body of the fruit.

'Delicious,' he pronounced. 'This tree is fine.'

I went to take a plum myself but the larger German, called Müller, pushed past me. 'I vill take the next plum now that the tree is shown to be good,' said the irritating man. He took a large bite from the ripe fruit and swallowed hard.

'Zat was very bitter,' he remarked and then grabbed his stomach. 'Vot haf you done to me? You haf tricked me.'

Müller fell to the ground clutching his abdomen.

'Quick,' cried the nurse. 'Drink some salty water. We must make you sick.'

But before salt could be added to our meagre supply of water the man was dead.

Hitler pulled the nurse off and warned us that he still intended to kill her if we did not help him through the next part of the ordeal.

'The quest must go on,' screamed the little dictator.

'You stupid man,' drawled Scott the secret agent. 'Do you think we did that on purpose? We have no idea why that happened anymore than you do. If we knew how to get through this hazard don't you think we would do so?'

'For your insolence,' snarled Hitler. 'You vill be the next to sample the fruit.'

Scott shrugged his still-powerful shoulders. I craned forward to see what was going to happen.

'I'll use my double-headed penny,' said Scott. 'I tend to get the call right if I do that.'

Chapter 28

I've been moving around in the boot and have found the toolkit. Now to saw through these bindings.

OK, that's done and lets see if I can get a little light in here. I watched Jimmy playing with the boot light switch on his car not long ago and I reckon I could jerry rig this one. Damn, it's harder to do in the dark than I thought.

Let there be light and there was light! Now to pull up the carpet, reveal the battery.

There it is. Let's see if I can undo the cables. Some thoughtful soul has put some vinyl gloves in with the toolkit so I can undo the battery connections without getting an electric shock.

That seems to have done it though the car is still running.

OK. Next I'll try the fuel pump. I'll have to pull away some of this padding.

No, wait a minute, I won't need to, the car is slowing down.

✶

'What's the problem Jankers? Why are you slowing down?' asked Robin Goodfellow, the sprite Puck.

'There is some sort of electrical failure, sir,' replied the chauffeur. 'The battery is not charging.'

'Then how come we are still going along?'

'There is a back-up system, sir, but it works for only a short distance.'

'Can we reach the service station?'

'I think we will have to pull on to the hard shoulder. I'm only coasting now.'

'Do it, Jankers. I bet it is something to do with that bitch Sienna Scott. Pull over now.'

'I'm doing so, sir. No choice I'm sorry to say.'

*

'Their car is pulling over,' I could see very clearly from my position on the wyvern.

'We'll land and tackle them,' said the dwarf, signalling to the other wyvern.

'Can we still surprise them?' I asked. 'Or can they see us?'

'We're still invisible but won't be when we land,' said the tall magician, Zhang, tremulously. 'I've got a bad feeling about this. The Puck I used to know was not powerful or clever enough to have pulled off the stunts we've been talking about.'

'But he could be malicious?' I suggested.

'Yes but he was just a mischievous sprite. He must have powerful friends. Oh dear, oh dear me. I'm not really a fighting man.'

'Bear up Zhang, old pal,' I remarked. 'We've had a lovely time chasing them with the wyverns and we can now save the girl. Couldn't be better.'

'I'm not a fighter,' whined the huge but timorous wizard. 'I've enjoyed my life doing simple conjuring tricks these last few hundred years.'

'And before that?' I asked, thinking that my short time as a fighter pilot did not add up to much.

'He was our foremost magician in Faerie,' the venerable dwarf answered for him.

'But I could not fight against the elemental, Parsifal X,' said the big wizard. 'He was just too scary. So I came over to Earth and started eating.'

'Eating for two, I'd say,' remarked the dwarf. 'Or even three or four.'

*

'Stop! Do not toss your coin. Although my erstwhile colleague has died I am still in charge,' screamed Hitler. 'I will not waste another human being on this fruit. The albatross will just go in on its own.'

'Why not let it fly above the orchard, or should I say Garden of Eden?' I enquired laconically, flicking an imaginary speck of dust off my once more immaculate dinner jacket.

'Vy not. Zat is a goot idea. Friar Tuck, make the albatross do it,' commanded Hitler.

The fat friar looked as if he was going to complain and them whispered in the ear of the huge seabird. Our feathered friend stretched out its huge wings and soared up above the orchard. It soon returned and squawked in Tuck's ear.

'It can't go over the orchard. There is some sort of invisible barrier,' reported Tuck.

'Then it will haf to fly straight into the orchard and we vill follow,' ordered Hitler, his gun pointed at Florence Nightingale.

'No. Don't make the bird do that,' shouted Tuck and tried to stop the bird from entering the garden.

'You, fat monk, are expendable,' screamed Hitler and before any of us could intervene he had shot Friar Tuck with his extremely powerful air gun. Tuck looked at his stomach incredulously and then saw that there were three holes that had started to bleed profusely.

'I'm damaged,' cried Tuck, lying down on the ground. 'The man's shot me.'

Nightingale pulled free from Hitler and went to Tuck's side.

'You'll be OK,' said the nurse. 'We'll get help for you.'

'You vill not,' cried Hitler and kicked Tuck hard in the head. I leapt at the German and, with the help of Robin Hood subdued him, removing his weapon.

'You've done enough harm,' I told the evil man. 'We will make sure you do no more.'

Despite his predicament the nasty German dictator laughed in our faces.

'You haf seen nothing yet.'

I took a piece of the monomolecular rope that I had retrieved earlier and started to bind the dictator's arms but his skin blackened and shrunk away. The clothes fell off and from within the carcass of the Nazi leader there emerged the dark shape of a bat. I got the distinct impression that this was not the dictator in transmuted form but a parasite that had been feeding on Hitler's very soul. This creature from the depths of hell flew up from the ground in a flickering, irregular flight and disappeared into the darkening sky. The albatross let out a startled cry and chased after the flying mammal.

Florence looked up from tending the friar.

'He's dead,' she tearfully reported. 'Friar Tuck has died.'

*

'Get her out of the boot, Jankers,' commanded Robin Goodfellow. 'She's done something to the battery.'

'Certainly, sir,' replied the chauffeur and he strode round to the back of the car. I leapt at the man from my perch on the invisible wyvern which was hovering over the car. I knocked the man over but in an instant he was back on his feet. I let him have a straight left but he did not go down.

'It's another golem,' I shouted to the people still on the wyverns but no response came.

The chauffeur came back at me again and I attempted, unsuccessfully, to topple him using a judo throw.

'Thank you Wizard Zhang,' Goodfellow shouted into the air. 'Using Sienna as bait was a good idea. You have delivered Jimmy Jiggles Scott into my hands.'

From seemingly thin air, the dwarf, the Captain and Maxwell Devonport tumbled to the ground.

'I've wanted some real dragons for a while,' came an invisible voice. 'I'll take them as my payment.'

'Not if I can help it,' came a surprisingly low-pitched female voice. The old car had caught up and Kristiana de Morgaine le Fay stood waving her hands and muttering. The wyverns appeared in front of us with a quivering Zhang holding onto the largest.

'Don't hurt me,' he cried. 'I was forced to double-cross you by Puck. I'll help you if you'll forgive me.'

Puck looked at the assembled company and decided that, despite having a golem on his side and his own mischievous magic he might not prevail. Grabbing one of the wyverns he jumped onto its back, kicking Zhang off as he did so.

'Come Jankers,' he shouted. 'Take the other wyvern. We will return with back up'

So saying the two dragons took off commanded by Puck and disappeared into the distance with a sharp and piercing cry.

I ran to the boot of the Rolls Royce and opened it. Sienna sprang up and out.

'Jimmy,' she exclaimed and hugged me tight. 'You're back.' She then grabbed the two boys and hugged them also.

'In a way,' I replied. 'But not completely I'm duty bound to say.'

'Why what's wrong?' she looked at me critically, holding me at arm's length.

'I keep thinking I'm a World War II fighter pilot called Jimmy Jiggles Scott and I can only remember all this,' I waved my hands around at my surroundings. 'As if I've read it in a book.'

'Is it some sort of amnesia?' asked Sienna. 'Have you had another head injury?'

✷

'So there is no-one to say a prayer for Tuck,' I remarked with a saturnine smile. I felt the reassuring presence of my Walter PPK inside my DJ. I hadn't used the gun because I had discovered earlier that it would not work but once I had a chance I would strip it down and discover why it was not functioning. I knelt down and picked up the heavy air pistol that Hitler had used to kill Tuck. I examined it closely. This machine would certainly not be legal in

England...it was far too powerful.

If this place really is an alien world that may be the reason my gun does not function. So how did Hitler know that and come forewarned and forearmed?

'Oh dear,' remarked Holmes who was standing next to me observing the albatross through his binoculars. 'That bat has just devoured the albatross whole.'

'How could it do that?' asked Robin Hood.

'Perhaps it's some sort of metaphysical vampire,' I suggested.

'You could be right,' agreed Holmes. 'We have to embrace the impossible. It is the only way to understand what is going on.'

'There's one good thing,' I pointed out. 'We have discovered how to go through this forest of fruit.'

'Have we? How?' asked Robin Hood.

'Just toss a coin each time we are prevented from moving through the orchard and eat whatever is presented to us. What the toss reveals can't be important or my double-headed coin would have upset the system. It is simply the act of tossing the coin that renders the fruit safe.'

'Are you sure, James?' asked Florence Nightingale, who looked completely recovered from her ordeal at the hands of the Nazis.

'About ninety percent certain,' I replied. 'I'm willing to try again to see if I am right.'

'We could have some salt water ready in case you are wrong or we could make up some emetic from tree bark,' suggested the nurse.

'I don't think that would work,' I answered. 'This place does not obey the usual rules and you either get it right and live or wrong and die.'

Chapter 29

'Head injury?' I felt my nodder. 'No. I don't think so, not since the incident on the Isle of Skye.'

'So you can remember that?' asked Sienna.

'Clearly,' I replied. 'But as if it applied to someone else.'

'There is a problem here,' agreed Maxwell Devonport. 'But one of the perpetrators is getting away. Puck has stolen the dragons.'

'Don't worry about that,' replied the venerable Arch Chancellor and, so saying, the dwarf took a whistle from his pocket and gave it a long blow. Nothing could be heard at all but the Arch Chancellor explained. 'This is a magical ultrasonic whistle. My wyvern will hear it wherever it has got to and fly back with the other wyvern. With a bit of luck they will bring Puck and his chauffeur back here. We have to get ready to receive them.'

★

The Prime Minister was looking in again at the large offices in Number 10 that were occupied by Robin Goodfellow and his workers. Lord Robert was still not there but the assistants were busy scribbling away. Darcy Macaroon went over to one desk where a man was busy writing in longhand on a sheet of plain paper. He leant over to see what the fellow was scribing.

In extremely clear and precise writing that closely resembled Darcy's own he could see that the assistant was writing a resignation letter addressed to the Queen. Macaroon, ignored by the assistant, looked on in amazement as he read the letter. It was written as if coming from himself, Darcy Macaroon, the Prime Minister of the United Kingdom!

Darcy quickly jumped back and the man still did nothing except forge the letter. The assistant reached the end of the epistle and signed it with a flourish using a perfect copy of Darcy's own signature. The man then sat back, his work accomplished.

The Prime Minister tiptoed up to the next desk. Once again the occupant ignored Macaroon. This fellow was writing a longer letter in which Macaroon confessed to a series of crimes against the United Kingdom, begged for forgiveness and stated that the usual political processes should be suspended in view of the fact that all the opposition leaders were implicated in the crimes also. In the last paragraph the assistant was suggesting that Lord Robert Goodfellow, in view of his unstinting service and total lack of involvement in any of the crimes, should be made interim Prime Minister. Horrified, Macaroon moved to a further desk where yet another assistant was writing a letter, this time a suicide note from Macaroon, explaining that he could not go on living a lie!

'Stop this!' shouted Macaroon. 'Stop this nonsense at once. You are all writing complete lies and I won't permit it. If this is yours or Lord Robert's idea of a joke I am not amused.'

The Prime Minister grabbed the suicide note and tore it into pieces.

'That's what I think of your stupid joke so stop this at once!'

'Time for stage two,' said one of the workers who was clearly co-ordinating the others. 'Arrange for Macaroon's death.'

'No way,' shouted Macaroon as he ran out of the room and slammed the door behind him. He could hear all of the assistants getting up from their desks and following him.

The basement and the secret tunnel to the subterranean headquarters, that's where I'll go, thought Macaroon feverishly. *I'll be able to get the blast doors closed. That should keep them out.*

He hurried down the small back staircase and switched on the light. Five identical assistants to those in the offices rose from the gloom.

God, how many are there? murmured Macaroon as he backed up the stairs. *Out the front door. Obvious solution.*

He ran through the corridors towards the front only to see two more assistants rise from chairs situated, inside, to either side of the door. Macaroon felt panic rise in his gullet and ran for the smaller staircase that took him to the flat. The safe room was his only hope...the place where he had sheltered from the Armageddon Prophets....the fortified toilet off his bedroom!

*

I tossed my double-headed coin in the air and, not surprisingly, it came down heads. I picked a piece of fruit and it tasted truly delightful. It was nectar of the gods. The trees parted and we were able to enter the garden that purported to be Eden. From then on we took it in turns to toss the coin and eat our way through the fruit jungle, thus serving to nourish us and allow egress.

In the centre of the overgrown orchard was a huge tree with attractive fruit. Curled round that tree was a very large, multi-coloured serpent.

'Hello!' said the serpent, looking straight at Florence Nightingale. 'What do we have here? A latter day Eve?'

'Don't be silly,' replied the Lady with the Lamp. 'I'm Florence Nightingale, a simple nurse. I am not Eve.'

'But I can tell that you are not party to carnal knowledge,' said the snake. 'So you should eat of my tree.'

'No thanks,' said Florence. 'I've heard what happened to the first Eve.'

'This is the Tree of the Knowledge of Good and Evil,' said the tempter. 'You should eat. Indeed you should!'

'I think we know enough about Good and Evil without eating fruit from your tree, thank you very much,' replied Florence.

'Then you will all stay in this garden for ever,' countered the serpent. 'The only way out of the Garden of Eden is to be expelled after eating the fruit of this tree. One person will do for all but at least one must eat.'

'Ignore the snake,' I counselled. 'We've done OK so far. Let's just move on.'

Agreeing with my suggestion we started towards the trees on the other side of the clearing but found our way was barred by intertwined branches. After some ineffective attempts at clearing a route we went back to the large tree and the snake.

'There is no way out except by eating the fruit,' whispered the snake.

'Oh, I'll do it,' I said in exasperation. 'Give me an apple!'

'Please,' hissed the snake, 'Say please!'

Even more exasperated by the whole episode I muttered the word "please" through gritted teeth. A branch of the tree bent down towards me and I put out a hand to take the fruit.

'I'll take it, thank you,' said Florence, somewhat primly. 'I am a grown adult even if I am but a feeble woman. This is my challenge and I shall meet it.'

She took the rosy apple in her hand and took a large bite. Her eyes widened and she looked round in alarm.

'This is not what we think it is. It is all wrong,' she cried. 'It is not.......'

Before she could finish her sentence a black shape appeared in a flutter of wings and attached itself to her neck. Robin Hood and I leapt forward to pull the metaphysical bat off the poor nurse but the damage was done. Florence fell in a heap to the floor and the bat fluttered away. Our unfortunate Nightingale was gone. Now there were just three of us.

*

'If you do not help us you will be turned into a rat,' said Morgan le Fay to Zhang. 'And this is what it will feel like.'

Suddenly the large American-Chinese magician shrank and became a pink-nosed rodent with long whiskers and tail. I could recall somebody else doing similar magic when I first appeared in Faerie. Almost as quickly the rat turned back into the magician.

'I will help, oh Jeeee, honest I will,' burbled the man, now a quivering wreck.

'Then your invisibility spell would be useful for a start,' said Morgan. 'And the three of us together could use a constraining spell on both Puck and his driver.'

'I hit the chauffeur really hard to no effect,' I remarked. 'I suspect that the driver is another golem.'

'If he is a golem that should make life even simpler,' remarked Morgan. 'I'll try the clay-firing spell on him. It won't harm a human being but it immobilises all golems.'

'Do you have your spells ready?' asked Maxwell Devonport, looking at the sky. 'Because I think I can see the two wyverns.'

✶

That's it, thought Darcy Macaroon. *I'm safe now. They won't get through the steel panic room doors.*

He quickly locked the door then slumped to the floor next to the toilet in total exhaustion. He could hear the gathering sound of multiple feet in the bedroom outside his room. Next a crashing noise started on the steel door of the bathroom. To Macaroon's amazement and horror the door started to buckle. Fist-shaped dents appeared in the centre of the door and a jagged hole opened up. Macaroon cringed back against the further wall of the bathroom and a towel fell of the rail onto his head.

'No' cried the Prime Minister of the United Kingdom. 'No. Stay out. I'll resign. I'll do anything but don't kill me. I don't want to die!'

A hand pushed through the hole in the solid steel door and groped around for the inside handle and lock. Finding the key still in the keyhole the hand undid the lock and the door was silently opened. Lord Robert Goodfellow's assistants walked over and picked up the crying Prime Minister and carried him to the middle of the room. Two of the assistants were attaching a noose to the flex of the central light in the room and the others started to lift Macaroon into the noose.

*

Two large angels appeared and escorted us out of the orchard and we found ourselves expelled from the garden but standing in front of the dirty grey castle that Merlin had shown us at the beginning of the quest. We could see the window of the room that Lady Aradel was trapped in.

'Do we go inside or do we climb up the outside?' asked Robin Hood. 'Those are the only alternatives.'

'Or we could do both,' suggested Holmes. 'That is the third possibility. We could create a diversion by attempting to go inside whilst one of us climbs up the outside.'

'Are you particularly good climbers?' I asked and both Robin Hood and Holmes shook their heads.

'I fell over the falls and only just made it out alive,' said Holmes. 'I'm very happy to be the diversion.'

'I'm good at trees but no good on castle walls,' added Hood. 'You'd better be the hero who climbs the walls freestyle and saves the girl. We'll do our best to create a suitably diversionary diversion.'

Using Holmes' binoculars I looked critically at the walls of the castle with the overhanging buttresses and balconies which I would have to get past. It might be better to climb up to a different turret and swing across. I considered the options and then decided it was time for action.

'OK,' I said quietly. 'You create the diversion. I'll be climbing up the right hand tower then swinging across to the window of the tower on the left using my remaining piece of monomolecular rope. I'll lower the prisoner out of the tower and then we all skedaddle out of here. Is that a plan?'

'It's a plan or at the very least an outline of a plan,' agreed Sherlock Holmes. 'Whether it will succeed is another matter.'

'We'll try it,' concluded Hood. 'You get into position and after you have counted to one hundred we'll start to distract whoever is guarding this place.'

The water and alligators I had seen in the initial vision were conspicuously absent from the moat. I climbed down into the dry channel surrounding the castle and readied myself to climb the wall that I had selected. Hood and Holmes made a bold approach to the drawbridge and crossed to the portcullis. I counted to one hundred and then started to climb. I could hear the two of them shouting through the portcullis at guards who were standing on duty but I was concentrating on finding fingertip handholds on the nearly smooth wall. Gradually I ascended the keep, my fingers aching and my toes spreading. This was an easier climb than the tower Lady Aradel was trapped in but it was still not simple by any manner or means. I could not rely on my watch to save me this time.... the compressed air that provided the explosive charge to control the wire was spent and the only thing I could do now with the watch was tell the time!

I could still hear a kerfuffle going on at the front of the building when I reached the apex of the tower. I carefully attached the monomolecular rope to the top of the turret and, with just a wave to Lady Luck, leapt from the building towards the window of the opposite tower. I swung out towards the opening but missed by a matter of inches. The pendulum swung back towards the other tower and I had to land against the wall on my feet.

No damage done, I decided on inspection, so I climbed back to the top and launched myself off again. This time I reached the window and was able to grab the sill. Down below I heard a sickening noise and then felt a pain in my chest. Robin Hood was down. Minutes later I felt a similar sensation in my abdomen. Holmes had gone. It was just me now. Would I be able to free Lady Aradel from her bonds?

✶

'Immobilisorum,' muttered Morgan le Fay, the Arch Chancellor and Wizard Zhang together as the wyverns landed. Puck was surrounded in his own protective coruscating barrier of light but the force of the joint spell from Morgan le Fay and the Arch Chancellor was such that the barrier broke and the mischievous sprite was held locked in position. The chauffeur leapt off his wyvern and ran to attack Morgan le Fay but the sorceress just waved her right arm nonchalantly. The driver was indeed a golem for it stopped dead in its tracks.

'You can't beat me,' said Puck.

'I think we just have,' I remarked. 'Or perhaps your definition of being beaten is different from mine?'

'It's who wins in the end that matters, fool,' replied Puck, spitefully.

'Good will triumph over evil,' I replied. 'It eventually always does because evil turns in on itself whilst good continues to work towards the benefit of all.'

'Oh spare me your cod philosophy,' sneered the sprite. 'If that's true how do you account for centuries of oppression by the Catholic Church? Or the frequent triumph of evil dictators over good leaders? It is just not a fact that good triumphs over evil. It is strength that triumphs over weakness. That's the real law of the jungle.'

'Lord Robert Goodfellow,' the chief constable spoke in a commanding voice. 'I am arresting you on the charge of murder most foul. I must warn you that anything you say may be taken down and used in evidence against you.'

'So whose murder are you arresting me for?'queried Puck, haughtily.

'The murder of the soothsayer gnome, henceforth known as John Doe,' answered Maxwell Devonport.

'You are out of your jurisdiction, old fellow,' replied Puck. 'Anything I did in Faerie is irrelevant whilst I am here in this reality.'

'Not so,' interjected the Arch Chancellor. 'A treaty was signed immediately after the Stonehenge debacle making cross-reality extradition legal. In addition I personally invited the chief constable to act on behalf of the Faerie realm and I undoubtedly have the authority to instruct him in that way.'

'Curse and damn,' shouted Puck, still unable to move his arms or legs. 'It will be too late for you to do anything very soon. I have a small army of golems arranging for the "suicide" of Darcy Macaroon. A letter appointing me as Prime Minister will have been written by now and I will be able to dismiss any and all charges against myself.'

'Puck,' answered the venerable dwarf. 'You always were a garrulous idiot. Quite why you told us that I have no idea but if it is true and the Prime Minister has been harmed you will be terminated.'

I looked at the Arch Chancellor in alarm. 'We don't have the death penalty here, Arch Chancellor.'

'I think you will find that it was reinstated during the State of Emergency,' replied the dwarf. 'And it is automatic for treason..... it can be commuted to life imprisonment but if he has arranged for the death of Macaroon I expect he will be hanged, drawn and quartered.'

'You can't do that!' screamed the sprite. 'My protector will save me!'

'Really?' asked the dwarf. 'And who might that be?'

'Lucifer, the Prince of Darkness,' whimpered the sprite. 'He'll sort you all out.'

'But he is bound in Hell,' I replied. 'No-one can free him except Saint Michael himself.'

'Hee hee hee,' giggled the mischievous sprite. 'And that's exactly what Saint Michael is doing right now.'

'But if I'm correct I'm right here,' I stated. 'I am James Michael Scott, alias Jiggles but also alias Saint Michael.'

'But you're not all here, are you?' giggled the sprite. 'You're certainly not all here!'

'This is immaterial,' said Devonport. 'You are under arrest and you will be taken to prison to await trial or extradition.'

'Nooooo!' screamed the sprite and, making an enormous mental and physical effort, he broke free of the restraining spell. I immediately thumped the overweight politico extremely hard on the chin with my best right hook. He fell down unconscious.

'Sometimes old-fashioned ways are the best,' I remarked.

'It may be that the spells predate your boxing style in which case they would be the old-fashioned method,' suggested the Arch Chancellor. 'Whatever, he is now well and truly out so we can tie him up with the ropes he had tied Sienna with and take him off to the nearest police station.'

'Morgan le Fay and myself need to get back to 1944 using Goodfellow's machine,' I remarked. 'I have to retrieve Red, the talking dog.'

'And then you will need to use the machine to find out what is happening with the rest of Saint Michael,' suggested Zhang. 'I am sure that Jimmy Jiggles Scott should meet the other aspects of his person.'

'So how do you know about the machine?' I asked, suspicious of the magician.

'Because Puck told me about its almost unlimited scope for mischief. That was why I helped him,' said Zhang and then added quickly. 'But not as much as I helped you.'

'And you believe that the machine can get us to the right place just as soon as I have picked up Red?'

'Of course,' said Zhang. 'The co-ordinates will be easy to find and act on.'

Chapter 30

One second the hands were pushing Darcy Macaroon up towards the noose and the next they froze in position as if the will that animated Robin Goodfellow's assistants had been turned off at source. Macaroon was still gripped firmly by hands that were as strong as steel and he was several inches from the floor. By twisting round and gradually easing a bedside chair towards him the Prime Minister managed to put his feet onto a support and then wriggle out of the grip of his assailants.

I've never seen anything like this before, thought the PM as he stared at the assistants who were now all completely stationary. He climbed off the chair, walked out of the room and down the stairs. The two people he had earlier seen at the front door were also immobile.

Outside it was night but the streetlights lit the scene. A policeman was standing guard and he turned and saluted as the prime minister emerged from Number 10.

'Evening sir,' said the constable. 'Is everything in order?'

'Not entirely,' replied the PM. 'Although it is certainly more in order than it was a few moments ago.'

'Really sir?' queried the policeman. 'I've not heard any disturbance.'

'I think you'd better call for back up,' suggested Darcy Macaroon. 'And I'll stand next to you whilst you do so, if you don't mind. I certainly don't fancy going back in there on my own.'

The constable raised his eyebrows but immediately pressed a number on his mobile phone, as instructed.

'Back up will be along in just a few moments,' he said to the PM. 'You can tell me what has been happening while we wait.'

✳

I was standing on the broad sill on the outside of the window which would lead me to Lady Aradel's incarceration. Unfortunately I could not enter straight away as there were iron bars in the way. In my emergency kit HQ had packed a small diamond coated flexible saw that curled up into a tiny ball. This I could insert between the bars and out again around one of them. I could then pull on the ends alternately and work my way through a bar. This would take considerable time but no-one had discovered my presence and I had space on the sill to get into a good position to undertake the task. I needed to remove at least three bars in order to get inside. I did not know whether I would have to saw through at top and bottom of the bars. It was possible that I could bend a bar down once I had cut the top but I was not certain as yet.

I looked into the room but all I could see in the gloom was a shape, presumably naked and tied to a bed. Lady Aradel had not yet seen me and I did not want to create any noise for fear of discovery. So I just set to work slowly sawing through the top of the first bar. Backwards and forwards, backwards and forwards. The flexible saw slowly bit into the metal and iron filings began to tumble onto the sills both inside and out.

All the time I had the horrible feeling that something was creeping up on me. Was it the nasty black bat? Was it the elusive follower that had been dogging us since the crossing of the gorge? Or was it both of them? I did not know which of the two had some how climbed up the wall after me but I was certain that they were there just at the edge of my peripheral vision.

✳

'There is only one prison cell in the UK that is at all capable of holding magically-gifted prisoners as powerful as Robin Goodfellow,' stated Maxwell Devonport. 'And that, sadly, is in London.'

'How does it work?' I asked. 'They seem to be able to open

locks with just a wave of the hands.'

'They can. But not if the cell is made of mild steel and a magnetic field is induced in it,' replied the chief constable. 'You gave us the idea when you told us about the magnetic monopoles in Hades.'

I searched my memory and found the appropriate section.

'I remember,' I said, nodding my head. 'The magnetic field can negate the magical force. But does it work?'

'Some representatives from Faerie have tested it and they reported that it was a sobering experience. They certainly could not break out but whether somebody quite as powerful as Sir Robert can overcome the negating effect of the magnetic field I just do not know.'

'So we all go to London,' I decided. 'Morgan le Fay and I have unfinished work to do in Occupied France and we can only get there via the machine in Puck's study.'

Sienna angrily jumped up. 'Jimmy Scott!' she exclaimed. 'If you think you can go traipsing off to France in your damaged mental state without me and the boys you have another think coming. You will have to take us all up to London with you.'

'I've called for a police van to come from Bristol with motorcycle outriders,' reported Maxwell Devonport. 'They should be here very soon. We should all go up in convoy.'

'Well,' interrupted Steve. 'Do you need me still?'

'Probably not,' said Maxwell. 'Will your car get back to Bristol?'

'It's fine,' said Steve defensively. 'I can take the boys with me.'

'They stay with me now I'm here,' protested Sienna. 'We'll go with the police to London.'

'Morgan le Fay and Zhang can maintain the constraining spell until Puck is in the Faerie cell. It will be perfectly adequate now that the sprite has been knocked unconscious. The Captain will have to look after the wyverns,' remarked the Arch Chancellor. 'They have had some very hard flights and need somewhere to recuperate. '

'There are some police stables at Bower Ashton and if you are in agreement I could spare an officer to take one of the wyverns. The Captain could ride on the other wyvern and follow the officer to the stables,' suggested Maxwell Devonport. 'My one worry is that they might spook the horses.'

'Not a problem if I use a perception filter spell,' replied the venerable dwarf. 'They will look like a pair of large shire horses.'

'I'm sure that the officer would enjoy a ride on one of the wyverns, so that is sorted,' remarked Devonport, raising his voice as it was almost drowned out by the sound of sirens from the rapidly approaching police cars.

✶

'This is a very strange thing,' said the detective inspector who had just arrived at Number Ten with the back up team requested by the Downing Street policeman. The detective was tapping on the face of one of the assistants which had been immobilised the moment Puck had been rendered unconscious and then   inadvertently baked when Morgan le Fay set off a powerful anti-golem spell.

'There are plenty more upstairs,' replied the Prime Minister. 'You can see what they were trying to do to me. It's obvious.'

'What I can't understand is how a solid baked clay statue such as this,' the detective flicked the golem with his index finger and the ringing sound of ceramic could be heard. 'How this statue, this artwork, could threaten anyone. Are you sure you are quite well, sir?'

'Only just,' replied the PM. 'But come upstairs and you'll be less sanguine about it all.'

'If you don't mind, sir, I'd rather take your statement down here before I do anything else.'

'I do mind and I'll remind you that I am the person who appoints the chief commissioner. If you don't do what I say I will feel obliged to contact him,' answered Macaroon, haughtily.

'Ok sir, I'll come and have a look,' agreed the policeman reluctantly.

'If you think they were strange,' said Macaroon, leading the detective away from the front door of the building. 'Wait until you see the group in the bedroom of my flat.'

✶

I had eventually sawn through just one bar and I now donned a pair of gloves before holding onto the rod and giving it a hefty tug. No go. The bar was too strong to bend with simple muscle power. I would have to cut at least part way through the bottom of the bar and that was becoming a tiring chore.

I sat for a moment with my back against the bars and rested with my feet over the sill. Once again I saw a flickering in my peripheral vision. There was something out there not far away but just keeping out of sight. It was time for me to start sawing again.

✶

The Captain from Faerie had left with the wyverns. Sienna, the boys, myself and Morgan le Fay were in a large police minibus being driven by a uniformed sergeant who kept up a running commentary with his base and the other vehicles on the police radio. The chief constable and the arch chancellor were sitting in the back of a police car with their prisoner, Puck, between them. Zhang was with them as the front seat passenger. It had been agreed that the entire convoy would first drop Puck at the holding cell and then go to his property in Hampstead.

I needed all the back-up I could get and I was sure that the Arch Chancellor would be able to understand the workings of the matter transmitter with the help of Morgan le Fay and reluctant assistance of Zhang. Maxwell Devonport wished to search the house for more evidence of Robin Goodfellow's criminal activity.

On the M4 towards London Joshua dropped off to sleep then woke up with a start.

'They're going to take Red to a secure Nazi base in St Malo and then they think she can lead them to the Communist Resistance,' he suddenly said.

'I had the same dream,' agreed Sam. 'It's because the soldier who has been looking after Red thinks she was given that name because she is a communist not because she is a red setter dog.'

'He's a really confused man, the soldier,' said Joshua 'And he's now calling her à la Red.'

'Because he thinks she will lead him to the resistance,' said Kristiana de Morgaine le Fay. 'To the Reds. It makes a kind of sense peculiar. But the Communists were mainly working dans le Sud.'

The police minibus continued in the convoy to London. We were delayed at the police station at Charing Cross, where the magnetic cell had to be turned on and set up for Puck's detainment. Maxwell Devonport insisted on doing things properly and obtaining a search warrant to enter Lord Robert's house took some wrangling. In our favour was an alert from the Downing Street police with a garbled story about the Prime Minister having been assaulted by Lord Robert Goodfellow's assistants.

But at last we were swinging our way northwards to Hampstead and the large house that belonged to Puck. More than ever I was certain that I needed to retrieve Red from her present guardianship which could otherwise lead to disaster.

*

I'm inside the room in the tower and I have not been discovered. I'm standing on the internal window sill surveying the scene. Lady Aradel is lying naked, bound to the bed. She is dozing gently like the Sleeping Beauty in the Chamber of Horrors of Madame Tussaud's in Marylebone Road, London.

Her bosom is gently rising and falling with each breath and despite her incarceration in chains she looks peaceful and more alluring than I can ever remember from my time as Jimmy Scott in Faerie. Quite why the sawing noise as I worked my way through the bars did not wake her I do not know but the longer she is silent the better.

There are electronic intruder alarms in this room which is something that has surprised me and I am just figuring out a way of getting round them. They are a pattern that I have seen before so it should not take too much consideration. More worrying was the horrible feeling that when I had entered the room so had a couple of other intruders. Maybe one was the evil bat but what the other was I had no idea.

Chapter 31

'So what are your views now?' the Prime Minister triumphantly asked the detective inspector. 'Do you still think I'm bonkers?'

Seeing the policeman's hesitation in answering the question Darcy Macaroon rephrased it.

'Do you still think that I was making up the story about these guys attacking me? Do you?' he demanded.

'No sir but I really don't know what to make of it,' answered the detective. 'I've reported your belief that Lord Robert Goodfellow was behind it all and I am receiving reports that Lord Robert has been arrested on a completely different charge.'

'Well there you go,' said Macaroon triumphantly. 'That proves it. The man's a crook!'

'But he's in your Government he's part of the Cabinet, sir,' protested the policeman.

'Not for long! Not for long!' replied the prime minister.

The house in Hampstead was almost exactly as we had left it. We knocked but there was no reply. Eventually a uniformed policeman "gained entry" by breaking a window and undoing the lock .... the work of a moment. Inside there were two stationary servants who were clearly golems that I supposed had baked in position when the spell against golems was enacted by Morgan le Fay or perhaps due to my success in knocking Lord Robert unconscious.

We had to wait while the police searched the ground floor but eventually we were permitted to enter Lord Robert's study. The letters addressed to him were still on the desk and the machine was hidden behind the false wall. Once again Morgan le Fay was able to open the hidden door with a wave of her hands and an "open sesame" spell.

'So this is the machine you say started as a Nazi invention?' Maxwell Devonport asked me.

'That's what Morgan Le Fay told me,' I replied. 'You should ask her.'

Maxwell turned to Morgan and she immediately corroborated what I said.

'Yes,' she replied to Maxwell's implied question. 'This is the exact copy of the original machine.'

'How do you know all this?' asked Maxwell suspiciously.

'I too was captured by this machine,' she answered. 'But I broke free and appeared at the machine's source in Occupied France. It was that machine that I showed to Jiggles and we used it to transmat to here.'

'How do you know whether you are whole or if you are a partial person like Lord James?' asked the Arch Chancellor.

For a moment Kristiana de Morgaine le Fay was confused.

'I am Kristiana de Morgaine le Fay,' she muttered incoherently. 'Take away from that I fake in a stingy mix up the remainder. That's what I am and we shall not be whole until we are mixed à la Red.'

By this time I had become used to Morgan le Fay muttering spells but this was a little different. She was chanting as if possessed, as if it was against her will. She repeated the same chant over and over again and then suddenly snapped out of it.

'What happened?' she asked.

'You were chanting a spell,' replied Maxwell Devonport.

'I don't think it was a spell,' interjected Samuel in his clear piping voice. 'She was trying to tell us something.'

'It was not any spell I know,' agreed the Arch Chancellor.

'I have never, ever chanted spells without knowing it,' stated Morgaine. 'I do not believe it is possible. Ce n'est pas possible!'

I looked at her steadily. *What was she trying to impart? What was*

her subconscious trying to establish?
Was it directly communicating with us because she could not do so consciously?

*

I sat on the sill not moving, looking at the alarm sensors and studying their pattern. They looked as if they were the type that responded to movement but they were ignoring Lady Aradel's breathing. So the area of the room where she was bound to the bed could not be alarmed, or, at least, not in the same way. The sensors were angled so that the floor between the bed and the window was the area in which movement would be detected. The detectors had not noticed me because the sill was above the level.

Can't stay here all day, I told myself.

I had decided that an athletic jump over the top of the area scanned would be the answer. Then I realised that even such a jump would not suffice....I would either have to do a forward flip, landing on my hands or a backflip, a flick-flack. Neither of these had I performed since childhood.

Perversely I concluded that the backflip in a form of Fosbury Flop from standing was the method which would permit me to move closest to the ceiling without my legs trailing and setting off the alarms. I went into a stretching routine that I had not practised since my days in the gymnastics team then stepped to the edge of the sill as if I was about to do a dive off the high board.

*

'Hello, this is Darcy Macaroon.....oh...it's you Robin......yes, I know that you have been incarcerated......no, I will not arrange for you to be let out.......pardon?.... Yes....I will arrange for you to be let out ..... straight away.'

Rather useful, getting a person to obey me by the use of post-hypnotic commands triggered by hearing an unusual word, thought Robin Goodfellow as he put the telephone down.

He had persuaded the police guarding him to bring the phone into the cell thus permitting him to arrange for the Prime Minister to speak to the Home Office who would then tell the Chief Commissioner to override all other instructions and to release him.... and no real magic required at all. Certainly nothing that the magnetic cell could prevent.

★

'The Chief Commissioner has just called me and has said that immense pressure has been put on him from above to let Goodfellow out on bail,' remarked Maxwell Devonport. 'I tried very hard to persuade him not to do so but I failed. Thus we can expect Goodfellow here at any moment, undoubtedly bringing with him a contingent of golems or other magical servants.'

'Could you persuade the police guarding this place to prevent his entry on the grounds that it is a crime scene?' I asked. 'They do that in the films every day.'

'I suggested that to the Chief Commissioner,' answered Devonport. 'He promised to do his best but I'm not holding out much hope.'

'So how long have we got?' Sienna queried.

'Ten minutes at the best,' replied Maxwell.

Joshua and Samuel had been busily searching around the machine. Joshua let out a cry.

'Have a look at what Sam has found!'

We all switched attention from the chief constable to the boys. Samuel was standing next to a console that had appeared from the side of the machine.

'There's an identical console inside the machine,' said Samuel proudly.

'You've been inside without asking?' asked Sienna. 'How do we know that it is safe?'

'It's OK, Mum,' replied Sam. 'We've worked out how it works.'

'We didn't even know that there were controls inside the

machine,' I said, surprised.

'They were hidden behind a panel but there was a small mark on it,' said Sam. 'A lot of electronic equipment is like that these days.'

'It's no wonder I can't understand any of this,' I answered. 'Put me in a Spitfire and I'm fine. All the controls are self explanatory.'

'I don't think so, Dad,' replied Joshua. 'It's just that you are into old tech. You always have been.'

'The controls on this machine are like Google Earth,' said Sam. 'You can zoom in, get street view, zoom out. Look at maps etcetera.'

'And all the co-ordinates you have been to are stored in a list, look!' exclaimed Joshua excitedly, pointing at the console.

We crowded over to look at the list. Place and time were clearly shown next to a small picture. The last place shown was Occupied France, 1944.

✴

I jumped, backwards, over the alarm beams and landed rather untidily by the bed. I stood still and waited to see if the game was up but to my relief no alarm was raised. Lady Aradel stirred in the bed, opened her eyes and looked over at me. I put my finger to my lips in the universal signal for silence. She tried, unsuccessfully, to sit up against the restraints but said not a word. Next I would have to work out how to undo her bindings but that should be the simplest task so far. Then, of course, I would need to get her out. That might not be so simple.

✴

'Only Jiggles and myself can go back to 1944,' announced Morgaine le Fay.

'I want to go as well,' said Sienna, to my dismay.

I did not want Sienna to be put into yet more danger.

'It is a matter of displacement,' said le Fay. 'I have thought about this a lot and if you do not wish to change the past and hence affect the present only that which came from the period should go back.'

'That can't be the case,' argued Sienna. 'If it was the case every time Robin Goodfellow used the machine he would be changing history.'

'He doesn't mind if he changes history but wc do,' said Morgaine. 'It is for that reason that I did not use magic when we were in France. Except une petitie peu to persuade the guard to give me a key.'

'So why are you happy to use magic now?' asked Sienna suspiciously and I waited to hear the answer.

Was there any sensible reply to that question?

'C'est trés facile,' replied Morgaine. 'I can answer that very easily. We are making history as we speak. That is how we live. But travelling in time, either real or imaginary, can alter the present and we do not wish to do that. Our friends and relatives might cease to exist.'

'Or even ourselves,' I suggested.

'That way lies a paradox which probably cannot be broken, mon ami,' replied Morgaine. 'But I do not wish to test that theory.'

'What do you mean by imaginary time travel?' asked Sienna, still very suspicious of Morgaine. 'How can that possibly affect the present?'

'Imaginary time is probably not as you think,' said Morgaine. 'I'm sure that the Arch Chancellor has more to say on this.'

We all turned to look at the venerable dwarf who was busy chanting away and waving his hands about.

'I've just put a thaumaturgical barrier around the house so that nobody can get in. It will hold up Robin Goodfellow,' remarked the dwarf when he saw us all looking at him. 'Now what was that about imaginary time?'

'Morgaine referred to travel in imaginary time and Sienna was wondering how that is possible,' I explained. 'I know that we use it in quantum mechanics but I don't know about time travel.'

'Yes,' agreed the dwarf. 'It is a concept derived from quantum theory, at right angles, perhaps to real time and analagous to imaginary numbers. But in this case Morgaine may be more accurately referring to fictional or literary time as discussed by my fellow magician, Wizard Zhang.'

The dwarf pointed to the tall Chinese-American wizard.

Suddenly I was fascinated.

'I don't think I was party to this discussion and it may hold the clue as to what has been happening to me,' I said. 'But do we have time for this? Won't the hordes of Puck be here soon?'

'Yes but they can't get in,' said the dwarf. 'Come on Zhang, tell Jiggles Scott your big idea.'

The tall magician looked abashed for a moment.

'It is a joint effort between the Arch Chancellor and myself but I'm not sure that it is true,' he mumbled. 'And I don't want to mislead an archangel.'

'Come on you old rogue,' I grinned. 'I want to hear your idea.'

*

Lady Aradel was lying naked on the bed, comprehensively bound with tight knotted ropes. I stepped towards her and was stopped by an invisible barrier. This was something new to me and, still keeping away from the alarm detectors, I moved around the bed examining the extent of the barrier. This could take some time....

Aradel stirred slightly again, straining against her bonds but she was, mercifully, keeping quiet. Whoever these Gods or Lords of Chaos were they certainly had imprisoned Aradel securely and, not for the first time, I wondered why they had done this. *Had Aradel strayed into the Chaos worlds when teleporting around the Multiverse?* Whoever they were I did not want to meet them....they had to be extremely powerful if they could catch and retain a shape-changing elf who was also a golden dragon.

✦

When Zhang had finished explaining the idea of the combined Allegorical Cave and Literati spell I looked at him with considerable interest.

'That might imply that I am a fictional character,' I concluded.

'Partially fictional at least,' agreed the Arch Chancellor.

'Then how am I here in the flesh?' I asked. 'I can understand how a person could be kept in a comatose state being fed stories from books but how do the ideas become real?'

'By utilising your inbuilt creative ability,' Zhang replied. 'You are the single most powerful creature in the two or three realms. You are the leader of the armies of Heaven.'

'...And your name means "Who is like God?",' added the dwarf. 'And you have the power to embody ideas.'

'So I created Jiggles out of a synthesis of James Scott and some fictional character?' I asked, bewildered.

'And the entirety of the 1944 Germany and France you visited,' said the dwarf.

'But what is this quest that my other avatars are embarked upon?' I asked.

'According to the boys and Sienna's dreams they are trying to free Lady Aradel,' replied the Arch Chancellor.

'It's a generic form of quest really,' added Zhang. 'Trekking across countryside to a tower where the lady is imprisoned.'

'Yes,' I agreed. 'But why?'

✦

I have examined the invisible force shield and found no way in, around, above or under. Lady Aradel has woken completely and is struggling against her bonds. I have told her to calm down. I will find a way to free her, of that I am sure.

No barrier is perfect.

✦

'Robin Goodfellow is outside with a gathering crowd of people some of whom are probably his acolytes,' announced Maxwell Devonport. 'How long will your spell hold?'

'I've reinforced it with the help of Zhang here,' replied the Arch Chancellor. 'Even still I reckon it can only hold for fifteen minutes more at best.'

'Then we should get on with whatever you wish to do with this machine,' said the chief constable.

'If the past you are going to is fictional it can't matter if I come too with the boys,' argued Sienna.

'You believe that changing literature does not affect the present?' asked Morgaine. 'Not that I necessarily accept that moving in imaginary time is fictional.'

'Surely it can't matter?' queried Sienna. 'If it is fictional it is simply made up.'

'It's not as simple as you think,' replied the venerable dwarf. 'Some of the Literati spell is related to fiction but much is biographical. Changing biographies is tantamount to changing history itself. What if the story being changed was in some revered text such as the Bible or the Koran? Changing it could hugely affect the present.'

'OK,' agreed Sienna. 'But what do we do? Just wait for Goodfellow to break through your barrier spell?'

'No!' I interjected. 'Send Morgaine and myself back to 1944 then if the boys are right you can choose to move anywhere you like so you could safely take everybody else in real time to Bristol where the chief constable holds sway. We will retrieve Red and then join you in Bristol.'

'All this for a dog!' exclaimed Sienna animatedly. 'A ruddy dog!'

'Non, non. It is much more than that!' protested Morgaine then started muttering again. 'I am Kristiana de Morgaine le Fay and we are mixed à la Red.'

'Not that again,' protested Sienna. 'I prefer rational discussion to incomprehensible talking in tongues.'

'Quite so,' I tried to cool the atmosphere. 'But time is pressing, real or imaginary. The two of us will go back to France and we will meet you in Bristol.'

Before there could be any further argument Le Fay and I jumped into the machine, opened the controls and adjusted the parameters as suggested by the boys. The same sensations occurred as previously when we had travelled in the machine. The walls vibrated and a sound screeched into the ultrasonic range only to return within seconds in a decrescendo of reducing pitch. The walls stopped vibrating.

Using the destination finder like Google Earth was an extremely easy thing to do and I had chosen exactly the time that we had left but located outside the Nazi installation. We would wait there to rescue Red when she came out of the place with the guard she had befriended. I was counting on the Occupiers refusing to believe in the sentience of the dog. I was sure that she would soon make a disturbance to indicate her need to go outside...all dogs do and they would expect Red to do so!

✶

'Hurry,' remarked the Arch Chancellor in a voice that quivered slightly, indicating his worry. 'The spell has been broken quicker than I expected and Puck is on his way in.'

The Arch Chancellor looked quizzically at Zhang as if he felt that the tall magician's contribution to the spell had not proved as substantial as he had expected and then ushered everybody towards the matter transmitter.

Sienna, the boys, Zhang, Maxwell Devonport and the venerable dwarf all clambered into the machine. It was a very tight squeeze but the dwarf managed to close the door and Joshua spun the dials such that Bristol was selected. He pushed the button for the machine to start and the walls immediately vibrated. Jiggles had warned them of the terrible screeching noise but it still surprised them as the machine took them away from London and off to the Scott home in Bristol.

✷

The barrier has gone! I can reach Aradel now and I've started to undo her bindings. The knots are unusual but I've used similar myself in the past. It is important to untie the ropes as cutting them is likely to set off alarms. Anyhow, that is the way I would have boobie-trapped the ropes so I'm carefully undoing each and every knot. It is taking a very long time and Lady Aradel is more impatient than I can recall. She was usually very patient but she is getting annoyed every time I fumble a knot which does happen occasionally because my fingers are very tired from the climbing and the sawing.

She also smells unusual, to say the least, but that is not surprising considering her incarceration. I've smelt worse.

✷

Red came out with a guard and we now had a chance to free her. I called out to Red from behind a tree and she bounded away from the soldier pulling him over as she did so. Morgaine secured the guard and gagged him.

'Hello Red,' I said happily as I tousled the hair around her neck and slapped her back.

'Hi Jiggles,' she replied. 'You've not been gone long. The button pushing must have worked.'

'We'll need to get back in there to use the machine but I thought it was safer if we met outside,' I explained.

'I reckon there is a chance right now,' replied my talking dog. 'Let's do it.'

'Mes amies,' said Morgaine, rejoining us. 'I still have the key to the installation.'

We followed her to the outer gate.

✷

'So the birds have flown the nest,' remarked the sprite, Robin Goodfellow, as he entered his study. 'I can, however, follow them using the same technique and the same co-ordinates.'

The hobgoblin opened the machine door and beckoned for a couple of his golems to follow. These were emergency forces he had kept previously inactive. He had discovered the destruction of his Downing Street contingent and had cursed profusely. But now he was hot on the heels of the people who had so annoyingly frustrated him. The golems had been hardened against the heat spell used to bake the other assistants. Puck was determined that he would not be caught by the same trick again. It had become necessary to kill the Scott family, every single one of them, and he would consider it a pleasure to do so.

✶

'Look!'

Morgaine pointed to the image on the console of the machine. We had entered the establishment with no difficulty. The scientists were still bound in the cupboard and the other guards were nowhere to be seen. On the screen we could see a man in a castle keep. His appearance was very much like my own and he was carefully untying the knots which were binding someone I recognized as Lady Aradel.

'He's almost freed Aradel!' cried Morgaine. 'Except that cannot be Aradel.'

'That is not Aradel,' barked Red.

'It's not?' I was confused. 'And is that me?'

'Yes. That's another version of Jimmy Scott,' explained Morgaine. 'And you must go there and persuade him to stop undoing the knots. There is only one explanation as to who is bound and why the quest has been enacted.'

'I see it! I understand what is happening,' I cried. 'You must send me there immediately.'

I stepped into the machine, Morgaine punched in the

co-ordinates and I arrived instantly in the tower.

All the alarms started ringing.

'Stop undoing the cords,' I cried.

I looked up from loosing the last knot. Aradel sat up and her face changed into a wide but disturbing grin.

'FREE!'

*

'Robin Goodfellow has followed us,' said the Arch Chancellor. 'I can tell it by the disturbance in the magical plane.'

'That and the fact that he is standing outside the front door with two large golems,' said Maxwell Devonport, looking out of the window.

'That as well,' admitted the Arch Chancellor. 'And unfortunately they are not responding to my baking spell.'

'Is it my imagination or is the sprite growing in size?' asked the chief constable. 'He was always quite large for a sprite but he seems visibly larger.'

'He is actually increasing in size as we watch,' murmured the dwarf. 'That is not a good sign.'

Now they were all looking out of the window at the extraordinary sight of Puck, the erstwhile politician known as Lord Robert Goodfellow, increasing in size until his head reached the level of the first floor window they were staring out from.

Then the sprite roared. 'My protector has been freed and I will receive my reward. I now control this world. So give yourselves up or don't bother. I will kill you either way. My power is almost infinite.'

He was larger still, fully thirty foot in height. Perversely his clothes had not grown with him and he had burst out of his suit like a middle aged Hulk. His skin was hairy and his feet were misshapen, his ears had become pointed and the likeness to the politician was rapidly disappearing.

'There is no point in any of us trying to run away,' said Zhang, cringing with fear. 'Look at the golems!'

The golems were splitting in two, dividing rapidly into a small army of clay men adding to their form from the claggy soil in the garden. They started to move around the outside of the house.

'I put a spell on the house to protect us as soon as we arrived,' said the Arch Chancellor. 'It will work for a while but Puck has far too much power. He will eventually overwhelm my spell. I do believe we are trapped.'

'We could try to reason with him,' suggested the chief constable. 'It might buy time. I will call my police force for back-up. '

'I doubt it will work but it's worth a try,' replied the venerable dwarf. 'I'm curious to know what has really been going on.'

'And why Puck should have become so malignant,' suggested Sienna. 'I always got the impression from the books I have read that Puck was a cheerful soul who played mischievous tricks rather than an evil monster.'

'Good point,' agreed the Arch Chancellor. 'And if we delay him enough the cavalry might just come, though where from I've no idea.'

'Dad will come and save us,' said Samuel. 'He always does.'

'I'm glad that you have faith in him,' said Zhang in tremulous tones. 'But I suspect that he is a lost cause. I think we should surrender.'

'I bet you my best game console that he does save us,' replied Sam. 'It won't be long now.'

Chapter 32

I woke up with a thick, muggy feeling in my head. I looked round the room. It was very small and overwhelmingly a creamy, off-white. The walls were padded and the floor carpeted. I was lying on a dirty foam mattress on the floor and standing above me was an overweight nurse who looked remarkably like Jo Brand. In her hand she held a large syringe full of a murky looking fluid.

'Do you need another injection dearie?' she asked me, in an almost kindly manner.

'What is it?' I asked. 'And for that matter, where am I?'

'Ah,' she grinned. 'That's better. You've come back to your senses. No more babbling about angels and devils, robots and centaurs.'

Babbling? Had I been doing that? I looked around again. It looked a bit like a hospital but what sort of institution would have padded cells? There was a smell of antiseptic and an underlying odour that could not be completely obscured by the chemicals, perhaps a mixture of old urine and vomit. In the distance I could hear wailing and shrieking coming from another room.

Where was I? Was I in a secure ward of a psychiatric hospital?

'Am I in hospital?' I asked.

'Yes dear,' she said. 'That's very good. You've been ill but you are a lot better. Now we'll see if you are orientated in time. What date do you think it is?'

'About 2017 or thereabouts,' I answered.

'No dear,' she countered. 'It is 1997.'

'So it's not even the twenty-first century yet?'

'No dear, not for another two and a half years.'

But I could remember the celebrations at the Millennium, surely I could? And the great big tent they spent a billion pounds on and called the dome. Was that all a lie, the imagining of a sick mind? A delusional hallucination? Then marriage, children, fighting the elemental called Parsifal X, defeating the devil. Fairies, gnomes, elves, dragons. As I thought about it I realised it could not be real. I could not be an archangel. It was daft. But most of all it was the dome. That was the daftest of all....nobody in their right mind would spend a billion on a tent and then sell it off for a fraction of the cost. The nurse was obviously right. I had been ill.

'So how old am I?'

'You can work that out, can't you dearie.'

I thought for a second. *I should be twenty four. There should be no scar on my left knee from the cartilage operation. I pulled up my pyjama leg and exposed the knee. Unscarred!*

No signs of an operation.

'I'm twenty-four,' I replied.

'Very good indeed,' she smiled and I felt happy in her radiance.

'What has happened to me?' I asked. 'What illness have I had?'

'You have had acute schizophrenia,' replied the nurse. 'You have been hallucinating wildly for the last few months and we have been trying to control you with chlorpromazine. You've been talking about elves and dragons, werewolves, devils and golems. Lots of things that don't exist and I'm sorry to say that at times you have been quite violent.'

'Have I hurt someone? Murdered anybody?'

My mind spun with the possibilities.

'Don't worry about that dear,' smiled the nurse. 'We can talk about those things at a later time. There are lots of people who want to talk to you.'

I bet there are, I thought. *Police, lawyers, psychiatrists.*

'What has happened to my degrees?' I asked. 'I remember doing Physics and then Astronomy. Have I finished the second degree?'

'It was the University that contacted us dear and arranged for you to be committed,' answered the Jo Brand look-alike.

'What brought the schizophrenia on?' I asked.

'Possibly it was just inherently in your make-up,' said the nurse. 'But we think that you may have been dabbling in LSD or mescaline. Something like that.'

'I never take drugs,' I replied dogmatically and then added. 'Except alcohol, of course.'

'Have you been to any wild parties?'

'Of course,' I replied. 'One or two.'

Who hadn't? I thought.

'Perhaps someone spiked your drinks. That could explain the acute onset.'

'So what happens now?' I asked, the practical side of my nature coming to the fore.

'We gradually get you better and you can then go back to your Astronomy course. They are holding the course open for you and you may be able to take your finals from in here,' she smiled and then held up a menu. 'You can start making decisions for yourself by choosing your menu. Just go down this list, tick the things you want and then sign it at the bottom.'

'What about things like my phone, my wallet? That sort of thing.'

'They are all here, dear, except the rather large scout knife that you were carrying. That could be dangerous so it has been confiscated.'

'Sorry, where are the phone and wallet?'

'In the bedside cabinet, dear,' said the nurse. 'Now have a quick look at the menu and make a choice then pop your signature at the bottom.'

I quickly glanced at the list but found that I could not make my mind up that easily. Start on the dessert and work backwards. That had been a trick of my father's when he was out at a restaurant ...tended to drive my mother bonkers. I'd choose ice cream but I could not see it on the menu.

'Isn't there any ice cream?' I asked, frantically reading the list again.

'No dear. There isn't any ice cream,' replied the friendly, smiling nurse.

'Why not?' I queried. 'Surely people like ice cream?'

'It's too messy and too cold,' she replied, rather crossly. 'We don't do ice cream.'

The words of a song by Dr Jazz, the Bristol Jazz band, popped incongruously into my head and quite stopped me from signing the paper.

The devil don't do no ice cream
The devil don't do no ice cream
He like it hot and he barbecue a lot
But the devil don't do no ice cream
The devil don't do no ice cream

I looked down the list again. Sure enough barbecued food featured prominently. Barbecued spare ribs, barbecued chicken, barbecued sausages....the list seemed endless.

'There's a lot of barbecued food,' I pointed out in a slightly squeaky voice. 'Is there any reason for that?'

'The patients like barbecued food,' she replied, looking at me strangely. 'Is there a problem in that? Tomorrow is a carvery. There will be a full roast rather than barbecue food.'

'I don't think I can make my mind up right now,' I said. 'Can you leave the list here. I'll make a my mind up and sign it by the time you come back.'

'No problems dear,' she said. 'By the way. The phone won't work in here. It is out of battery and there is no signal in here, anyway. If you want to make a phone call you have to book it through me.'

'Thank you,' I replied. 'Are there any books I can read?'

'Plenty of those dear,' she replied. 'What would you like?

Adventure books?'

She reached into a trolley that was hidden behind her and brought out a clutch of books. 'What have I got here?' she said. 'Robin Hood and his Merry Men. Probably too young for you. Here's a spy novel. Or would you like a biography?'

She picked out a hardback. 'This is the life of Einstein and there's another here about Archimedes. Here is something about the Greek myths. Or perhaps science fiction or fighter pilots?'

My head was spinning.

'Stop, stop!' I exclaimed. 'It's too much.'

'I'm sorry,' she said. 'I'll choose a book for you and leave it here and you can make your own choice tomorrow. But be sure to select your own menu and sign it. I'll be back for it soon.'

'Before you go can you tell me which mental hospital I am in?'

'Of course dear,' replied the nurse. 'Now don't be shocked. It's only because of your condition but you are in Broadmoor Hospital.'

'But isn't that a prison for nutters? The place where they've got the worst cases. People like Ronald Kray and Charles Bronson?'

'Ronald died two years ago dear but Charles is still here. But it's not a prison. It's definitely a hospital. Now you are recovering we can soon let you out of the room and you'll be able to meet some of the other patients. They'll all be pleased to meet you.'

The nurse smiled at me again and it reminded me of the smile on the face of a crocodile.

'You will soon be able to take part in group therapy,' said the over-friendly and overweight nurse before waddling out of the room and locking the door behind her.

Though she was gone I had the distinct impression that I was still being observed. Perhaps through a part of the wall that looked solid but contained a small grill or via a small closed circuit TV camera. Constantly observed. The sensation could, of course, all be part of my paranoia, my illness.

I was locked up, inside a padded room, incarcerated in a mental hospital that was more like a prison than a hospital. In fact, from what I remembered about Broadmoor it was more like a prison than many prisons and to cap it all they wanted me to take part in group therapy with Bronson, reputed to be the most violent man in Britain! Was this what it was all about? Had I hallucinated all the adventures based on things I had read in books? Was I a schizophrenic who had to be locked up for my own safety and the safety of others? Had I murdered someone thinking that they were the devil or one-eyed monsters?

I thought of all the things that had happened to me. Falling down a hole and landing in Faerie was just like Alice in Wonderland. Then all those different characters on a quest. They could all have been in books. Saint George, Sherlock Holmes, Robin Hood, Jonah, Chiron, dragons, devils, angels....all in books.

I looked at the book the nurse had left on my bedside cabinet next to the Gideons Bible. It was the spy novel. When I picked it up it fell open due to a faded newspaper cutting folded inside the covers. This was from page three of the Telegraph and was a short resume' of a court case. I read the report with growing alarm.

James Michael Scott, 24, of Bristol, England has been declared unfit to plead at his trial for the murder of both his parents and a family friend. The psychiatrist's report indicated that Scott is a violent schizophrenic with multiple personality disorder and had been in a severe delusional state when he committed the murders using a large ornamental sword he had bought at an antique shop. "Scott is still hallucinating about demons, dragons and dwarves," said a police spokesman. "He is a very sick man and will be kept indefinitely in a secure hospital."

I sat miserably on the side of the bed with my head in my hands and a horrible sinking feeling in my stomach which rapidly progressed to overwhelming nausea. I retched heavily and brought up bile-stained fluid. This was a complete disaster. My life was in ruins. Where I had thought I was being a hero I was in fact undertaking the most terrible crimes. I deserved to die, not to sit in a comfortable room and contemplate group therapy.

I picked up the white Gideons Bible thinking that I might gain some comfort from a verse in it. As I did so it fell open on Exodus Chapter 20 and someone had underlined two consecutive verses:

12. Honor thy father and thy mother that thy days may be long upon the land which the LORD thy God giveth thee

13. Thou shalt not murder.

I had failed on both counts. Was there any way I could kill myself? I looked about me. Perhaps I could tear strips from the bedding and hang myself from the light fitting? No, the lamp was set flush with the ceiling.

I sat contemplating the possibilities and the exact way to enact such a suicide. Most of the methods were not possible here. I had no belt to hang myself with, there were no pills to overdose on, no building to jump off, no train to leap in front of.

I opened the drawer of my bedside cabinet.......There was a collection of pills at the back of the drawer, at least thirty of them of different shapes and sizes! I must have been collecting them rather than swallowing them... hiding them in my mouth and building up enough to kill myself...and now I could do it. No wonder they could not stabilise my condition, I was not taking the medicine! I resolved to swallow the first tablet and keep going until they had all gone. How easy the decision had become. I stretched out my hand.

The mobile telephone rang. I looked at it in amazement. The nurse had said that the phone was dead and here it was ringing. Before I could answer it I saw two little mechanical legs protrude from the end of the phone and the object righted itself. A further appendage appeared from the top of the phone and a camera swivelled round to look at me.

'Good,' said the phone. 'She's gone. We can get to work.'

I turned away from the phone. The hallucinations had started again. Would they never stop?

Chapter 33

'Now stop sitting there moping and attend to what I am saying,' said the phone.

I ignored it. Phones do not develop legs, I told myself, and they do not work if the batteries are flat. I resolved to get on and choose my food for the next day. I picked up the pen and the menu list.

'Stop, stop!' cried the phone. 'I thought you had already realised that the list is all wrong.'

'OK,' I replied resignedly. 'I'll talk to you, mister phone, but only as long as you understand that I don't really think that this is happening. I don't believe that phones can sprout legs.'

'Just look at that list and read it properly,' said the phone. 'Then you'll believe that phones grow legs.'

I looked down the list. I had only briefly examined it before but now I looked more closely.

Menu choice from James Scott
Tuesday 3rd June
Devilled kidneys on toast
Devilled eggs
Devilled biscuits
Barbecued spare ribs
Barbecued sausage
Barbecued loin
Grilled or barbecued soul

'They're fine,' I said. 'It just means spicy barbecued food.'

'Does it say from what?' asked the phone.

'What do you mean from what?' I asked, getting irritated by this hallucination, this apparition.

'What animal it is from? Does it say?'

'No, not as such,' I replied.

'Look at the top,' said the phone. 'What does it say there?'

'Menu choice for James Scott,' I replied.

'No it doesn't,' countered the phone, contradicting me. 'Read it again.'

'Oh,' I realised. 'It actually says menu choice from James Scott. That's just a typo.'

'So you think it's just a mistake.'

'I do.'

'And the "Grilled or barbecued soul"?'

'Another typing error.'

'Well it's not,' the phone contradicted me again. 'You sign that and you are selling your body and soul to the devil.'

I stood up and picked up the phone.

'I won't listen to you. This is just more delusion. More mania.' I tried to smash the phone into pieces but found that I could not move it.

'James Scott,' said the phone. 'Do not try to harm me for doing so you will harm yourself.'

'Who are you?' I asked, letting go of the phone and watching it hover in midair. 'You can't be an old phone so who or what are you?'

'I'm the robot Jimmy Scott,' replied the phone. 'I'm the robot who went with you on the quest to save Lady Aradel. Only it wasn't Aradel we were saving as you well know if you care to remember.'

Not Aradel? Who is Lady Aradel?

Wasn't she just part of my schizophrenic ramblings, my flights of ideas, my hallucinations and split personality?

'No,' said the phone. 'You were undoing metaphysical and physical bonds, OK, but they were not surrounding Lady Aradel were they?'

'No they weren't,' I agreed.

'So who and what did she look like when you finally loosened the bonds?'

'I don't remember.'

'Yes you do. Your subconscious is just rebelling against what you saw.'

'What did I see? Don't make me think about it. It was all imaginary.'

'No, Lord James Michael Scott. This hospital is imaginary. That was real.'

'Stop it, stop it. You're driving me crazy. I won't listen. I won't.'

I sat hunched forward with my hands over my ears and closed my eyes. I did not want to hear the phone and I did not want to see it either. How long I sat like that I have no idea. I went through the history of my life that the nurse had told me was delusional.

My romance with Sienna, the wedding, the two wonderful children, Joshua and Samuel. My mother-in-law, the witch. I opened my eyes and looked around. Surely I would not have dreamt up a mother-in-law who was so acerbic? Then I slumped back again. Maybe I would....it was, after all, a stereotype.

But following that were the adventures in Faerie, the clashing of realities, the rise of the money god and fall of the devil. And now here I was in a mental hospital. I suppose it made sense.

'Have you finished feeling sorry for yourself?' asked the phone.

I looked at it again. It had now changed shape and was busy sawing at the hinges of the bedside cabinet.

'What do you think you are doing?' I asked. 'Who told you to disrupt my cupboard?'

'I need the metal,' explained the phone.

'What for?' I asked. 'You're a phone.'

'I need to regrow some facilities,' explained the phone. 'And, as I said, I'm not a phone. I am the robot.'

'OK,' I answered. 'Let me pretend again that you are there talking to me and that it is not my overwrought imagination. I saw the robot crash to its death in the gorge.'

'There you go,' replied the phone. 'You do remember the quest. Of course you do because so do I.'

'But I just said that I saw you destroyed by the fall. The monomolecular rope was cut and you fell to destruction. So you cannot be the robot. Get out of that one.'

I was rather proud of myself managing to find a flaw in the delusion. The phone seemed to flinch as if it had human feelings.

'Don't seem so pleased about my perceived destruction,' it complained peevishly. 'You are wrong. I was not destroyed.'

'I saw it happen,' I parried. 'The robot fell fully five hundred feet and exploded into pieces on the rocks and was then washed away by the river in full spate.'

'Correct,' the phone agreed. 'That is what you saw.'

'Then I must be right. You cannot be the robot.'

'I am not the totality of the robot but I am its core,' replied the phone. 'But quiet for just a moment I am trying to attach an important section.'

I looked over at the phone with some annoyance. How could you put up with a phone that shushed you up when it was busy? Then to my astonishment the phone, still hovering in mid-air, suddenly twisted inside out and expanded five-fold.

'That's much more comfortable,' it declared.

I stared. It now did look like the robot that had accompanied us on part of the quest.

'How can you be such an advanced model?' I asked. 'There are no robots as advanced as you.'

'There are in fiction,' replied the phone. 'I'm from a series of books about a Galaxy-wide community that is run by extremely advanced, highly intelligent and benign machines that look after the human beings. Even the wetware can be backed up.'

'So how does the physical reality of fictional robots occur?' I asked, puzzled. 'And what is wetware.'

'You really are the archangel Saint Michael who has godlike powers and you have been fooled into creating your own reality,' replied the robot. 'And wetware is simply biological life.'

'Godlike powers?'

'Second only to his nibs himself so that's decidedly godlike,' answered the robot.

'So how do you know what I saw when we released Lady Aradel?' I was still firing questions at the robot, trying to find a crack, a flaw in the argument it was putting to me. I continued. 'You weren't there! It must be delusion. I'm the only one still living who saw what happened. Robin Hood and Sherlock Holmes were the only others there and they are both dead.'

'I was there,' replied the robot. 'I followed you all the way through the clashing rocks and through the garden of forbidden delights, the so-called Garden of Eden. I kept well back behind the Germans but I was always there.'

'How did you survive and why did you not rejoin us?' I demanded to know, thumping my fist on the bedside cabinet. 'We needed all the help we could get.'

'I decided that something was wrong with the story we were being told by Merlin and later I realised I was right,' replied the robot. 'Can you recall what Jiggles discovered?'

'Jiggles!' I exclaimed. 'One of my delusional personalities.'

'No,' countered the robot. 'A very brave part of yourself. So what did he discover?'

'That Merlin was Puck and that Puck killed the gnome,' I said, amazed that I knew it.

'Correct,' the robot agreed. 'But we did not find that out until you, the secret agent Scott, and you, Jiggles the fighter pilot, were both physically and mentally reunited. This happened just as you thought you were releasing Lady Aradel.'

'But how did you escape destruction,' I asked again.

'I could not fly because my anti-gravity unit was

malfunctioning,' replied the robot. 'So I fell into the chasm when the mono-molecular rope was cut.'

'I know that,' I replied. 'I saw it with my own eyes. How did you escape?'

'My teleportation device was still functioning in a minor way and I teleported a small escape pod to the other side of the gorge. It was that which followed you.'

'But I still don't understand why you did not intervene. We needed your help,' I argued.

'I knew that it could not be Lady Aradel,' replied the robot. 'You see, I was Jimmy Scott the robot and I had all your memories as well as my mechanical ones all contained in a quantum computer.'

'So how could they tell you that it was not Aradel who was a prisoner?' I asked. 'I need to know!'

'As I fell I went rapidly through all my memories to see if any could help me in that situation and one thing stood out.'

'What was that?'

'Lady Aradel never called you Jimmy in public, only at the most intimate moments and then only telepathically.'

'What does that prove?' I asked.

'She would have called for help from Lord James not from Jimmy,' said the robot. 'I knew then it was absolutely vital that I survived so I tried my teleportation devices on my smallest viable escape pod and they worked.'

I looked at the robot critically.

'So can you help now?' I asked.

'I probably can,' replied the robot. 'I have recoded the quantum state of all the versions of Jimmy Scott that died after the gorge crossing. The intelligence, the memories the abilities.'

'And those before the gorge crossing?'

'Lost, I'm sorry to have to report,' stated the robot.

'And can the memories you have stored be reconnected with mine?' I asked. 'Would it make me whole again?'

'I believe, with an eighty-eight percent likelihood that it would. Minus the abilities of the avatars that fell before the gorge. I only recorded them in partial detail,' answered the robot.

'And if it doesn't, then what happens?' I asked.

'Then we both die,' replied the robot, nonchalantly. 'And the entirety of existence goes under the sway of Lucifer for at least a thousand years. If not more.'

'What do we need to start the re-integration?' I asked.

'You must recall what you saw when you released the prisoner,' demanded the robot. 'Unless you do that re-integration will be blocked.'

'I can't,' I shook my head. 'I really can't. It's all a blur. A horrifying blur.'

'That's it. Concentrate on the horror. That's the key,' cried the robot.

'I saw a strange shape. A dragon....but then Lady Aradel is a dragon isn't she?' I pleaded with the robot. In my mind I was saying over and over again ...please let it be Lady Aradel I freed but I knew it wasn't.

'It was the shape of a dragon but it wasn't Aradel and it wasn't Drak. Tell me what you saw!' The robot screamed the last demand at me.

'It was the devil. I saw the devil. I had freed the devil from his captivity in hell!'

Abruptly as I said this the door of the hospital room was roughly unlocked and two white clad men entered followed by the nurse. The men grabbed me and pinned me down on the bed.

'It looks as if I will have to give you the injection after all!' she exclaimed, squirting some fluid from the end of the needle and then jabbing me in the leg. 'You have started to hallucinate again. We heard you talking to yourself and shouting about the devil.'

One of the white uniformed attendants noticed the damage to the hinges of the bedside cabinet and pointed this out to the nurse.

'You have been a naughty boy, damaging hospital property,' she scolded me. 'No ice cream for you!'

'There isn't any ice cream on the menu anyway so...' I started to protest but my voice had become jumbled, my tongue was too big and my mouth was going dry.

'I shall get the psychiatrist to see you immediately!' threatened the nurse. 'He has some novel ways to deal with awkward patients. He'll speak to the neurosurgeon!'

God help me, I thought. *They're going to lobotomise me.*

The trio traipsed out of the room and locked the door behind them. I lay like a quivering mass of jelly. Whatever she had injected into me it was certainly slowing me down at the same time as creating horrible sensations all over my body.

I lay looking at the phone which was lying unchanged on the bedside table. So, yet another hallucination, I surmised.

As soon as I had thought that the phone did the peculiar unfolding I had seen earlier and once more became the robot.

'This has to be done quickly before they return and before the serum has a full effect upon you,' explained the robot, touching me with an extendable arm as it did so. There was a blinding flash. I looked around. I was James Michael Scott and I knew that I was the Archangel Michael. However I was chained in hell in the place of the devil. Deep inside me I realised I still had all the capabilities of the robot, capabilities that had all along been mine, so I could teleport out of there.

I had not been hallucinating. It was the other way round... the quest had indeed been real and the hospital was a Lucifer-induced delusion.

It was time to kick arse and I knew whose arse I needed to kick. When I was on the rampage in my full archangel guise the devil would not know what hit him.

Satan, here I come, it's clobbering time!

Then I sobered down a little. I was still not at full capacity.

My healing powers were diminished, I did not have my sword, my armour was only partially present and I could not change shape and meet the devil in an equal form such as a dragon. I knew inherently that these powers, lost with my avatars before the gorge, would eventually return but could take a thousand years, during which time Satan would be running havoc throughout the twin realities of Earth and Faerie. There may be no Earth to save once my full powers had returned.

Then I recalled Lady Aradel.

Not the false one who was the devil in disguise but my friend the queen of the elves and dragons. If she and her husband could help I might have sufficient fire power to defeat Lucifer. Lady Aradel was missing but I knew where she was. She was still stuck in 1944 ...... in two parts. She was both Kristiana de Morgaine le Fay, the sorceress and Red, the talking dog. "à la Red" an obvious anagram for Aradel. "Kristiana de Morgaine le Fay, minus I fake in a stingy." Meaningless except as another anagram to eventually give More Aradel.

So I needed to get back to the 1944 gestalt. I knew the co-ordinates and I had the robot's ability to teleport. At least I thought I did but I had never used it myself.

'Robot?' I looked inside myself and the robot replied.

'Yes St Michael. How can I help?'

'Can I rely on you to control the teleportation of Saint Michael?'

'Of course,' came the internal reply.

'Then take us to the place and time that we left Red and Morgaine, please,' I commanded and no sooner had I said it than it happened. We teleported.

Red barked a welcome but Morgaine looked less pleased.

'How can you have dealt with the problem so quickly?' she asked with some annoyance. 'You have been gone but for a moment.'

'I need the two of you to co-ordinate thought,' I said, ignoring her displeasure.

'Pourquoi?' asked Morgaine at the same moment as Red barked. 'Why?'

'Because you are two sides of the same person,' I stated. 'You are both Lady Aradel.'

In a blinding flash the space occupied by the dog and the French Resistance worker was taken by a huge shape.....the golden dragon that was one aspect of Lady Aradel. This then transmogrified into the shape of Lady Aradel.

'Lord James Scott,' she gasped, giving me a big hug. 'Otherwise known as Saint Michael, chief of all the angels ....am I pleased to see you?!'

Chapter 34

'Next we have to find Lucifer and restrain him,' I said to Lady Aradel.

'If we go back to Bristol where your family are going I have no doubt that Puck will have followed them, Lord James,' replied the elf queen. 'And when we put Puck under stress Lucifer is bound to appear. He has sworn to help Puck in return for arranging for his freedom.'

'You are right,' I agreed. 'But first we must destroy this machine by going back and preventing its initial construction.'

'Which will prevent them from being used but won't stop Lucifer from whatever evil he intends.'

'As long as the machines are in existence and in the hands of Puck and his friends they will be a problem.'

'So we destroy this one. I agree.'

My internal robot set the parameters and Lady Aradel and I teleported back to destroy the machine at its instigation.

*

'Puck,' cried the Arch Chancellor. 'We need to talk.'

The venerable dwarf was standing on a chair and leaning out of the upstairs window, looking up at the hobgoblin.

'What is there for us to talk about?' asked the huge manifestation of the sprite as it peered down at the head and shoulders of the tiny figure.

'You could tell me why you have done all this,' suggested the dwarf.

'Or I could tell you how I am going to kill you by slicing your belly down the middle and ripping out your guts,' stated the monstrosity.

'Puck, Puck,' answered the venerable dwarf. 'You used to be fun. You used to amuse us all with your escapades.'

'Such as?'

'Misleading midnight wanderers, blowing out the candles to kiss the girls in the dark, taking the shape of an animal or making someone look like an ass,' replied the dwarf. 'Harmless pranks. Not this serious stuff. Not murder.'

'And did you respect me, dwarf? Did you?'

'For what you were, yes,' replied the Arch Chancellor.

'Which was?'

'Oberon's emissary and a harmless prankster.'

'Harmless prankster? Is that it?' demanded Puck, angrily shaking a street light as if it were simply a toy.

'No, no, no. That's not all. I said you were Oberon's emissary,' said the dwarf, trying to placate the huge and angry sprite.

'But mostly you saw me as Oberon's jester, no doubt,' retorted Puck.

'That is the role you always played so why have you changed?' asked the dwarf.

'Because Oberon is missing and you no longer thought of me,' answered Puck, alias Robin Goodfellow. 'I was a major character in all the plays, a significant figure in the ballads, the subject of books and of people's dreams. But now I am forgotten.'

'You were never forgotten, Puck.....' started the dwarf, still shouting out of the window.

'Just passed over. Is that what you were going to say?' asked Puck.

'No, no. We all loved you,' cried the dwarf.

'Spare me the sentimental crap,' cried Puck. 'You ignored me. I was forgotten by the real world and ignored by the Faerie kingdom. But I have proven myself worthy!'

'To whom, Puck?' asked the dwarf. 'What are you trying to prove and to whom?'

'I've proven my worth and I have faith that I will be rewarded,' cried Puck. 'My power is clear for all to see and that is because of my success.'

'The greater the faith the closer the devil,' muttered Maxwell Devonport.

'The devil is always closer than you think!' exclaimed Puck. 'He is nearer to you now than you can imagine. The devil is everywhere! My work has succeeded.'

Maxwell whispered in the dwarf's ear. 'Try to find out exactly what he has done.'

'I could hear that,' shouted the enormous figure of Puck. 'You want to know what I have done? I made a pact with the devil. That's what I have done.'

'Don't say these things lightly,' cautioned the Arch Chancellor, leaning out further as he spoke. 'Pacts with the devil come back to bite the hand that feeds that evil creature. Look what happened to Parsifal X!'

'Parsifal X was a simple elemental who was too big for his boots,' cried Puck. 'I am a trickster and I am equal to the devil's whiles. Sometimes I have even been mistaken for him.'

'I'm not sure that you should be proud of that,' answered the dwarf.

'Proud? Of course I'm proud,' Puck shouted back. 'No one else could have done what I have done.'

'Which is?' queried the dwarf.

'I tricked Saint Michael into freeing the devil. No one else could have done that!'

'But why?' asked the dwarf.

'And how?' asked Devonport.

'As you have no doubt worked out by now I used the machine to capture James Scott as he went under the bridge. I then did something you won't have thought about. I used a powerful Allegorical Cave spell kept active by the use of a Literati spell. You won't have thought of that!'

'Actually we did,' replied the dwarf, truthfully though unwisely.

'But how did that unleash the devil?'

'You can't have thought of the spells,' cried Puck in rage, smashing the street light down on the roof of the house.

Despite the Arch Chancellor's protective spell a few tiles were dislodged, crashing to the ground.

'It took us a long time and many great wizards,' said the dwarf, still playing for time. He looked round at the assembled company. The tall wizard, Zhang, was cowering in one corner, hands over his ears, trying to ignore the proceedings. The dwarf was too busy to worry about him right now. Sienna and the boys were paying close attention to the conversation with Puck. Devonport was busy on his mobile.

'But you still don't know quite what I made him do,' said Puck in a snidely satisfied voice.

'Will you tell us?' asked the dwarf.

'Why not?' answered Puck. 'I will tell you.'

The dwarf and the others trapped in the house waited for Puck's explanation and after a few minutes silence, during which they could hear distant sirens, he started talking again.

'Lucifer visited me, or rather I conjured him, sometime after he had last been defeated by Saint Michael, that pompous, stuffed-up, righteous angel you call Jimmy Scott.'

Sienna and the boys started to bristle with indignation at the slight to Jimmy's name but they were calmed down by the Arch Chancellor and the chief constable. Puck continued oblivious to the offence he had caused.

'He asked me if I could think of any way of freeing him. I, of course, replied that yes I could.'

Puck paused, considering how to phrase the next sentence.

'In return he promised me dominion over the entire world for eternity.'

The captives in the house looked on in horror and Puck took up his narrative again.

'So of course I accepted. Who wouldn't?' he looked in at the captives. 'Any of you would have been tempted! Don't try to deny it!'

When no denials were forthcoming the angry sprite continued.

'The trick was to fool Saint Michael into believing he was multiple characters, each with a facet or two of his abilities.... flight, power, healing, intelligence etcetera etcetera. His godlike creative powers would make these facets come true and then they could be directed to unlock Lucifer, who was chained in Hell.'

'Why would they release Lucifer?' asked Sienna. 'Surely they would refuse to do that?'

'Not if they thought that they were saving a maiden in distress,' laughed Puck, hooting "hee hee hee" in an evil manner.

'And did they fall for that?' asked Maxwell, fascinated by the confession.

'They did. You see it was not just any maiden. We made the devil look like Lady Aradel, who Saint Michael is rather fond of, I believe.'

'What do you mean by that?' prickled Sienna and Puck just laughed and continued to praise himself.

'I had very cleverly made the real Aradel disappear by using the same spells used on Scott. Then multiple aspects of Saint Michael went on a quest tearing down the very structures he had put in place himself to guard and imprison the devil for all of eternity. Don't you admire the ingenuity? Don't you enjoy the irony? It is my best jape!'

'And did it all pan out as you expected?' asked the chief constable.

'Better than I expected,' chortled the enormous Puck. 'Better even than I could ever have hoped. Many of the avatar attributes died on the way leaving a shadow of Saint Michael's abilities in just one Jimmy Scott. He freed Lucifer thinking it was Aradel and has himself been easily imprisoned or should I say incarcerated?'

The sprite laughed his mad and maddening chuckle. The captive audience looked on in horror. The sprite was still growing and becoming more ugly and demonic as it did so. The ears had grown longer and hairy and a large, prehensile tail had protruded from the remains of Puck's pants.

'What is happening to you, Puck?' asked the dwarf. 'Your shape is changing.'

'I am evolving into an angel,' cried Puck with delight as scaly wings burst from his shoulders. 'I will single-handedly be the equal to any army that Heaven sends against me.'

'And what will this role give you that you could not have anyway?' asked the dwarf.

'I will be the sole commander of the whole world,' roared Puck. 'Not an overlooked jester, not a purveyor of japes. I am the ruler!'

Puck rained blows on the house with the street lamp and the whole property started to wobble and shake. The roof was giving way and the Arch Chancellor's spell was clearly failing.

'Help me,' he pleaded with Zhang, the whimpering magician, but the tall man just huddled in the corner of the room, looking out at the captives with terrified eyes.

Trying for more time the dwarf leant out of the window again. 'Tell us why you killed the gnome,' suggested the dwarf.

'Does it matter why?' roared the huge demonic Puck. 'I did. That's all there is to it.'

'You must have had some reason,' argued the Arch Chancellor,

'That diminutive speck kept predicting the future, that's all,' replied Puck. 'He knew what I was doing so he had to go before he told anyone.'

'He told us that you were the killer,' said the dwarf.

'How did he do that?' asked Puck, intrigued. 'I put a spell on him so that he could not write or say any of my names.'

'He left a puck in his hidey-hole. The place he knew you would stow his body,' answered the venerable dwarf.

'A Puck?' queried the gigantic demonic figure. 'A statue of me?'

'Not exactly a statue. In fact it was a round disk.'

'A disk? Was it a coin with my face on it?' the grotesque sprite preened himself.

'No, no,' replied the dwarf truthfully. 'It was a disk used in hockey, or more accurately ice hockey. They hit it around with wooden sticks.'

'A Puck that is smacked around with sticks!' the overgrown sprite spoke indignantly. 'The insult. How dare they? I will destroy anyone who is practising this "ice hockey." Where can I find them?'

'Mostly in North America, I think,' answered the Vice Chancellor. He turned to the other occupants of the house. 'Is that right?'

'Yes,' agreed Sienna. 'A different continent completely.'

'I will find them and eradicate such blasphemers.'

The gigantic figure moved as if to go away from the house and pursue the players of ice hockey and then slowly rotated his head so that he was once again looking straight into the upstairs room where the Scotts, the venerable dwarf, Maxwell Devonport and Zhang, the cowardly magician were trapped.

'So how did the gnome get hold of such an abused Puck?' asked the sprite, with a suspicious look on its face.

Nobody replied and Puck started smashing the roof and kicking the door.

'Tell me. Tell me. Tell me!' he cried, louder and louder.

'He was given it by Jimmy Scott,' shouted Zhang, to the dismay of the others.

'So I have to kill the Scotts first then go after the so-called hockey players,' smiled Puck, with a hideous grin that further contorted his bloated demonic face. 'Hand them over to me now and it will go better for you.'

'We will do no such thing,' stated the dwarf. 'We have no intention whatsoever of surrendering to a self-seeking, jumped-up, toad of a capering, idiotic jackanapes.'

Puck picked up the street lamp again and started beating on the roof whilst simultaneously kicking the front door as he did so. All round the house they could hear the sound of breaking glass as hardened golems smashed the windows.

'I'm not so sure that your last reply helped very much,' said Maxwell Devonport, the chief constable. 'But I can entirely understand why you said it.'

Chapter 35

'So this is the very first teleportation matter transmission machine,' I said, looking at the set up in a small laboratory in the Kaiser-Wilhelm Institut, Heidelburg. 'It looks as if Herr Doktor Walter Bothe is in charge.'

'And it appears that they have just six physicists here measuring nuclear constants,' remarked Lady Aradel, reading a rota of experimenters.

'But the crucial piece of apparatus is this one,' I pointed to a complex laser set-up. 'I did not know they had developed lasers let alone experiments like this. They are looking into entangled pairs. Quantum entanglement, a condition identified in a thought experiment by Einstein in association with Podolsky and Rosen. The basis of conventional, non-magical teleportation.'

'So if we disrupt the experiment ...' started Aradel.

'Then they will never know that it is possible and they will not make the machine that Puck and Lucifer converted into a full-blown time and space matter transmitter.'

I quickly consulted my robotic self and realised that a slight misalignment of the mirrors would suffice coupled with a minor rearrangement of the detectors.

'It is done,' I said, just a little smugly. 'So now we can go back to Bristol and save the day. If of course we are needed.'

My robotic self gave a little alert. 'Sorry to have to report this but the parameters for transmission to Bristol have just disappeared from my memory banks. I do not know how to teleport anymore.'

✻

'The house protection spell is giving way,' said the Arch

Chancellor. 'We will have to arm ourselves and fight hand-to-hand against the invaders.'

'Told you there would be no cavalry,' remarked Zhang to Samuel. 'First you hand over your game console then I'm going to surrender.'

'Wait,' shouted Sienna. 'Something is happening out there!'

The besieged captives looked out of the windows and could see in the distance police cars and vans. In front of the cars were two large police horses. As the captives watched the police horses approach the demonic Puck and one of the policemen on horseback put a loud hailer to his mouth.

'Put down your weapons and surrender. We have you surrounded.'

'Surrender? To a policeman on horseback? When I can do this?' cried Puck leaping into the air and unfurling his wings. Puck was now a full blown demon and was flying over the top of the police cordon.

'Why should I worry about police horses?' laughed the demon. 'I can fly!'

To the surprise of the besieged onlookers the horses changed into two large wyverns. It was clear that one of the riders was the Captain from the Eastern Mainland of Faerie. In his hand he had a huge sword. Both wyverns flapped their gigantic wings and attacked the demon. Initially they had considerable success due to Puck's inexperience at flying but gradually the superior might of the demon began to tell. The sprite was able to draw on Lucifer's immense and hideous strength and he grew larger and more misshapen. Eventually Puck threw one wyvern to the ground with a broken wing and sliced the head off the other. The captain tumbled off the fallen wyvern and ran to attack Puck but was pinned down by an army of golems.

Puck picked up a large foot and crushed the nearest, luckily empty, police van. Policemen scattered in every direction away from the rampaging monster.

'Now to finish the business with Scott's house,' cried the evil Puck. 'Now it is time for the Scotts to die.'

✱

'I can't teleport,' I told Lady Aradel. 'Destroying the experiment has interfered with my robotic capacity to teleport. It must have relied on a variant of the transmat machine mechanism.'

'Never mind,' replied Aradel. 'I can take both of us. Don't forget that I can also teleport and I don't need a machine.'

I watched as Lady Aradel changed into the beautiful and huge, silvery-gold dragon, perhaps one hundred feet in total length. I climbed onto her back and we winked out of wartime Germany and arrived to a Bristol battle scene.

There was destruction everywhere and I could see an enormous demon attempting to crush my house. The structure was barely standing up to the load the demonic monster was putting on it and I could tell that it was going to collapse any second. I felt myself grow as my righteous anger flared and I leapt off the flying dragon and onto the back of the demon. We were now matched size for size as I pulled the creature from the house and wrestled it to the ground in a clearing in the middle of the road. Lady Aradel was breathing fire and this was immobilising the army of golems.

Faintly I could hear a high-pitched triumphal cry from within the house.

'You owe me a game console, Zhang,' shouted Samuel. 'That's my Dad. I told you he would come.'

'You're not going to get a console from me,' snarled Zhang. 'You would only win the bet if your father saved the day and he hasn't yet. He has to beat me!'

The Chinese American magician grabbed Samuel in a claw-like hand, opened the window and jumped from the upper storey of the house. To my amazement he did not crash to the ground but grew immensely and then sprouted wings, horns and a tail. I could see that Zhang had turned into the medieval conception of the devil. He was Lucifer.

'Tables have turned, Jimmy boy,' shouted Lucifer as he kicked me hard in the side. 'You might be able to beat my sidekick but in your weakened state you are no match for me.'

I fell heavily to the ground but not before I had managed to knock Samuel from his grasp. I carefully caught my son and placed him inside the house. I then turned back to fight the devil who had now sprouted a trident in one hand and a whip in the other. The silvery gold dragon was attacking Lucifer from behind but we were incrementally being outgunned by the power of the devil. Without my sword and without my instant regenerative healing ability I was understrength and hurting.

Puck had managed to wriggle free from captivity and was helping the devil to fight both of us and they were slowly but surely winning. The powers of Hell were beating the armies of Heaven and I could not tell where any assistance might come from.

'WHO IS HURTING MY WIFE?' came an enormously loud voice. A tall, dark, handsome man was suddenly standing in the road looking up at Satan and Puck in a very aggressive manner.

'Who are you, puny mortal?' asked Lucifer in a disparaging manner, picking one clawed foot off my body and looking down at the man from his huge height.

'Puny mortal?' shouted the man, in slightly quieter but still stentorian tones. 'How dare you address me that way? I am Clawfang, the Dragon King.'

The Dragon King took a large sword from his belt and threw it to me.

'Here you are Lord Scott,' he said nonchalantly. 'I think you need this more than I do. It is yours.'

I caught the weapon. It was indeed my own sword. In the pommel I could see the telltale diamond. This was Morning Star, the biter of demons. When I looked up the tall figure of a man had gone and an enormous golden dragon at least one hundred and fifty feet long had taken its place.

The dragon was battling with Lucifer who had now taken the form of an equal sized dragon.

I jumped up and unfurled my large white wings. I helped Lady Aradel to once more subdue Puck and then turned to the fight between Lucifer and Clawfang. It was a maelstrom of angry dragons and I was not certain which way the conflict would go. Taking Morning Star in my right hand I was careful to bide my time then struck at the speed of light. I had clipped the wings of the devil and he fell to the ground. I stamped on his body and held the sword against his neck.

'It's over, Lucifer,' I said quietly. 'You've had your evil fun and now it is back to captivity for you. You cannot beat me now I have regained most of my power.'

The devil just spat and hissed.

'You've spoilt my revenge,' said the Dragon King ruefully, taking human form again. 'I had him there. A second more and I would have got him.'

'You're probably right but he can't actually be killed,' I explained. 'The best we can do is lock him up again and I will need your assistance and that of Lady Aradel to teleport him to Hell where we must bind both Lucifer and Puck.'

'He owes me a game console,' came a shout from the house and Samuel came running out.

'Don't accept a game console from Satan,' I warned. 'He only makes bad bargains.'

'Lucifer had agreed to put Puck in control of the whole world for eternity,' said Sam. 'What would he really have done if he had won?'

The devil laughed.

'You've beaten me again,' said Lucifer in an almost pleasant voice. 'But Puck here would have got what I offered him. It's just that I was going to finish what Parsifal X started and use all the energy in this world to bolster Faerie. I would then have ruled that fair kingdom as a hellish paradise. Puck would have been left in charge of a burnt out, dead hulk. For all eternity. That was to be his reward for freeing me from being chained in hell!'

The devil laughed and Puck just groaned.

✳

Once Satan was firmly locked in Hell we returned to Earth. Taking human form the two dragons and myself arrived in Bristol just moments after we had left. Sienna, the boys, the chief constable and the Arch Chancellor were stumbling out of the ruins of my house. I suggested that we should regroup at Steve's house. Maxwell Devonport agreed to follow us there just as soon as he had debriefed his police force. The Captain from the Eastern Mainland limped over to us. One wyvern was dead and the other was injured but would recover. To the dwarf's delight the live dragon was Caroline, his faithful transport, but the Arch Chancellor was saddened when he thought about the other wyvern.

'Such a waste,' he said, shaking his head. 'Such a cruel waste.'

We walked, hobbled and limped round to Steve's house where the television was playing a news broadcast loudly.

"**.....The fighting in Bristol has come to an end and the apparitions of demons, dragons and angels have stopped. Now for other news... Astronomers are reporting a series of unusual coincidences in the solar system.**

A large comet has plunged into the atmosphere of Saturn and one of the moons of Jupiter has moved out of alignment. One astronomer likened the appearances to that of a giant hand shifting things around in the heavens. The astronomer royal rebuked the astronomer for using such fanciful language....."

'So our activities on Earth have been matched in the Cosmos,' said Lady Aradel.

'It would seem so,' I agreed. 'But let's talk about what happened here. I missed a few things and so did we all. For example, where did Zhang come from? I thought he was a friend of the Arch Chancellor.'

'He was, he was,' moaned the dwarf. 'I really can't understand it. He was always such a nice guy.'

'Could the devil have taken his place?' asked Joshua. 'I thought he was supposed to be able to do that sort of thing.'

'Very probably,' I concurred. 'Where did you meet him?'

'He is an old companion from Faerie but this time we met in Kiev,' answered the dwarf.

'Where he was extremely fat,' added Sam.

'He was tall but skinny when I met him here in Bristol,' I said.

'Well, he magically lost weight in order not to be too heavy for the wyvern,' said the Arch Chancellor. 'I thought it was a most useful spell.'

'Is there a magical way of losing weight?' I asked. 'I thought it required careful portion control and that magic was not much use. Could that have been the time that the devil took over?'

'Very probably,' agreed the dwarf. 'In which case we may well find Zhang's dead carcass in Kiev.'

'It would explain why he first helped us by pointing the finger at Robin Goodfellow and then turned against us and tried to betray us,' I surmised.

'Perhaps Zhang had dealings with Lucifer thus giving the devil an easy inroad?' suggested Lady Aradel.

'I have a question for Clawfang,' I spoke up.

'Go ahead,' said the Dragon King. 'Shoot.'

'I heard that you were in a coma and could not be roused so how did you get out of that? Oh yes, just one more. Thank you for my sword but where did you find it?'

'I was never in a coma,' replied the golden dragon. 'I was searching for Aradel. I realised that she was lost somewhere and I sent multiple avatars throughout the Multiverse looking for a trace of her. To do that I had to leave my body in an unconscious state.

It was heavily guarded.'

'So how did you find my sword?' I asked, genuinely puzzled.

'My avatar discovered from the mirror in the basement of Chiron's castle where Chiron had gone. The mirror also told me that Chiron was a double personality....Lord James Scott and the centaur. I thought that Lady Aradel might have followed you or you might have been following her,' explained Clawfang.

'What happened next?' I asked.

'The avatar followed the Spartans down the Path of the Dead to the outer reaches of Limbo on the way to Hell and took the sword from one of them. The Spartan had taken it off Saint George,' answered the dragon. 'I could not fly over the gorge into Hell because your strong protective spells prevented me.'

'And you detected where Lady Aradel was when her two parts were reunited?'

'Straight away and the trail led me here to Redland in Bristol.'

'Thank you so much for looking for me' cried Lady Aradel, more in love with her husband than ever before. 'And how are the baby dragons.'

'Doing just fine,' replied Clawfang with the proud smile of a happy father.

'I have one small question for Lady Aradel,' I smiled. Sienna looked at me quizzically, almost worriedly but I did not know why. 'If I may be permitted to ask you?'

'Of course, Lord James,' replied Lady Aradel in her usual formal manner.

'When I was Jiggles you told me that you knew the voice purporting to be Merlin was not the real McCoy because you had seen Merlin die.'

'That's right,' agreed Aradel. Sienna relaxed.

'But how did you know that given that you were not really Kristiana de Morgaine le Fay but a severed version of Lady Aradel?'

'I did see Merlin die,' replied Aradel. 'I was visiting the real world at the time back in the sixth century.'

'If you knew all this and knew you were Lady Aradel why couldn't you tell us?'

This had perplexed me since Red and Kristy had united as Aradel.

'There was a strong spell on me preventing such a disclosure,' replied Lady Aradel . 'I presume the same as that applied to the seer gnome. We could not tell anybody but could only leave oblique clues.'

The chief constable appeared at the door with another policeman.

'I've brought the superintendent from the Southmead police station,' explained Devonport. 'He needs to sit in on our discussion.'

We sat down and the conversation ranged widely until we had worked out as far as possible what had happened to whom and where. Finally, when we were about to leave to have another look at the ruined house, we received a telephone call.

'Hello, this is Darcy Macaroon,' the prime minister was on the line. 'I wanted to apologise to Jimmy Scott.'

'Hello Darcy,' I replied, slightly bemused. *Why did he have to apologise?*

'It was my fault that you were sent to Faerie to collect the fairy gold.'

'Certainly,' I agreed. 'But it was Robin Goodfellow who imprisoned me.'

'I feel that was my fault too. I did ask him to do whatever he wanted to stabilise the pound. I didn't think for a minute he would make a pact with the devil and attack you.'

'But the pound stabilised without the fairy gold.'

'Yes,' replied the prime minister. 'Goodfellow said that it was because you were missing. He believed that your presence was against the financial interest of the country. I was worried that he had killed you to save the pound.'

'I'm difficult to kill,' I answered.

'Thank goodness for that,' replied Macaroon. 'But you can understand how guilty it made me feel. And then he made me release him from jail even after his own clay men had tried to kill me. Me!'

'How did he make you do that?' I asked.

'It was some strange word he used. After he had said the word I just had to obey him. I could watch myself doing it but I could not stop myself.'

'A post-hypnotic command,' I concluded. 'I wonder how many of those he has left around the place.'

'So no hard feelings?'

'None whatsoever,' I said. 'But you could do something for me.'

'What would you like. Your house mended? ...I understand it's in ruins. A pay rise?'

'A new game console for my son,' I answered. 'He's owed one but I forbade him from accepting it from the devil. You could pay off the devil's bet!'

The End

But the stories continue in *Tsunami* and *Change* and the Scotts will return in an attempt to save the planet yet again in the next trilogy, *The Witches' Brew*:

"Hubble Bubble,
Toil
and Trouble"